Hull College Group Libraries

This book must be returned on or before the
latest date stamped below

D0230726

The Werewolf Pack

an Anthology

*Selected and introduced
by Mark Valentine*

WORDSWORTH EDITIONS

In loving memory of
MICHAEL TRAYLER
the founder of Wordsworth Editions

I

Readers who are interested in other titles from
Wordsworth Editions are invited to visit our website at
www.wordsworth-editions.com

For our latest list and a full mail-order service contact
Bibliophile Books, Unit 5 Datapoint,
South Crescent, London E16 4TL
Tel: +44 020 74 74 24 74
Fax: +44 020 74 74 85 89
orders@bibliophilebooks.com
www.bibliophilebooks.com

This edition published 2008 by
Wordsworth Editions Limited
8B East Street, Ware, Hertfordshire SG12 9HJ

ISBN 978 1 84022 087 2

Typeset in Great Britain by Roperford Editorial
Printed by Clays Ltd, St Ives plc

CONTENTS

INTRODUCTION

Tales of shapeshifting, changing from human to beast form, are as old as storytelling itself. Even some of our prehistoric cave paintings may depict the idea. The earliest religions, involving animism and shamanic practices, often feature a close affinity between man and the animal world. In magical rites, involving trance states, ceremonial dance, masks, speaking in strange tongues, and visions, the seer encounters totem animals or becomes identified with potent, powerful beast forms. Something of this ancient practice may survive in folk and fairy tales, where animals may be wise guides or sly tricksters.

Of all animals, the wolf was one of the most invoked, celebrated and feared. In Dark Age times, kings offered rewards, or pardons for wrongdoings, to those who collected sacks of wolves' tongues. January, the leanest and harshest time of year, was known as 'wolf-month'. Saxons and Danes used the word wolf as part of the personal names of warriors and leaders, such Aethelwulf or Cynewulf. A wolf was associated with St Edmund, the tenth-century East Anglian king and martyr, who was for long the unofficial patron saint of the English. It was said to have guarded his head and helped monks and the king's followers to find it. Despite this, the wolf was usually reviled by church scribes, carvers and illuminators. It is depicted as a sly and slinking beast, and as a symbol of evil and sin. But its fierceness and prowess was also acknowledged. Medieval lords took the wolf as their emblem in heraldry, while outlaws and renegades might be likened to wolves, and relish the comparison.

The wolf died out in Britain in the early eighteenth century, but folk memories of the wily, sinister predator who howls and hunts in packs under the moon, were slow to die. Many places in England still vie to be known as the lair of the last wolf, with picturesque legends of its fate. From Humphrey Head, a promontory in Cumbria, the last wolf is said to have been chased by knights from the nearby tower house, disappearing for ever as it leapt into the sea. A cave or deep pit on the headland is said to be its last den. But tales from the Peak District, Northamptonshire, Devon, Sussex, Charnwood Forest, and elsewhere all lay claim to the last wolf accolade too. There have even been suggestions that the wolf should be reintroduced into the wild in the Scottish Highlands.

As fairy tales began to be fashioned out of traditional and courtly fabric from the eighteenth century onwards, the wolf's loping form was seldom far away. What else is *Little Red Riding Hood* than a kind of werewolf story? And *Beauty and the Beast* draws from the same inspiration. In this collection, we acknowledge these origins by including an excellent example of wolf transformation in a fairy tale, F. J. Harvey Darton's brocaded story of 'William and the Werewolf' from *A Wonder Book of Old Romance* (1907). The tale itself, of course, has older roots and may ultimately derive from French medieval romance.

Also included are two stories collected by Andrew Lang, the Victorian Scottish equivalent of Hans Andersen and the Grimm brothers. Brought up in the Border country, he was attracted by the local ballads and folk tales, and this led him to gather similar material from many periods, cultures and countries. They were presented in gift books for children named after the colour of their binding, but the quality of his prose and the fact that his tales were presented purely for their own virtues (and not as improving texts) made them popular with readers of all ages. Here, from the *Grey Fairy Book* (1900), we offer 'The White Wolf', an archetypal tale which blends many well-known motifs in a tale of magic, beauty, wisdom and pity. And from the *Yellow Fairy Book* (1906), there is 'The Boy and the Wolves', a brief, chilling story which achieves unsentimental pathos.

Wolves, along with ruined abbeys or castles, saturnine villains, immurement, phantoms, graveyards, decay and wronged heroines, were part of the macabre landscape of the Gothic novel in the early nineteenth century. Even that master storyteller Sir Walter Scott, influenced by the Gothic in several of his novels, played with hints of the werewolf theme. In *The Bride of Lammermuir* (1819), the noble young Master of Ravenswood, cheated out of his ancient family estates, lives instead in a lonely tower, Wolf's Crag. When his sweetheart is forced to marry another, breaking her promises to him, her new husband is found dreadfully mauled and the bloodstained bride has been driven out of her wits. A werewolf's revenge is not, in fact, the explanation, but the lupine implications in the book remain.

Scott's contemporary G. W. M. Reynolds tackled the theme more directly in his massive and complex *Wagner, the Wehr-wolf* (1846–7), in which a Faustian pact causes the protagonist to change each month to wolf form. A beautiful *femme fatale*, a Rosicrucian prophet, the Inquisition, all become embroiled, and there are many other sub-plots and bloodthirsty scenes. Although central to the novel, the werewolf is just one of many macabre images that Reynolds uses. It was Captain Frederick Marryat, famous for his *Children of the New Forest*, who produced the first fully successful evocation of a were-wolf in English. Writing with a more subtle touch, in his episode of 'The Werewolf: Krantz's Tale', also known as 'The White Wolf of the Hartz Mountains', he captured all of the key elements and a careful balance of terror and tragedy. This was included in his novel *The Phantom Ship* (1839) but is a complete tale in itself. It has rightly been described by E. F. Bleiler, author of *The Guide to Supernatural Fiction* (1983), as 'the first significant werewolf tale in English, and still one of the best', and so it is an essential inclusion here. Incidentally, the tale, with its Transylvanian characters and scenes of nocturnal feasting upon innocent souls, is also an im-portant precursor of *Dracula*.

As well as this thematic association with the classic vampire novel, the werewolf can also be seen working in the shadows of another great classic of the macabre, Robert Louis Stevenson's *Strange Case of Dr Jekyll and Mr Hyde* (1886). The story's theme of the struggle between civilised man and a monstrous form within has an obvious affinity, even though the novel itself is much more subtle in its depiction of the beast than the snarling, hairy-palmed film versions.

Sir Gilbert Campbell's tale of a spectral wolf prowling the Russian steppes, 'The White Wolf of Kostopchin', from his collection *Wild and Weird, Tales of Imagination and Mystery* (1889), is one of the most traditional renditions in the field, with all the blood-curling charac-teristics and tragic elements that we have come to expect. In similar classic folkloristic vein is 'A Werewolf of the Campagna' by Mrs Hugh Fraser, the older sister of fantasy novelist F. Marion Crawford. She was later the author of a highly effective novel of diabolism, *The Satanist* (1912).

An elegant and melancholy rendition of the werewolf theme was provided by Count Eric Stenbock, author of the rare volume of Decadent stories, *Studies of Death* (1894). His tale 'The Other Side' was not collected in that book but appeared in the Oxford journal *The Spirit Lamp* a year earlier. Although described as a 'Breton legend', the story bears all the mark of the Count's fervent imagin-ation. Stenbock, scion of an Estonian noble family, came to England in his youth and made a name for himself as an eccentric figure, who kept animal familiars (a toad, an owl or a snake), worshipped strange gods, and spent lavishly.

The Count was not alone in being inspired by the lupine theme. Few writers in the field of dark fiction have been able to resist the lure of the wolf. Arthur Machen, author of the classic horror works *The Great God Pan* (1894) and *The Three Impostors* (1895), wrote a werewolf yarn around the same time as these, which regrettably he destroyed. Algernon Blackwood, the master ghost-story teller, made his psychic investigator Dr John Silence investigate a case of lycanthropy in 'The Camp of the Dog' (1908). Arthur Conan Doyle's *The Hound of the Baskervilles* (1902) has many affinities with the werewolf theme – a family legend and curse, a ferocious attack by night, a baying figure, swirling mists and a weird luminosity around the apparently supernatural creature – and the great wolfhound is every bit as fierce and frightening as the wolf of legend could be. However, a most singular fact is that the friend who gave Conan Doyle the idea for the book was himself the author of a wolf curse story which has many similar ingredients.

Bertram Fletcher Robinson outlined the theme for *The Hound of the Baskervilles* to Conan Doyle during a holiday in Norfolk in 1901, and the two men then spent time together in Dartmoor plotting it out further and going over the scenes where the story was to take place. The creator of Sherlock Holmes was delighted by the strange tale, and even offered to credit the book as a collaboration. Though this was declined, he dedicated the book to his friend in recognition of his important role in its inspiration. In fact, though, Robinson was to go on a few years later to publish his own yarn involving a mysterious white wolf killed centuries ago in a Norfolk country estate, which still stalks the grounds – a case investigated by his own detective, Addington Peace. 'The Terror of the Snow' is an effective and evocative piece well worth reviving, and not just for its Sherlock Holmes connections. Sadly, Fletcher Robinson died not long after, in 1907, before his reputation could be further established.

We also include here examples from three fine Edwardian authors. Barry Pain is remembered today, if at all, as the author of books of cockney humour, such as the Eliza stories (from 1900 onwards), and he was much in demand as a parodist who could be relied upon to produce quick mockeries of the bestsellers of the day. But he was a prolific writer for the Edwardian story magazines and he also wrote a surprisingly strong body of macabre tales which are deft examples of the form. In 'The Undying Thing' (from *Stories in the Dark*, 1901),

Pain makes excellent use of the family curse theme, often associated with werewolf stories, and is also one of the first to bring the wolves in from the distant German or Balkan fastnesses to closer to home, setting his tale in an English country estate.

Hector Hugh Munro, who wrote under the pen-name of Saki, also liked to let loose wild creatures in the peaceful demesnes of Edwardian England, with his black-humoured satires with their cool dark wit and savage repartee: many were collected in *Beasts and Super-Beasts* (1914). It is a pleasure to include two of his sardonic pieces here. Saki's sympathies are always with the beasts of the wild; he clearly appreciated the amorality and direct satisfaction of appetites that they represented, and liked those of his characters who possessed the same qualities. As bibliophile Charles Cox has observed, Saki is 'as easy in the society of a werewolf as in that of a duchess'.

Bernard Capes was a popular author of historical novels and stories in the same period, whose work was praised by G.K. Chesterton as comparable to that of Stevenson: he said he could make a penny-dreadful read as though it were worth a pound. He could also be a willing and accomplished practitioner in the macabre. His 'The Thing in the Forest' (from *The Fabulists*, 1915) is a pithy but excellent example, with an unusual choice of character for the werewolf possession.

It was only a matter of time before an author was bound to try their hand at a modern length treatment of the werewolf theme. In some ways, the werewolf idea has been diminished by the absence of a single classic text, the instantly recognisable book, as in *Dracula* for the figure of the vampire. Perhaps the nearest British example would be *The Undying Monster, a Tale of the Fifth Dimension* by Jessie Douglas Kerruish (1922). The critic and poet Edward Shanks thought that it 'takes a credible place by the side of *Dracula*'. Set in Sussex, the novel involves a family curse, mysterious inscribed stone, and the intrusion of strange dimensions of time. Somewhat overlooked now, Kerruish was well-versed in archaeology, mythology and the occult and uses all three to great effect. A close rival, however, is Gerald Biss's *The Door of the Unreal* (1919), also set in Sussex. Both make good use of cliff-hanging horror and several intertwining mysteries investigated by a sturdy detective. The comparable American classic must be Guy Endore's *The Werewolf of Paris* (1933), a bold, brutal yarn of madness, murder and cannibalism in nineteenth-century France.

The fantastic tales of the Romanian doctor Vasile Voiculescu deserve to be much better known among English-speaking readers. During the post-World War Two period, until something of a thaw in the nineteen-sixties, he was unable to publish his work in the Communist-ruled country. The settings of his stories, among nineteenth-century estates, his scholarly or landed characters, and his willingness to explore ideas in parapsychology and the occult, all would have made his work unwelcome. As 'Amongst the Wolves' shows, however, he was a fine storyteller who knew how to use folk stories well and balance these through the voice of an ironic but morbidly interested observer.

The cinema has been unable to resist the dramatic (and special effects) opportunities offered by the transformation of a man into a beast, and by night-time attacks and pursuits. With an excellent cast of Lon Chaney Jr, Claude Rains and Bela Lugosi, *The Wolf Man* (1941) made good use of all the traditional elements of the werewolf theme. There is an old family estate, a gypsy's warning, a mist-shrouded battle against the wolf, psychological uncertainty, suppressed sexuality, and much else. It was unsurpassed until *Curse of the Werewolf* (1961), based on Guy Endore's novel, with Oliver Reed, to the manner born, in the lead role. Many inferior imitations followed, until all of them were comprehensively undermined by *An American Werewolf in London* (1981), which affectionately parodies and encapsulates the genre while still delivering some stark thrills of its own. And by 1985 (*The Company of Wolves*) a more symbolic and nuanced version of the legend, acknowledging its primeval origins and the power and allure of these nocturnal creatures, was possible.

Contemporary writers, while still fascinated by the werewolf legend, have often been led to explore new and different facets of the theme, sometimes overturning traditional expectations. I am pleased to include in this volume several examples, including Ron Weighell's excellent tribute to the Sherlock Holmes tales, Steve Duffy's fine relocation of the werewolf to the wastelands of the Wild West, R. B. Russell's enigmatic tribute to French art cinema, and Gail-Nina Anderson's insightful return to the folk story form.

MARK VALENTINE

THE WEREWOLF PACK

The White Wolf of the Hartz Mountains

CAPTAIN FREDERICK MARRYAT

Before noon Philip and Krantz had embarked, and made sail in the peroqua.

They had no difficulty in steering their course; the islands by day, and the clear stars by night, were their compass. It is true that they did not follow the more direct track, but they followed the more secure, working up through the smooth waters, and gaining to the northward more than to the west. Many times were they chased by the Malay proas, which infested the islands, but the swiftness of their little peroqua was their security; indeed the chase was, generally speaking, abandoned, as soon as the smallness of the vessel was made out by the pirates, who expected that little or no booty was to be gained.

One morning, as they were sailing between the isles, with less wind than usual, Philip observed: 'Krantz, you said that there were events in your own life, or connected with it, which would corroborate the mysterious tale I confided to you. Will you now tell me to what you referred?'

'Certainly,' replied Krantz; 'I have often thought of doing so, but one circumstance or another has hitherto prevented me; this is, however, a fitting opportunity. Prepare therefore to listen to a strange story, quite as strange, perhaps, as your own.

'I take it for granted, that you have heard people speak of the Hartz Mountains,' observed Krantz.

'I have never heard people speak of them that I can recollect,' replied Philip; 'but I have read of them in some book, and of the strange things which have occurred there.'

'It is indeed a wild region,' rejoined Krantz, 'and many strange tales are told of it; but, strange as they are, I have good reason for believing them to be true. I have told you, Philip, that I fully believe in your communion with the other world – that I credit the history of your father, and the lawfulness of your mission; for that we are surrounded, impelled, and worked upon by beings different in their nature from ourselves, I have had full evidence, as you will acknowledge, when I state what has occurred in my own family. Why such malevolent beings as I am about to speak of should be permitted to interfere with us, and punish, I may say, comparatively unoffending mortals, is beyond my comprehension; but that they are so permitted is most certain.'

'The great principle of all evil fulfils his work of evil; why, then, not the other minor spirits of the same class?' inquired Philip. 'What matters it to us, whether we are tried by, and have to suffer from, the enmity of our fellow-mortals, or whether we are persecuted by beings more powerful and more malevolent than ourselves? We know that we have to work out our salvation, and that we shall be judged according to our strength; if then there be evil spirits who delight to oppress man, there surely must be, as Amine asserts, good spirits, whose delight is to do him service. Whether, then, we have to struggle against our passions only, or whether we have to struggle not only against our passions, but also the dire influence of unseen enemies, we ever struggle with the same odds in our favour, as the good are stronger than the evil which we combat. In either case we are on the 'vantage ground, whether, as in the first, we fight the good cause single-handed, or as in the second, although opposed, we have the host of Heaven ranged on our side. Thus are the scales of Divine Justice evenly balanced, and man is still a free agent, as his own virtuous or vicious propensities must ever decide whether he shall gain or lose the victory.'

'Most true,' replied Krantz, 'and now to my history.

'My father was not born, or originally a resident, in the Hartz Mountains; he was the serf of an Hungarian nobleman, of great possessions, in Transylvania; but, although a serf, he was not by any means a poor or illiterate man. In fact, he was rich, and his intelligence and respectability were such, that he had been raised by his lord to the stewardship; but, whoever may happen to be born a serf, a serf must he remain, even though he become a wealthy man; such was the condition of my father. My father had been married for about five years; and, by his marriage, had three children – my eldest brother Caesar, myself (Hermann), and a sister named Marcella. You know, Philip, that Latin is still the language spoken in that country; and that will account for our high-sounding names. My mother was a very beautiful woman, unfortunately more beautiful than virtuous: she was seen and admired by the lord of the soil; my father was sent away upon some mission; and, during his absence, my mother, flattered by the attentions, and won by the assiduities, of this nobleman, yielded to his wishes. It so happened that my father returned very unexpectedly, and discovered the intrigue. The evidence of my mother's shame was positive: he surprised her in the company of her seducer! Carried away by the impetuosity of his feelings, he watched the opportunity of a meeting taking place between them, and murdered both his wife and her seducer. Conscious that, as a serf, not even the provocation which he had received would be allowed as a justification of his conduct, he hastily collected together what money he could lay his hands upon, and, as we were then in the depth of winter, he put his horses to the sleigh, and taking his children with him, he set off in the middle of the night, and was far away before the tragical circumstance had transpired. Aware that he would be pursued, and that he had no chance of escape if he remained in any portion of his native country (in which the authorities could lay hold of him), he continued his flight without intermission until he had buried himself in the intricacies and seclusion of the Hartz Mountains. Of course, all that I have now told you I learned afterwards. My oldest recollections are knit to a rude, yet comfortable cottage, in which I lived with my father, brother, and sister. It was on the confines of one of those vast forests which cover the northern part of Germany; around it were a few acres of ground, which, during the summer months, my father cultivated, and which, though they yielded a doubtful harvest, were sufficient for our support. In the winter we remained much indoors, for, as my father followed the chase, we were left alone, and the wolves, during that season, incessantly prowled about. My father had purchased the cottage, and land about it, of one of the rude foresters, who gain their livelihood partly by hunting, and partly by burning charcoal, for the purpose of smelting the ore from the neighbouring mines; it was distant about two miles from any other habitation. I can call to mind the whole landscape now: the tall pines which rose up on the mountain above us, and the wide expanse of forest beneath, on the topmost boughs and heads of whose trees we looked down from our cottage, as the mountain below us rapidly descended into the distant valley. In summertime the prospect was beautiful; but during the severe winter, a more desolate scene could not well be imagined.

'I said that, in the winter, my father occupied himself with the chase; every day he left us, and often would he lock the door, that we might not leave the cottage. He had no-one to assist him, or to take care of us – indeed, it was not easy to find a female servant who would live in such a solitude; but, could he have found one, my father would not have received her, for he had imbibed a horror of the sex, as the difference of his conduct towards us, his two boys, and my poor little sister, Marcella, evidently proved. You may suppose we were sadly neglected; indeed, we suffered much, for my father, fearful that we might come to some harm, would not allow us fuel, when he left the cottage; and we were obliged, therefore, to creep under the heaps of bears'-skins, and there to keep ourselves as warm as we could until he returned in the evening, when a blazing fire was our delight. That my father chose this restless sort of life may appear strange, but the fact was that he could not remain quiet; whether from remorse for having committed murder, or from the misery consequent on his change of situation, or from both combined, he was never happy unless he was in a state of activity. Children, however, when left much to themselves, acquire a thoughtfulness not common to their age. So it was with us; and during the short cold days of winter we would sit silent, longing for the happy hours when the snow would melt, and the leaves burst out, and the birds begin their songs, and when we should again be set at liberty.

'Such was our peculiar and savage sort of life until my brother Caesar was nine, myself seven, and my sister five, years old, when the circumstances occurred on which is based the extraordinary narrative which I am about to relate.

'One evening my father returned home rather later than usual; he had been unsuccessful, and, as the weather was very severe, and many feet of snow were upon the ground, he was not only very cold, but in a very bad humour. He had brought in wood, and we were all three of us gladly assisting each other in blowing on the embers to create the blaze, when he caught poor little Marcella by the arm and threw her aside; the child fell, struck her mouth, and bled very much. My brother ran to raise her up. Accustomed to ill-usage, and afraid of my father, she did not dare to cry, but looked up in his face very piteously. My father drew his stool nearer to the hearth, muttered something in abuse of women, and busied himself with the fire, which both my brother and I had deserted when our sister was so unkindly treated. A cheerful blaze was soon the result of his exertions; but we did not, as usual, crowd round it. Marcella, still bleeding, retired to a corner, and my brother and I took our seats beside her, while my father hung over the fire gloomily and alone. Such had been our position for about half-an-hour, when the howl of a wolf, close under the window of the cottage, fell on our ears. My father started up, and seized his gun: the howl was repeated, he examined the priming, and then hastily left the cottage, shutting the door after him. We all waited (anxiously listening), for we thought that if he succeeded in shooting the wolf, he would return in a better humour; and although he was harsh to all of us, and particularly so to our little sister, still we loved our father, and loved to see him cheerful and happy, for what else had we to look up to? And I may here observe, that perhaps there never were three children who were fonder of each other; we did not, like other children, fight and dispute together; and if, by chance, any disagreement did arise between my elder brother and me, little Marcella would run to us, and kissing us both, seal, through her entreaties, the peace between us. Marcella was a lovely, amiable child; I can recall her beautiful features even now – Alas! poor little Marcella.'

'She is dead then?' observed Philip.

'Dead! Yes, dead! – but how did she die? – But I must not anticipate, Philip; let me tell my story.

'We waited for some time, but the report of the gun did not reach us, and my elder brother then said, 'Our father has followed the wolf, and will not be back for some time. Marcella, let us wash the blood from your mouth, and then we will leave this corner, and go to the fire and warm ourselves.'

'We did so, and remained there until near midnight, every minute wondering, as it grew later, why our father did not return. We had no idea that he was in any danger, but we thought that he must have chased the wolf for a very long time. 'I will look out and see if father is coming,' said my brother Caesar, going to the door.

'Take care,' said Marcella, 'the wolves must be about now, and we cannot kill them, brother.'

My brother opened the door very cautiously, and but a few inches; he peeped out. – 'I see nothing,' said he, after a time, and once more he joined us at the fire.

'We have had no supper,' said I, for my father usually cooked the meat as soon as he came home; and during his absence we had nothing but the fragments of the preceding day.

'And if our father comes home after his hunt, Caesar,' said Marcella, 'he will be pleased to have some supper; let us cook it for him and for ourselves.'

Caesar climbed upon the stool, and reached down some meat – I forget now whether it was venison or bear's meat; but we cut off the usual quantity, and proceeded to dress it, as we used to do under our father's superintendence. We were all busied putting it into the platters before the fire, to await his coming, when we heard the sound of a horn. We listened – there was a noise outside, and a minute afterwards my father entered, ushering in a young female, and a large dark man in a hunter's dress.

'Perhaps I had better now relate, what was only known to me many years afterwards. When my father had left the cottage, he perceived a large white wolf about thirty yards from him; as soon as the animal saw my father, it retreated slowly, growling and snarling. My father followed; the animal did not run, but always kept at some distance; and my father did not like to fire until he was pretty certain that his ball would take effect: thus they went on for some time, the wolf now leaving my father far behind, and then stopping and snarling defiance at him, and then again, on his approach, setting off at speed.

'Anxious to shoot the animal (for the white wolf is very rare), my father continued the pursuit for several hours, during which he continually ascended the mountain.

'You must know, Philip, that there are peculiar spots on those mountains which are supposed, and, as my story will prove, truly supposed, to be inhabited by the evil influences; they are well known to the huntsmen, who invariably avoid them. Now, one of these spots, an open space in the pine forests above us, had been pointed out to my father as dangerous on that account. But, whether he disbelieved these wild stories, or whether, in his eager pursuit of the chase, he disregarded them, I know not; certain, however, it is, that he was decoyed by the white wolf to this open space, when the animal appeared to slacken her speed. My father approached, came close up to her, raised his gun to his shoulder, and was about to fire; when the wolf suddenly disappeared. He thought that the snow on the ground must have dazzled his sight, and he let down his gun to look for the beast – but she was gone; how she could have escaped over the clearance, without his seeing her, was beyond his comprehension. Mortified at the ill success of his chase, he was about to retrace his steps, when he heard the distant sound of a horn. Astonishment at such a sound – at such an hour – in such a wilderness, made him forget for the moment his disappointment, and he remained riveted to the spot. In a minute the horn was blown a second time, and at no great distance; my father stood still, and listened: a third time it was blown. I forget the term used to express it, but it was the signal which, my father well knew, implied that the party was lost in the woods. In a few minutes more my father beheld a man on horseback, with a female seated on the crupper, enter the cleared space, and ride up to him. At first, my father called to mind the strange stories which he had heard of the supernatural beings who were said to frequent these mountains; but the nearer approach of the parties satisfied him that they were mortals like himself.

'As soon as they came up to him, the man who guided the horse accosted him. "Friend Hunter, you are out late, the better fortune for us: we have ridden far, and are in fear of our lives, which are eagerly sought after. These mountains have enabled us to elude our pursuers; but if we find not shelter and refreshment, that will avail us little, as we must perish from hunger and the inclemency of the night. My daughter, who rides behind me, is now more dead than alive, – say, can you assist us in our difficulty?"

' "My cottage is some few miles distant," replied my father, "but I have little to offer you besides a shelter from the weather; to the little I have you are welcome. May I ask whence you come?"

' "Yes, friend, it is no secret now; we have escaped from Transylvania, where my daughter's honour and my life were equally in jeopardy!"

'This information was quite enough to raise an interest in my father's heart. He remembered his own escape: he remembered the loss of his wife's honour, and the tragedy by which it was wound up. He immediately, and warmly, offered all the assistance which he could afford them.

' "There is no time to be lost, then, good sir," observed the horseman; "my daughter is chilled with the frost, and cannot hold out much longer against the severity of the weather."

' "Follow me," replied my father, leading the way towards his home. "I was lured away in pursuit of a large white wolf," observed my father; "it came to the very window of my hut, or I should not have been out at this time of night."

' "The creature passed by us just as we came out of the wood," said the female in a silvery tone.

' "I was nearly discharging my piece at it," observed the hunter; "but since it did us such good service, I am glad that I allowed it to escape."

'In about an hour and a half, during which my father walked at a rapid pace, the party arrived at the cottage, and, as I said before, came in.

' "We are in good time, apparently,' observed the dark hunter, catching the smell of the roasted meat, as he walked to the fire and surveyed my brother and sister, and myself. "You have young cooks here, Mynheer."

' "I am glad that we shall not have to wait," replied my father. "Come, mistress, seat yourself by the fire; you require warmth after your cold ride."

' "And where can I put up my horse, Mynheer?" observed the huntsman.'

' "I will take care of him," replied my father, going out of the cottage door.

'The female must, however, be particularly described. She was young, and apparently twenty years of age. She was dressed in a travelling dress, deeply bordered with white fur, and wore a cap of white ermine on her head. Her features were very beautiful, at least I thought so, and so my father has since declared. Her hair was flaxen, glossy and shining, and bright as a mirror; and her mouth, although somewhat large when it was open, showed the most brilliant teeth I have ever beheld. But there was something about her eyes, bright as they were, which made us children afraid; they were so restless, so furtive; I could not at that time tell why, but I felt as if there was cruelty in her eye; and when she beckoned us to come to her, we approached her with fear and trembling. Still she was beautiful, very beautiful. She spoke kindly to my brother and myself, patted our heads, and caressed us; but Marcella would not come near her; on the contrary, she slunk away, and hid herself in the bed, and would not wait for the supper, which half an hour before she had been so anxious for.

'My father, having put the horse into a close shed, soon returned, and supper was placed upon the table. When it was over, my father requested that the young lady would take possession of his bed, and he would remain at the fire, and sit up with her father. After some hesitation on her part, this arrangement was agreed to, and I and my brother crept into the other bed with Marcella, for we had as yet always slept together.

'But we could not sleep; there was something so unusual, not only in seeing strange people, but in having those people sleep at the cottage, that we were bewildered. As for poor little Marcella, she was quiet, but I perceived that she trembled during the whole night, and sometimes I thought that she was checking a sob. My father had brought out some spirits, which he rarely used, and he and the strange hunter remained drinking and talking before the fire. Our ears were ready to catch the slightest whisper – so much was our curiosity excited.

' "You said you came from Transylvania?" observed my father.

' "Even so, Mynheer," replied the hunter. "I was a serf to the noble house of — — ; my master would insist upon my surrendering up my fair girl to his wishes; it ended in my giving him a few inches of my hunting-knife."

' "We are countrymen, and brothers in misfortune," replied my father, taking the huntsman's hand, and pressing it warmly.

' "Indeed! Are you, then, from that country?"

' "Yes; and I too have fled for my life. But mine is a melancholy tale."

' "Your name?" inquired the hunter.

' "Krantz."

' "What! Krantz of — — ! I have heard your tale; you need not renew your grief by repeating it now. Welcome, most welcome, Mynheer, and, I may say, my worthy kinsman. I am your second cousin, Wilfred of Barnsdorf," cried the hunter, rising up and embracing my father.

'They filled their horn mugs to the brim, and drank to one another, after the German fashion. The conversation was then carried on in a low tone; all that we could collect from it was, that our new relative and his daughter were to take up their abode in our cottage, at least for the present. In about an hour they both fell back in their chairs, and appeared to sleep.

' "Marcella, dear, did you hear?" said my brother in a low tone.

' "Yes," replied Marcella, in a whisper; "I heard all. Oh! brother, I cannot bear to look upon that woman – I feel so frightened."

'My brother made no reply, and shortly afterwards we were all three fast asleep.

'When we awoke the next morning, we found that the hunter's daughter had risen before us. I thought she looked more beautiful than ever. She came up to little Marcella and caressed her; the child burst into tears, and sobbed as if her heart would break.

'But, not to detain you with too long a story, the huntsman and his daughter were accommodated in the cottage. My father and he went out hunting daily, leaving Christina with us. She performed all the household duties; was very kind to us children; and, gradually, the dislike even of little Marcella wore away. But a great change took place in my father; he appeared to have conquered his aversion to the sex, and was most attentive to Christina. Often, after her father and we were in bed, would he sit up with her, conversing in a low tone by the fire. I ought to have mentioned, that my father and the huntsman Wilfred, slept in another portion of the cottage, and that the bed which he formerly occupied, and which was in the same room as ours, had been given up to the use of Christina. These visitors had been about three weeks at the cottage, when, one night, after we children had been sent to bed, a consultation was held. My father had asked Christina in marriage, and had obtained both her own consent and that of Wilfred; after this a conversation took place, which was, as nearly as I can recollect, as follows –

' "You may take my child, Mynheer Krantz, and my blessing with her, and I shall then leave you and seek some other habitation – it matters little where."

' "Why not remain here, Wilfred?"

' "No, no, I am called elsewhere; let that suffice, and ask no more questions. You have my child."

' "I thank you for her, and will duly value her; but there is one difficulty."

' "I know what you would say; there is no priest here in this wild country: true; neither is there any law to bind; still must some ceremony pass between you, to satisfy a father. Will you consent to marry her after my fashion? if so, I will marry you directly."

' "I will," replied my father.

' "Then take her by the hand. Now, Mynheer, swear."

' "I swear," repeated my father.

' "By all the spirits of the Hartz Mountains – "

' "Nay, why not by Heaven?" interrupted my father.

' "Because it is not my humour," rejoined Wilfred; "if I prefer that oath, less binding perhaps, than another, surely you will not thwart me."

' "Well, be it so then; have your humour. Will you make me swear by that in which I do not believe?"

' "Yet many do so, who in outward appearance are Christians," rejoined Wilfred; "say, will you be married, or shall I take my daughter away with me?"

' "Proceed," replied my father, impatiently.

' "I swear by all the spirits of the Hartz Mountains, by all their power for good or for evil, that I take Christina for my wedded wife; that I will ever protect her, cherish her, and love her; that my hand shall never be raised against her to harm her."

'My father repeated the words after Wilfred.

' "And if I fail in this my vow, may all the vengeance of the spirits fall upon me and upon my children; may they perish by the vulture, by the wolf, or other beasts of the forest; may their flesh be torn from their limbs, and their bones blanch in the wilderness; all this I swear."

'My father hesitated, as he repeated the last words; little Marcella could not restrain herself, and as my father repeated the last sentence, she burst into tears. This sudden interruption appeared to discompose the party, particularly my father; he spoke harshly to the child, who controlled her sobs, burying her face under the bedclothes.

'Such was the second marriage of my father. The next morning, the hunter Wilfred mounted his horse, and rode away.

'My father resumed his bed, which was in the same room as ours; and things went on much as before the marriage, except that our new mother-in-law did not show any kindness towards us; indeed, during my father's absence, she would often beat us, particularly little Marcella, and her eyes would flash fire, as she looked eagerly upon the fair and lovely child.

'One night, my sister awoke me and my brother.

' "What is the matter?" said Caesar.

' "She has gone out," whispered Marcella.

' "Gone out!"

' "Yes, gone out at the door, in her night-clothes," replied the child; "I saw her get out of bed, look at my father to see if he slept, and then she went out at the door."

'What could induce her to leave her bed, and all undressed to go out, in such bitter wintry weather, with the snow deep on the ground, was to us incomprehensible; we lay awake, and in about an hour we heard the growl of a wolf, close under the window.

' "There is a wolf," said Caesar; "she will be torn to pieces."

' "Oh, no!" cried Marcella.

'In a few minutes afterwards our mother-in-law appeared; she was in her night-dress, as Marcella had stated. She let down the latch of the door, so as to make no noise, went to a pail of water, and washed her face and hands, and then slipped into the bed where my father lay.

'We all three trembled, we hardly knew why, but we resolved to watch the next night: we did so – and not only on the ensuing night, but on many others, and always at about the same hour, would our mother-in-law rise from her bed, and leave the cottage – and after she was gone, we invariably heard the growl of a wolf under our window, and always saw her, on her return, wash herself before she retired to bed. We observed, also, that she seldom sat down to meals, and that when she did, she appeared to eat with dislike; but when the meat was taken down, to be prepared for dinner, she would often furtively put a raw piece into her mouth.

'My brother Caesar was a courageous boy; he did not like to speak to my father until he knew more. He resolved that he would follow her out, and ascertain what she did. Marcella and I endeavoured to dissuade him from this project; but he would not be controlled, and the very next night he lay down in his clothes, and as soon as our mother-in-law had left the cottage, he jumped up, took down my father's gun, and followed her.

'You may imagine in what a state of suspense Marcella and I remained, during his absence. After a few minutes, we heard the report of a gun. It did not awaken my father, and we lay trembling with anxiety. In a minute afterwards we saw our mother-in-law enter the cottage – her dress was bloody. I put my hand to Marcella's mouth to prevent her crying out, although I was myself in great alarm. Our mother-in-law approached my father's bed, looked to see if he was asleep, and then went to the chimney, and blew up the embers into a blaze.

' "Who is there?" said my father, waking up.

' "Lie still, dearest," replied my mother-in-law, "it is only me; I have lighted the fire to warm some water; I am not quite well."

'My father turned round and was soon asleep; but we watched our mother-in-law. She changed her linen, and threw the garments she had worn into the fire; and we then perceived that her right leg was bleeding profusely, as if from a gunshot wound. She bandaged it up, and then dressing herself, remained before the fire until the break of day.

'Poor little Marcella, her heart beat quick as she pressed me to her side – so indeed did mine. Where was our brother, Caesar? How did my mother-in-law receive the wound unless from his gun? At last my father rose, and then, for the first time I spoke, saying, "Father, where is my brother, Caesar?"

' "Your brother!" exclaimed he, "why, where can he be?"

' "Merciful Heaven! I thought as I lay very restless last night," observed our mother-in-law, "that I heard somebody open the latch of the door; and, dear me, husband, what has become of your gun?"

'My father cast his eyes up above the chimney, and perceived that his gun was missing. For a moment he looked perplexed, then seizing a broad axe, he went out of the cottage without saying another word.

'He did not remain away from us long: in a few minutes he returned, bearing in his arms the mangled body of my poor brother; he laid it down, and covered up his face.

'My mother-in-law rose up, and looked at the body, while Marcella and I threw ourselves by its side wailing and sobbing bitterly.

' "Go to bed again, children," said she sharply. "Husband," continued she, "your boy must have taken the gun down to shoot a wolf, and the animal has been too powerful for him. Poor boy! he has paid dearly for his rashness."

'My father made no reply; I wished to speak – to tell all – but Marcella, who perceived my intention, held me by the arm, and looked at me so imploringly, that I desisted.

'My father, therefore, was left in his error; but Marcella and I, although we could not comprehend it, were conscious that our mother-in-law was in some way connected with my brother's death.

'That day my father went out and dug a grave, and when he laid the body in the earth, he piled up stones over it, so that the wolves should not be able to dig it up. The shock of this catastrophe was to my poor father very severe; for several days he never went to the chase, although at times he would utter bitter anathemas and vengeance against the wolves.

'But during this time of mourning on his part, my mother-in-law's nocturnal wanderings continued with the same regularity as before.

'At last, my father took down his gun, to repair to the forest; but he soon returned, and appeared much annoyed.

' "Would you believe it, Christina, that the wolves – perdition to the whole race – have actually contrived to dig up the body of my poor boy, and now there is nothing left of him but his bones?"

' "Indeed!" replied my mother-in-law. Marcella looked at me, and I saw in her intelligent eye all she would have uttered.

' "A wolf growls under our window every night, father," said I.

' "Aye, indeed? – Why did you not tell me, boy? – Wake me the next time you hear it."

'I saw my mother-in-law turn away; her eyes flashed fire, and she gnashed her teeth.

'My father went out again, and covered up with a larger pile of stones the little remnants of my poor brother which the wolves had spared. Such was the first act of the tragedy.

'The spring now came on: the snow disappeared, and we were permitted to leave the cottage; but never would I quit, for one moment, my dear little sister, to whom, since the death of my brother,

I was more ardently attached than ever; indeed I was afraid to leave her alone with my mother-in-law, who appeared to have a particular pleasure in ill-treating the child. My father was now employed upon his little farm, and I was able to render him some assistance.

'Marcella used to sit by us while we were at work, leaving my mother-in-law alone in the cottage. I ought to observe that, as the spring advanced, so did my mother-in-law decrease her nocturnal rambles, and that we never heard the growl of the wolf under the window after I had spoken of it to my father.

'One day, when my father and I were in the field, Marcella being with us, my mother-in-law came out, saying that she was going into the forest to collect some herbs my father wanted, and that Marcella must go to the cottage and watch the dinner. Marcella went, and my mother-in-law soon disappeared in the forest, taking a direction quite contrary to that in which the cottage stood, and leaving my father and I, as it were, between her and Marcella.

'About an hour afterwards we were startled by shrieks from the cottage, evidently the shrieks of little Marcella. "Marcella has burnt herself, father," said I, throwing down my spade. My father threw down his, and we both hastened to the cottage. Before we could gain the door, out darted a large white wolf, which fled with the utmost celerity. My father had no weapon; he rushed into the cottage, and there saw poor little Marcella expiring: her body was dreadfully mangled, and the blood pouring from it had formed a large pool on the cottage floor. My father's first intention had been to seize his gun and pursue, but he was checked by this horrid spectacle; he knelt down by his dying child, and burst into tears: Marcella could just look kindly on us for a few seconds, and then her eyes were closed in death.

'My father and I were still hanging over my poor sister's body, when my mother-in-law came in. At the dreadful sight she expressed much concern, but she did not appear to recoil from the sight of blood, as most women do.

'"Poor child!' said she, 'it must have been that great white wolf which passed me just now, and frightened me so – she's quite dead, Krantz."

'"I know it – I know it!" cried my father in agony.

'I thought my father would never recover from the effects of this second tragedy: he mourned bitterly over the body of his sweet child, and for several days would not consign it to its grave, although frequently requested by my mother-in-law to do so. At last he yielded, and dug a grave for her close by that of my poor brother, and took every precaution that the wolves should not violate her remains.

'I was now really miserable, as I lay alone in the bed which I had formerly shared with my brother and sister. I could not help thinking that my mother-in-law was implicated in both their deaths, although I could not account for the manner; but I no longer felt afraid of her: my little heart was full of hatred and revenge.

'The night after my sister had been buried, as I lay awake, I perceived my mother-in-law get up and go out of the cottage. I waited some time, then dressed myself, and looked out through the door, which I half opened. The moon shone bright, and I could see the spot where my brother and my sister had been buried; and what was my horror, when I perceived my mother-in-law busily removing the stones from Marcella's grave.

'She was in her white night-dress, and the moon shone full upon her. She was digging with her hands, and throwing away the stones behind her with all the ferocity of a wild beast. It was some time before I could collect my senses and decide what I should do. At last, I perceived that she had arrived at the body, and raised it up to the side of the grave. I could bear it no longer; I ran to my father and awoke him.

' "Father! father!" cried I, "dress yourself, and get your gun."

' "What!" cried my father, "the wolves are there, are they?"

'He jumped out of bed, threw on his clothes, and in his anxiety did not appear to perceive the absence of his wife. As soon as he was ready, I opened the door, he went out, and I followed him.

'Imagine his horror, when (unprepared as he was for such a sight) he beheld, as he advanced towards the grave, not a wolf, but his wife, in her night-dress, on her hands and knees, crouching by the body of my sister, and tearing off large pieces of the flesh, and devouring them with all the avidity of a wolf. She was too busy to be aware of our approach. My father dropped his gun, his hair stood on end; so did mine; he breathed heavily, and then his breath for a time stopped. I picked up the gun and put it into his hand. Suddenly he appeared as if concentrated rage had restored him to double vigour; he levelled his piece, fired, and with a loud shriek, down fell the wretch whom he had fostered in his bosom.

' "God of Heaven!" cried my father, sinking down upon the earth in a swoon, as soon as he had discharged his gun.

'I remained some time by his side before he recovered. "Where am I?" said he. "What has happened? – Oh! – yes, yes! I recollect now. Heaven forgive me!"

'He rose and we walked up to the grave; what again was our astonishment and horror to find that instead of the dead body of my mother-in-law, as we expected, there was lying over the remains of my poor sister, a large, white she-wolf.

' "The white wolf!" exclaimed my father, "the white wolf which decoyed me into the forest – I see it all now – I have dealt with the spirits of the Hartz Mountains."

'For some time my father remained in silence and deep thought. He then carefully lifted up the body of my sister, replaced it in the grave, and covered it over as before, having struck the head of the dead animal with the heel of his boot, and raving like a madman. He walked back to the cottage, shut the door, and threw himself on the bed; I did the same, for I was in a stupor of amazement.

'Early in the morning we were both roused by a loud knocking at the door, and in rushed the hunter Wilfred.

' "My daughter! – Man – my daughter! – where is my daughter!" cried he in a rage.

' "Where the wretch, the fiend, should be, I trust," replied my father, starting up and displaying equal choler; "where she should be – in hell! – Leave this cottage or you may fare worse."

' "Ha – ha!" replied the hunter, "would you harm a potent spirit of the Hartz Mountains. Poor mortal, who must needs wed a weir wolf."

' "Out demon! I defy thee and thy power."

' "Yet shall you feel it; remember your oath – your solemn oath – never to raise your hand against her to harm her."

' "I made no compact with evil spirits."

' "You did; and if you failed in your vow, you were to meet the vengeance of the spirits. Your children were to perish by the vulture, the wolf – "

' "Out, out, demon!"

' "And their bones blanch in the wilderness. Ha! – ha!"

'My father, frantic with rage, seized his axe, and raised it over Wilfred's head to strike.

' "All this I swear," continued the huntsman, mockingly.

'The axe descended; but it passed through the form of the hunter, and my father lost his balance, and fell heavily on the floor.

' "Mortal!" said the hunter, striding over my father's body, "we have power over those only who have committed murder. You have been guilty of a double murder – you shall pay the penalty attached to your marriage vow. Two of your children are gone; the third is yet to follow – and follow them he will, for your oath is registered. Go – it were kindness to kill thee – your punishment is – that you live!"

'With these words the spirit disappeared. My father rose from the floor, embraced me tenderly, and knelt down in prayer.

'The next morning he quitted the cottage for ever. He took me with him and bent his steps to Holland, where we safely arrived. He had some little money with him; but he had not been many days in Amsterdam before he was seized with a brain fever, and died raving mad. I was put into the Asylum, and afterwards was sent to sea before the mast. You now know all my history. The question is, whether I am to pay the penalty of my father's oath? I am myself perfectly convinced that, in some way or another, I shall.'

On the twenty-second day the high land of the south of Sumatra was in view; as there were no vessels in sight, they resolved to keep their course through the Straits, and run for Pulo Penang, which they expected, as their vessel laid so close to the wind, to reach in seven or eight days. By constant exposure, Philip and Krantz were now so bronzed, that with their long beards and Mussulman dresses, they might easily have passed off for natives. They had steered during the whole of the days exposed to a burning sun; they had lain down and slept in the dew of night, but their health had not suffered. But for several days, since he had confided the history of his family to Philip, Krantz had become silent and melancholy; his usual flow of spirits had vanished, and Philip had often questioned him as to the cause. As they entered the Straits, Philip talked of what they should do upon their arrival at Goa, when Krantz gravely replied, 'For some days, Philip, I have had a presentiment that I shall never see that city.'

'You are out of health, Krantz,' replied Philip.

'No; I am in sound health, body and mind. I have endeavoured to shake off the presentiment, but in vain; there is a warning voice that continually tells me that I shall not be long with you. Philip, will you oblige me by making me content on one point: I have gold about my person which may be useful to you; oblige me by taking it, and securing it on your own.'

'What nonsense, Krantz.'

'It is no nonsense, Philip. Have you not had your warnings? Why should I not have mine? You know that I have little fear in my composition, and that I care not about death; but I feel the presentiment which I speak of more strongly every hour. It is some kind spirit who would warn me to prepare for another world. Be it so.

I have lived long enough in this world to leave it without regret; although to part with you and Amine, the only two now dear to me, is painful, I acknowledge.'

'May not this arise from over-exertion and fatigue, Krantz? Consider how much excitement you have laboured under within these last four months. Is not that enough to create a corresponding depression? Depend upon it, my dear friend, such is the fact.'

'I wish it were – but I feel otherwise, and there is a feeling of gladness connected with the idea that I am to leave this world, arising from another presentiment, which equally occupies my mind.'

'Which is?'

'I hardly can tell you; but Amine and you are connected with it. In my dreams I have seen you meet again; but it has appeared to me, as if a portion of your trial was purposely shut from my sight in dark clouds; and I have asked, "May not I see what is there concealed?" – and an invisible has answered, "No! 'twould make you wretched. Before these trials take place, you will be summoned away" – and then I have thanked Heaven, and felt resigned.'

'These are the imaginings of a disturbed brain, Krantz; that I am destined to suffering may be true; but why Amine should suffer, or why you, young, in full health and vigour, should not pass your days in peace, and live to a good old age, there is no cause for believing. You will be better tomorrow.'

'Perhaps so,' replied Krantz; – 'but still you must yield to my whim, and take the gold. If I am wrong, and we do arrive safe, you know, Philip, you can let me have it back,' observed Krantz, with a faint smile – 'but you forget, our water is nearly out, and we must look out for a rill on the coast to obtain a fresh supply.'

'I was thinking of that when you commenced this unwelcome topic. We had better look out for the water before dark, and as soon as we have replenished our jars, we will make sail again.'

At the time that this conversation took place, they were on the eastern side of the Strait, about forty miles to the northward. The interior of the coast was rocky and mountainous, but it slowly descended to low land of alternate forest and jungles, which continued to the beach: the country appeared to be uninhabited. Keeping close in to the shore, they discovered, after two hours' run, a fresh stream which burst in a cascade from the mountains, and swept its devious course through the jungle, until it poured its tribute into the waters of the Strait.

They ran close in to the mouth of the stream, lowered the sails, and pulled the peroqua against the current, until they had advanced far enough to assure them that the water was quite fresh. The jars were soon filled, and they were again thinking of pushing off; when, enticed by the beauty of the spot, the coolness of the fresh water, and wearied with their long confinement on board of the peroqua, they proposed to bathe – a luxury hardly to be appreciated by those who have not been in a similar situation. They threw off their Mussulman dresses, and plunged into the stream, where they remained for some time. Krantz was the first to get out; he complained of feeling chilled, and he walked on to the banks where their clothes had been laid. Philip also approached nearer to the beach, intending to follow him.

'And now, Philip,' said Krantz, 'this will be a good opportunity for me to give you the money. I will open my sash, and pour it out, and you can put it into your own before you put it on.'

Philip was standing in the water, which was about level with his waist.

'Well, Krantz,' said he, 'I suppose if it must be so, it must; but it appears to me an idea so ridiculous – however, you shall have your own way.'

Philip quitted the run, and sat down by Krantz, who was already busy in shaking the doubloons out of the folds of his sash; at last he said – 'I believe, Philip, you have got them all, now? – I feel satisfied.'

'What danger there can be to you, which I am not equally exposed to, I cannot conceive,' replied Philip; 'however – '

Hardly had he said these words, when there was a tremendous roar – a rush like a mighty wind through the air – a blow which threw him on his back – a loud cry – and a contention. Philip recovered himself, and perceived the naked form of Krantz carried off with the speed of an arrow by an enormous tiger through the jungle. He watched with distended eyeballs; in a few seconds the animal and Krantz had disappeared!

'God of Heaven! Would that Thou hadst spared me this,' cried Philip, throwing himself down in agony on his face. 'Oh! Krantz, my friend – my brother – too sure was your presentiment. Merciful God! have pity – but Thy will be done;' and Philip burst into a flood of tears.

For more than an hour did he remain fixed upon the spot, careless and indifferent to the danger by which he was surrounded. At last, somewhat recovered, he rose, dressed himself, and then again sat down – his eyes fixed upon the clothes of Krantz, and the gold which still lay on the sand.

'He would give me that gold. He foretold his doom. Yes! yes! it was his destiny, and it has been fulfilled. *His bones will bleach in the wilderness*, and the spirit-hunter and his wolfish daughter are avenged.'

The White Wolf of Kostopchin

SIR GILBERT CAMPBELL

A wide sandy expanse of country, flat and uninteresting in appearance, with a great staring whitewashed house standing in the midst of wide fields of cultivated land, whilst far away were the low sandhills and pine forests to be met with in the district of Lithuania, in Russian Poland. Not far from the great white house was the village in which the serfs dwelt, with the large bakehouse and the public bath which are invariably to be found in all Russian villages, however humble. The fields were negligently cultivated, the hedges broken down and the fences in bad repair; shattered agricultural implements had been carelessly flung aside in remote corners, and the whole estate showed the want of the superintending eye of an energetic master. The great white house was no better looked after, the garden was an utter wilderness, great patches of plaster had fallen from the walls, and many of the Venetian shutters were almost off the hinges. Over all was the dark lowering sky of a Russian autumn, and there were no signs of life to be seen, save a few peasants lounging idly towards the vodka shop, and a gaunt halt-starved cat creeping stealthily abroad in quest of a meal.

The estate, which was known by the name of Kostopchin, was the property of Paul Sergevitch, a gentleman of means, and the most discontented man in Russian Poland. Like most wealthy Muscovites, he had travelled much, and had spent the gold which had been amassed by serf labour, like water, in all the dissolute revelries of the capitals of Europe. Paul's figure was as well known in the boudoirs of the *demi-mondaines* as his face was familiar at the public gaming tables. He appeared to have no thought for the future, but only to live in the excitement of the mad career of dissipation which he was pursuing. His means, enormous as they were, were all forestalled, and he was continually sending to his intendant for fresh supplies of money. His fortune would not have long held out against the constant inroads that were being made upon it, when an unexpected circumstance took place which stopped his career like a flash of lightning. This was a fatal duel, in which a young man of great promise, the son of the prime minister of the country in which he then resided, fell by his hand. Representations were made to the Tsar, and Paul Sergevitch was recalled, and, after receiving a severe reprimand was ordered to return to his estates in Lithuania. Horribly discontented, yet not daring to disobey the Imperial mandate, Paul buried himself at Kostopchin, a place he had not visited since his boyhood. At first he endeavoured to interest himself in the workings of the vast estate; but agriculture had no charm for him, and the only result was that he quarrelled with and dismissed his German intendant, replacing him by an old serf, Michal Vassilitch, who had been his father's valet. Then he took to wandering about the country, gun in hand, and upon his return home would sit moodily drinking brandy and smoking innumerable cigarettes, as he cursed his lord and master, the emperor, for consigning him to such a course of dullness and ennui. For a couple of years he led this aimless life, and at last, hardly knowing the reason for so doing, he married the daughter of a neighbouring landed proprietor. The marriage was a most unhappy one; the girl had really never cared for Paul, but had married him in obedience to her father's mandates, and the man, whose temper was always brutal and violent, treated her, after a brief interval of contemptuous indifference, with savage cruelty. After three years the unhappy woman expired, leaving behind her two children – a boy, Alexis, and a girl, Katrina. Paul treated his wife's death with the most perfect indifference; but he did not put anyone in her place. He was very fond of the little Katrina, but did not take much notice of the boy, and resumed his lonely wanderings about the country with dog and gun. Five years had passed since the death of his wife. Alexis was a fine, healthy boy of seven, whilst Katrina was some eighteen months younger. Paul was lighting one of his eternal cigarettes at the door of his house, when the little girl came running up to him.

'You bad, wicked papa,' said she. 'How is it that you have never brought me the pretty grey squirrels that you promised I should have the next time you went to the forest?'

'Because I have never yet been able to find any, my treasure,' returned her father, taking up his child in his arms and half smothering her with kisses. 'Because I have not found them yet, my golden queen; but I am bound to find Ivanovitch, the poacher, smoking about the woods, and if he can't show me where they are, no-one can.'

'Ah, little father,' broke in old Michal, using the term of address with which a Russian of humble position usually accosts his superior; 'Ah, little father, take care; you will go to those woods once too often.'

'Do you think I am afraid of Ivanovitch?' returned his master, with a coarse laugh. 'Why, he and I are the best of friends; at any rate, if he robs me, he does so openly, and keeps other poachers away from my woods.'

'It is not of Ivanovitch that I am thinking,' answered the old man. 'But oh! Gospodin, do not go into these dark solitudes; there are terrible tales told about them, of witches that dance in the moonlight, of strange, shadowy forms that are seen amongst the trunks of the tall pines, and of whispered voices that tempt the listeners to eternal perdition.'

Again the rude laugh of the lord of the manor rang out, as Paul observed, 'If you go on addling your brain, old man, with these nearly half-forgotten legends, I shall have to look out for a new intendant.'

'But I was not thinking of these fearful creatures only,' returned Michal, crossing himself piously. 'It was against the wolves that I meant to warn you.'

'Oh, father, dear, I am frightened now,' whimpered little Katrina, hiding her head on her father's shoulder. 'Wolves are such cruel, wicked things.'

'See there, greybearded dotard,' cried Paul, furiously, 'you have terrified this sweet angel by your farrago of lies; besides, who ever heard of wolves so early as this? You are dreaming, Michal Vassilitch, or have taken your morning dram of vodka too strong.'

'As I hope for future happiness,' answered the old man, solemnly, 'as I came through the marsh last night from Kosma the herdsman's cottage – you know, my lord, that he has been bitten by a viper, and is seriously ill – as I came through the marsh, I repeat, I saw something like sparks of fire in the clump of alders on the right-hand side. I was anxious to know what they could be, and cautiously moved a little nearer, recommending my soul to the protection of Saint Vladimir. I had not gone a couple of paces when a wild howl came that chilled the very marrow of my bones, and a pack of some ten or a dozen wolves, gaunt and famished as you see them, my lord, in the winter, rushed out. At their head was a white she-wolf, as big as any of the male ones, with gleaming tusks and a pair of yellow eyes that blazed with lurid fire. I had round my neck a crucifix that had been given me by the priest of Streletza, and the savage beasts knew this and broke away across the marsh, sending up the mud and water in showers in the air; but the white she-wolf, little father, circled round me three times, as though endeavouring to find some place from which to attack me. Three times she did this, and then, with a snap of her teeth and a howl of impotent malice, she galloped away some fifty yards and sat down, watching my every movement with her fiery eyes. I did not delay any longer in so dangerous a spot, as you may well imagine, Gospodin, but walked hurriedly home, crossing myself at every step; but, as I am a living man, that white devil followed me the whole distance, keeping fifty paces in the rear, and every now and then licking her lips with a sound that made my flesh creep. When I got to the last fence before you come to the house I raised up my voice and shouted for the dogs, and soon I heard the deep bay of Troska and Bransköe as they came bounding towards me. The white devil heard it, too, and, giving a high bound into the air, she uttered a loud howl of disappointment, and trotted back leisurely towards the marsh.'

'But why did you not set the dogs after her?' asked Paul, interested, in spite of himself, at the old man's narrative. 'In the open Troska and Bransköe would run down any wolf that ever set foot to the ground in Lithuania.'

'I tried to do so, little father,' answered the old man, solemnly; 'but directly they got up to the spot where the beast had executed her last devilish gambol, they put their tails between their legs and ran back to the house as fast as their legs could carry them.'

'Strange,' muttered Paul, thoughtfully. 'That is, if it is truth and not vodka that is speaking.'

'My lord,' returned the old man, reproachfully, 'man and boy, I have served you and my lord your father for fifty years, and no-one can say that they ever saw Michal Vassilitch the worse for liquor.'

'No-one doubts that you are a sly old thief, Michal,' returned his master, with his coarse, jarring laugh; 'but for all that, your long stories of having been followed by white wolves won't prevent me from going to the forest today. A couple of good buckshot cartridges will break any spell, though I don't think that the she-wolf, if she existed any-where other than in your own imagination, has anything to do with magic. Don't be frightened, Katrina, my pet; you shall have a fine white wolf skin to put your feet on, if what this old fool says is right.'

'Michal is not a fool,' pouted the child, 'and it is very wicked of you to call him so. I don't want any nasty wolf skins, I want the grey squirrels.'

And you shall have them, my precious,' returned her father, setting her down upon the ground. 'Be a good girl, and I will not be long away.'

'Father,' said the little Alexis, suddenly, 'let me go with you. I should like to see you kill a wolf, and then I should know how to do so, when I grow older and taller.'

'Pshaw,' returned his father, irritably. 'Boys are always in the way. Take the lad away, Michal; don't you see that he is worrying his sweet little sister?'

'No, no, he does not worry me at all,' answered the impetuous little lady, as she flew to her brother and covered him with kisses. 'Michal, you shan't take him away, do you hear?'

'There, there, leave the children together,' returned Paul, as he shouldered his gun, and kissing the tips of his fingers to Katrina, stepped away rapidly in the direction of the dark pine woods. Paul walked on, humming the fragment of an air that he had heard in a very different place many years ago. A strange feeling of elation crept over him, very different to the false excitement which his solitary drinking bouts were wont to produce. A change seemed to have come over his whole life, the skies looked brighter, the spiculae of the pine trees of a more vivid green, and the landscape seemed to have lost that dull cloud of depression which had for years appeared to hang over it. And beneath all this exaltation of the mind, beneath all this unlooked-for promise of a more happy future, lurked a heavy, inexplicable feeling of a power to come, a something without form or shape, and yet the more terrible because it was shrouded by that thick veil which conceals from the eyes of the soul the strange fantastic designs of the dwellers beyond the line of earthly influences.

There were no signs of the poacher, and wearied with searching for him, Paul made the woods reëcho with his name. The great dog, Troska, which had followed his master, looked up wistfully into his face, and at a second repetition of the name 'Ivanovitch', uttered a long plaintive howl, and then, looking round at Paul as though entreating him to follow, moved slowly ahead towards a denser portion of the forest. A little mystified at the hound's unusual proceedings, Paul followed, keeping his gun ready to fire at the least sign of danger. He thought that he knew the forest well, but the dog led the way to a portion which he never remembered to have visited before. He had got away from the pine trees now, and had entered a dense thicket formed of stunted oaks and hollies. The great dog kept only a yard or so ahead; his lips were drawn back, showing the strong white fangs, the hair upon his neck and back was bristling, and his tail firmly pressed between his hind legs. Evidently the animal was in a state of the most extreme terror, and yet it proceeded bravely forward. Struggling through the dense thicket, Paul suddenly found himself in an open space of some ten or twenty yards in diameter. At one end of it was a slimy pool, into the waters of which several strange-looking reptiles glided as the man and dog made their appearance. Almost in the centre of the opening was a shattered stone cross, and at its base lay a dark heap, close to which Troska stopped, and again raising his head, uttered a long melancholy howl. For an instant or two, Paul gazed hesitatingly at the shapeless heap that lay beneath the cross, and then, mustering up all his courage, he stepped forwards and bent anxiously over it. Once glance was enough, for he recognised the body of Ivanovitch the poacher, hideously mangled. With a cry of surprise, he turned over the body and shuddered as he gazed upon the terrible injuries that had been inflicted. The unfortunate man had evidently been attacked by some savage beast, for there were marks of teeth upon the throat, and the jugular vein had been almost torn out. The breast of the corpse had been torn open, evidently by long sharp claws, and there was a gaping orifice upon the left side, round which the blood had formed in a thick coagulated patch. The only animals to be found in the forests of Russia capable of inflicting such wounds are the bear or the wolf, and the question as to the class of the assailant was easily settled by a glance at the dank ground, which showed the prints of a wolf so entirely different from the plantigrade traces of the bear.

'Savage brutes,' muttered Paul. 'So, after all, there may have been some truth in Michal's story, and the old idiot may for once in his life have spoken the truth. Well, it is no concern of mine, and if a fellow chooses to wander about the woods at night to kill my game, instead of remaining in his own hovel, he must take his chance. The strange thing is that the brutes have not eaten him, though they have mauled him so terribly.'

He turned away as he spoke, intending to return home and send out some of the serfs to bring in the body of the unhappy man, when his eye was caught by a small white object, hanging from a bramble bush near the pond. He made towards the spot, and taking up the object, examined it curiously. It was a tuft of coarse white hair, evidently belonging to some animal.'

'A wolf's hair, or I am much mistaken,' muttered Paul, pressing the hair between his fingers, and then applying it to his nose. 'And from its colour, I should think that it belonged to the white lady who so terribly alarmed old Michal on the occasion of his night walk through the marsh.'

Paul found it no easy task to retrace his steps towards those parts of the forest with which he was acquainted, and Troska seemed unable to render him the slightest assistance, but followed moodily behind. Many times Paul found his way blocked by impenetrable thicket or dangerous quagmire, and during his many wanderings he had the ever-present sensation that there was a something close to him, an invisible something, a noiseless something, but for all that a presence which moved as he advanced, and halted as he stopped in vain to listen. The certainty that an impalpable thing of some shape or other was close at hand grew so strong, that as the short autumn day began to close, and darker shadows to fall between the trunks of the lofty trees, it made him hurry on at his utmost speed. At length, when he had grown almost mad with terror, he suddenly came upon a path he knew, and with a feeling of intense relief, he stepped briskly forward in the direction of Kostopchin. As he left the forest and came into the open country, a faint wail seemed to ring through the darkness; but Paul's nerves had been so much shaken that he did not know whether this was an actual fact or only the offspring of his own excited fancy. As he crossed the neglected lawn that lay in front of the house, old Michal came rushing out of the house with terror convulsing every feature.

'Oh, my lord, my lord!' gasped he, 'is not this too terrible?'

'Nothing has happened to my Katrina?' cried the father, a sudden sickly feeling of terror passing through his heart.

'No, no, the little lady is quite safe, thanks to the Blessed Virgin and Saint Alexander of Nevskoi,' returned Michal; 'but oh, my lord, poor Marta, the herd's daughter – '

'Well, what of the slut?' demanded Paul, for now that his moment-ary fear for the safety of his daughter had passed away, he had but little sympathy to spare for so insignificant a creature as a serf girl.

'I told you that Kosma was dying,' answered Michal. 'Well, Marta went across the marsh this afternoon to fetch the priest, but alas! she never came back.'

'What detained her, then?' asked his master.

'One of the neighbours, going in to see how Kosma was getting on, found the poor old man dead; his face was terribly contorted, and he was half in the bed, and half out, as though he had striven to reach the door. The man ran to the village to give the alarm, and as the men returned to the herdsman's hut, they found the body of Marta in a thicket by the clump of alders on the marsh.'

'Her body – she was dead then?' asked Paul.

'Dead, my lord; killed by wolves,' answered the old man. 'And oh, my lord, it is too horrible, her breast was horribly lacerated, and her heart had been taken out and eaten, for it was nowhere to be found.'

Paul started, for the horrible mutilation of the body of Ivanovitch the poacher occurred to his recollection.

'And, my lord,' continued the old man, 'this is not all; on a bush close by was this tuft of hair,' and, as he spoke, he took it from a piece of paper in which it was wrapped and handed it to his master.

Paul took it and recognised a similar tuft of hair to that which he had seen upon the bramble bush beside the shattered cross.

'Surely, my lord,' continued Michal, not heeding his master's look of surprise, 'you will have out men and dogs to hunt down this terrible creature, or, better still, send for the priest and holy water, for I have my doubts whether the creature belongs to this earth.'

Paul shuddered, and, after a short pause, he told Michal of the ghastly end of Ivanovitch the poacher.

The old man listened with the utmost excitement, crossing himself repeatedly, and muttering invocations to the Blessed Virgin and the saints every instant; but his master would no longer listen to him, and, ordering him to place brandy on the table, sat drinking moodily until daylight.

The next day a fresh horror awaited the inhabitants of Kostopchin. An old man, a confirmed drunkard, had staggered out of the vodka shop with the intention of returning home; three hours later he was found at a turn of the road, horribly scratched and mutilated, with the same gaping orifice in the left side of the breast, from which the heart had been forcibly torn out.

Three several times in the course of the week the same ghastly tragedy occurred – a little child, an able-bodied labourer, and an old woman, were all found with the same terrible marks of mutilation upon them, and in every case the same tuft of white hair was found in the immediate vicinity of the bodies. A frightful panic ensued, and an excited crowd of serfs surrounded the house at Kostopchin, calling upon their master, Paul Sergevitch, to save them from the fiend that had been let loose upon them, and shouting out various remedies, which they insisted upon being carried into effect at once.

Paul felt a strange disinclination to adopt any active measures. A certain feeling which he could not account for urged him to remain quiescent; but the Russian serf when suffering under an access of superstitious terror is a dangerous person to deal with, and, with extreme reluctance, Paul Sergevitch issued instructions for a thorough search through the estate, and a general *battue* of the pine woods.

The army of beaters convened by Michal was ready with the first dawn of sunrise, and formed a strange and almost grotesque-looking assemblage, armed with rusty old firelocks, heavy bludgeons, and scythes fastened on to the end of long poles. Paul, with his double-barrelled gun thrown across his shoulder and a keen hunting knife thrust into his belt, marched at the head of the serfs, accompanied by the two great hounds, Troska and Bransköe. Every nook and corner of the hedgerows were examined, and the little outlying clumps were thoroughly searched, but without success; and at last a circle was formed round the larger portion of the forest, and with loud shouts, blowing of horns, and beating of copper cooking utensils, the crowd of eager serfs pushed their way through the brushwood. Frightened birds flew up, whirring through the pine branches; hares and rabbits darted from their hiding places behind tufts and hummocks of grass, and scurried away in the utmost terror. Occasionally a roe deer rushed through the thicket, or a wild boar burst through the thin lines of beaters, but no signs of wolves were to be seen. The circle grew narrower and yet more narrow, when all at once a wild shriek and a confused murmur of voices echoed through the pine trees. All rushed to the spot, and a young lad was discovered weltering in his blood and terribly mutilated, though life still lingered in the mangled frame. A few drops of vodka were poured down the throat, and he managed to gasp out that the white wolf had sprung upon him suddenly, and, throwing him to the ground, had commenced tearing at the flesh over his heart. He would inevitably have been killed, had not the animal quitted him, alarmed by the approach of the other beaters.

'The beast ran into that thicket,' gasped the boy, and then once more relapsed into a state on insensibility.

But the words of the wounded boy had been eagerly passed round, and a hundred different propositions were made.

'Set fire to the thicket,' exclaimed one.

'Fire a volley into it,' suggested another.

'A bold dash in, and trample the beast's life out,' shouted a third.

The first proposal was agreed to, and a hundred eager hands collected dried sticks and leaves, and then a light was kindled. Just as the fire was about to be applied, a soft, sweet voice issued from the centre of the thicket.

'Do not set fire to the forest, my dear friends; give me time to come out. Is it not enough for me to have been frightened to death by that awful creature?'

All started back in amazement, and Paul felt a strange, sudden thrill pass through his heart as those soft musical accents fell upon his ear.

There was a light rustling in the brushwood, and then a vision suddenly appeared, which filled the souls of the beholders with surprise. As the bushes divided, a fair woman, wrapped in a mantle of soft white fur, with a fantastically shaped travelling cap of green velvet upon her head, stood before them. She was exquisitely fair, and her long Titian red hair hung in dishevelled masses over her shoulders.

'My good man,' began she, with a certain tinge of aristocratic hauteur in her voice, 'is your master here?'

As moved by a spring, Paul stepped forward and mechanically raised his cap.

'I am Paul Sergevitch,' said he, 'and these woods are on my estate of Kostopchin. A fearful wolf has been committing a series of terrible devastations upon my people, and we have been endeavouring to hunt it down. A boy whom he has just wounded says that he ran into the thicket from which you have just emerged, to the surprise of us all.'

'I know,' answered the lady, fixing her clear, steel-blue eyes keenly upon Paul's face. 'The terrible beast rushed past me, and dived into a large cavity in the earth in the very centre of the thicket. It was a huge white wolf, and I greatly feared that it would devour me.'

'Ho, my men,' cried Paul, 'take spade and mattock, and dig out the monster, for she has come to the end of her tether at last. Madam, I do not know what chance has conducted you to this wild solitude, but the hospitality of Kostopchin is at your disposal, and I will, with your permission, conduct you there as soon as this scourge of the countryside has been dispatched.'

He offered his hand with some remains of his former courtesy, but started back with an expression of horror on his face.

'Blood,' cried he; 'why, madam, your hand and fingers are stained with blood.'

A faint colour rose to the lady's cheek, but it died away in an instant as she answered, with a faint smile: 'The dreadful creature was all covered with blood, and I suppose I must have stained my hands against the bushes through which it had passed, when I parted them in order to escape from the fiery death with which you threatened me.'

There was a ring of suppressed irony in her voice, and Paul felt his eyes drop before the glance of those cold steel-blue eyes. Meanwhile, urged to the utmost exertion by their fears, the serfs plied spade and mattock with the utmost vigour. The cavity was speedily enlarged, but, when a depth of eight feet had been attained, it was found to terminate in a little burrow not large enough to admit a rabbit, much less a creature of the white wolf's size. There were none of the tufts of white hair which had hitherto been always found beside the bodies of the victims, nor did that peculiar rank odour which always indicates the presence of wild animals hang about the spot.

The superstitious Muscovites crossed themselves, and scrambled out of the hole with grotesque alacrity. The mysterious disappearance of the monster which had committed such frightful ravages had cast a chill over the hearts of the ignorant peasants, and, unheeding the shouts of their master, they left the forest, which seemed to be overcast with the gloom of some impending calamity.

'Forgive the ignorance of these boors, madam,' said Paul, when he found himself alone with the strange lady, 'and permit me to escort you to my poor house, for you must have need of rest and refreshment, and – '

Here Paul checked himself abruptly, and a dark flush of embarrassment passed over his face.

'And,' said the lady, with the same faint smile, 'and you are dying with curiosity to know how I suddenly made my appearance from a thicket in your forest. You say that you are the lord of Kostopchin; then you are Paul Sergevitch, and should surely know how the ruler of Holy Russia takes upon himself to interfere with the doings of his children?'

'You know me, then?' exclaimed Paul, in some surprise.

'Yes, I have lived in foreign lands, as you have, and have heard your name often. Did you not break the bank at Blankburg? Did you not carry off Isola Menuti, the dancer, from a host of competitors; and, as a last instance of my knowledge, shall I recall to your memory a certain morning, on a sandy shore, with two men facing each other pistol in hand, the one young, fair, and boyish-looking, hardly twenty-two years of age, the other – '

'Hush!' exclaimed Paul, hoarsely; 'you evidently know me, but who in the fiend's name are you?'

'Simply a woman who once moved in society and read the papers, and who is now a hunted fugitive.'

'A fugitive!' returned Paul, hotly; 'who dares to persecute you?'

The lady moved a little closer to him, and then whispered in his ear: 'The police!'

'The police!' repeated Paul, stepping back a pace or two. 'The police!'

'Yes, Paul Sergevitch, the police,' returned the lady, 'that body at the mention of which it is said the very Emperor trembles as he sits in his gilded chambers in the Winter Palace. Yes, I have had the imprudence to speak my mind too freely, and – well, you know what women have to dread who fall into the hands of the police in Holy Russia. To avoid such infamous degradations I fled, accompanied by a faithful domestic. I fled in hopes of gaining the frontier, but a few versts from here a body of mounted police rode up. My poor old servant had the imprudence to resist, and was shot dead. Half wild with terror I fled into the forest, and wandered about until I heard the noise your serfs made in the beating of the woods. I thought it was the police, who had organised a search for me, and I crept into the thicket for the purpose of concealment. The rest you know. And now, Paul Sergevitch, tell me whether you dare give shelter to a proscribed fugitive such as I am.'

'Madam,' returned Paul, gazing into the clear-cut features before him, glowing with the animation of the recital, 'Kostopchin is ever open to misfortune – and beauty,' added he, with a bow.

'Ah!' cried the lady, with a laugh in which there was something sinister; 'I expect that misfortune would knock at your door for a long time, if it was unaccompanied by beauty. However, I thank you, and will accept your hospitality; but if evil come upon you, remember that I am not to be blamed.'

'You will be safe enough at Kostopchin,' returned Paul. 'The police won't trouble their heads about me; they know that since the Emperor drove me to lead this hideous existence, politics have no charm for me, and that the brandy bottle is the only charm of my life.'

'Dear me,' answered the lady, eyeing him uneasily, 'a morbid drunkard, are you? Well, as I am half perished with cold, suppose you take me to Kostopchin; you will be conferring a favour on me, and will get back all the sooner to your favourite brandy.'

She placed her hand upon Paul's arm as she spoke, and mechanically he led the way to the great solitary white house. The few servants betrayed no astonishment at the appearance of the lady, for some of the serfs on their way back to the village had spread the report of the sudden appearance of the mysterious stranger; besides, they were not accustomed to question the acts of their somewhat arbitrary master.

Alexis and Katrina had gone to bed, and Paul and his guest sat down to a hastily improvised meal.

'I am no great eater,' remarked the lady, as she played with the food before her; and Paul noticed with surprise that scarcely a morsel passed her lips, though she more than once filled and emptied a goblet of the champagne which had been opened in honour of her arrival.

'So it seems,' remarked he; 'and I do not wonder, for the food in this benighted hole is not what either you or I have been accustomed to.'

'Oh, it does well enough,' returned the lady, carelessly. 'And now, if you have such a thing as a woman in the establishment, you can let her show me to my room, for I am nearly dead for want of sleep.'

Paul struck a hand-bell that stood on the table beside him, and the stranger rose from her seat, and with a brief 'Good night', was moving towards the door, when the old man Michal suddenly made his appearance on the threshold. The aged intendant started backwards as though to avoid a heavy blow, and his fingers at once sought for the crucifix which he wore suspended round his neck, and on whose protection he relied to shield him from the powers of darkness.

'Blessed Virgin!' he exclaimed. 'Holy Saint Radislas protect me, where have I seen her before?'

The lady took no notice of the old man's evident terror, but passed away down the echoing corridor.

The old man now timidly approached his master, who, after swallowing a glass of brandy, had drawn his chair up to the stove, and was gazing moodily at its polished surface.

'My lord,' said Michal, venturing to touch his master's shoulder, 'is that the lady that you found in the forest?'

'Yes,' returned Paul, a smile breaking out over his face; 'she is very beautiful, is she not?'

'Beautiful!' repeated Michal, crossing himself, 'she may have beauty, but it is that of a demon. Where have I seen her before? – Where have I seen those shining teeth and those cold eyes? She is not like anyone here, and I have never been ten versts from Kostopchin in my life. I am utterly bewildered. Ah, I have it, the dying herdsman – save the mark! Gospodin, have a care. I tell you that the strange lady is the image of the white wolf.'

'You old fool,' returned his master, savagely, 'let me ever hear you repeat such nonsense again, and I will have you skinned alive. The lady is high-born, and of good family; beware how you insult her. Nay, I give you further commands: see that during her sojourn here she is treated with the utmost respect. And communicate this to all the servants. Mind, no more tales about the vision that your addled brain conjured up of wolves in the marsh, and above all do not let me hear that you have been alarming little Katrina with your senseless babble.'

The old man bowed humbly, and, after a short pause, remarked: 'The lad that was injured at the hunt today is dead, my lord.'

'Oh, dead is he, poor wretch!' returned Paul, to whom the death of a serf lad was not a matter of overweening importance. 'But look here, Michal, remember that if any inquiries are made about the lady, that no-one knows anything about her; that, in fact, no-one has seen her at all.'

'Your lordship shall be obeyed,' answered the old man; and then, seeing that his master had relapsed into his former moody reverie, he left the room, crossing himself at every step he took.

Late into the night Paul sat up thinking over the occurrences of the day. He had told Michal that his guest was of noble family, but in reality he knew nothing more of her than she had condescended to tell him.'

'Why, I don't even know her name,' muttered he; 'and yet somehow or other it seems as if a new feature of my life was opening before me. However, I have made one step in advance by getting her here, and if she talks about leaving, why, all that I have to do is threaten her with the police.'

After his usual custom he smoked cigarette after cigarette, and poured out copious tumblers of brandy. The attendant serf replenished the stove from a small den which opened into the corridor, and after a time Paul slumbered heavily in his armchair. He was aroused by a light touch upon the shoulder, and, starting up, saw the stranger of the forest standing by his side.

'This is indeed kind of you,' said she, with her usual mocking smile. 'You felt that I should be strange here, and you got up early to see to the horses, or can it really be, those ends of cigarettes, that empty bottle of brandy? Paul Sergevitch, you have not been to bed at all.'

Paul muttered a few indistinct words in reply, and then, ringing the bell furiously, ordered the servant to clear away the débris of last night's orgy, and lay the table for breakfast; then, with a hasty apology, he left the room to make a fresh toilet, and in about half an hour returned with his appearance sensibly improved by his ablutions and change of dress.

'I dare say,' remarked the lady, as they were seated at the morning meal, for which she manifested the same indifference that she had for the dinner of the previous evening, 'that you would like to know my name and who I am. Well, I don't mind telling you my name. It is Ravina, but as to my family and who I am, it will perhaps be best for you to remain in ignorance. A matter of policy, my dear Paul Sergevitch, a mere matter of policy, you see. I leave you to judge from my manners and appearance whether I am of sufficiently good form to be invited to the honour of your table – '

'None more worthy,' broke in Paul, whose bemuddled brain was fast succumbing to the charms of his guest; 'and surely that is a question upon which I may be deemed a competent judge.'

'I do not know about that,' returned Ravina, 'for from all accounts the company that you used to keep was not of the most select character.'

'No, but hear me,' began Paul, seizing her hand and endeavouring to carry it to his lips. But as he did so an unpleasant chill passed over him, for those slender fingers were icy cold.

'Do not be foolish,' said Ravina, drawing away her hand, after she had permitted it to rest for an instant in Paul's grasp, 'do you not hear someone coming?'

As she spoke the sound of tiny pattering feet was heard in the corridor, then the door was flung violently open, and with a shrill cry of delight, Katrina rushed into the room, followed more slowly by her brother Alexis.

'And are these your children?' asked Ravina, as Paul took up the little girl and placed her fondly upon his knee, whilst the boy stood a few paces from the door gazing with eyes of wonder upon the strange woman, for whose appearance he was utterly unable to account. 'Come here, my little man,' continued she; 'I suppose you are the heir of Kostopchin, though you do not resemble your father much.'

'He takes after his mother, I think,' returned Paul carelessly; 'and how has my darling Katrina been?' he added, addressing his daughter.

'Quite well, papa dear,' answered the child; 'but where is the fine white wolf skin that you promised me?'

'Your father did not find her,' answered Ravina, with a little laugh; 'the white wolf was not so easy to catch as he fancied.'

Alexis had moved a few steps nearer to the lady, and was listening with grave attention to every word she uttered.

'Are white wolves so difficult to kill, then?' asked he.

'It seems so, my little man,' returned the lady, 'since your father and all the serfs of Kostopchin were unable to do so.'

'I have got a pistol, that good old Michal has taught me to fire, and I am sure I could kill her if ever I got sight of her,' observed Alexis, boldly.

'There is a brave boy,' returned Ravina, with one of her shrill laughs; 'and now, won't you come and sit on my knee, for I am very fond of little boys?'

'No, I don't like you,' answered Alexis, after a moment's consideration, 'for Michal says – '

'Go to your room, you insolent young brat,' broke in the father, in a voice of thunder. 'You spend so much of your time with Michal and the serfs that you have learned all their boorish habits.'

Two tiny tears rolled down the boy's cheeks as in obedience to his father's orders he turned about and quitted the room, whilst Ravina darted a strange look of dislike after him. As soon, however, as the door had closed, the fair woman addressed Katrina.

'Well, perhaps you will not be so unkind to me as your brother,' said she. 'Come to me,' and as she spoke she held out her arms.

The little girl came to her without hesitation, and began to smooth the silken tresses which were coiled and wreathed around Ravina's head.

'Pretty, pretty,' she murmured, 'beautiful lady.'

'You see, Paul Sergevitch, that your little daughter has taken to me at once,' remarked Ravina.

'She takes after her father, who was always noted for his good taste,' returned Paul, with a bow; 'but take care, madam, or the little puss will have your necklace off.'

The child had indeed succeeded in unclasping the glittering ornament, and was now inspecting it in high glee.

'That is a curious ornament,' said Paul, stepping up to the child and taking the circlet from her hand.

It was indeed a quaintly fashioned ornament, consisting as it did of a number of what were apparently curved pieces of sharp-pointed horn set in gold, and depending from a snake of the same precious metal.

'Why, these are claws,' continued he, as he looked at them more carefully.

'Yes, wolves' claws,' answered Ravina, taking the necklet from the child and reclasping it round her neck. 'It is a family relic which I have always worn.'

Katrina at first seemed inclined to cry at her new plaything being taken from her, but by caresses and endearments Ravina soon contrived to lull her once more into a good temper.

'My daughter has certainly taken to you in a most wonderful manner,' remarked Paul, with a pleased smile. 'You have quite obtained possession of her heart.'

'Not yet, whatever I may do later on,' answered the woman, with her strange cold smile, as she pressed the child closer towards her and shot a glance at Paul which made him quiver with an emotion that he had never felt before. Presently, however, the child grew tired of her new acquaintance, and sliding down from her knee, crept from the room in search of her brother Alexis.

Paul and Ravina remained silent for a few instants, and then the woman broke the silence.

'All that remains for me now, Paul Sergevitch, is to trespass on your hospitality, and to ask you to lend me some disguise, and assist me to gain the nearest post town, which, I think, is Vitroski.'

'And why should you wish to leave this place at all,' demanded Paul, a deep flush rising to his cheek. 'You are perfectly safe in my house, and if you attempt to pursue your journey there is every chance of your being recognised and captured.'

'Why do I wish to leave this house?' answered Ravina, rising to her feet and casting a look of surprise upon her interrogator. 'Can you ask me such a question? How is it possible for me to remain here?'

'It is perfectly impossible for you to leave; of that I am quite certain,' answered the man, doggedly. 'All I know is, that if you leave Kostopchin, you will inevitably fall into the hands of the police.'

'And Paul Sergevitch will tell them where they can find me?' questioned Ravina, with an ironical inflection in the tone of her voice.

'I never said so,' returned Paul.

'Perhaps not,' answered the woman, quickly, 'but I am not slow in reading thoughts; they are sometimes plainer to read than words. You are saying to yourself, 'Kostopchin is but a dull hole after all; chance has thrown into my hands a woman whose beauty pleases me; she is utterly friendless, and is in fear of the pursuit of the police; why should I not bend her to my will?' That is what you have been thinking, – is it not so, Paul Sergevitch?'

'I never thought, that is – ' stammered the man.

'No, you never thought that I could read you so plainly,' pursued the woman, pitilessly; 'but it is the truth that I have told you, and sooner than remain an inmate of your house, I would leave it, even if all the police of Russia stood ready to arrest me on its very threshold.'

'Stay, Ravina,' exclaimed Paul, as the woman made a step towards the door. 'I do not say whether your reading of my thoughts is right or wrong, but before you leave, listen to me. I do not speak to you in the usual strain of a pleading lover, – you, who know my past, would laugh at me should I do so; but I tell you plainly that from the first moment that I set eyes upon you, a strange new feeling has risen up in my heart, not the cold thing that society calls love, but a burning resistless flood which flows down like molten lava from the volcano's crater. Stay, Ravina, stay, I implore you, for if you go from here you will take my heart with you.'

'You may be speaking more truthfully than you think,' returned the fair woman, as, turning back, she came close up to Paul, and placing both her hands upon his shoulders, shot a glance of lurid fire from her eyes. 'Still, you have but given me a selfish reason for my staying, only your own self-gratification. Give me one that more nearly affects myself.'

Ravina's touch sent a tremor through Paul's whole frame which caused every nerve and sinew to vibrate. Gaze as boldly as he might into those steel-blue eyes, he could not sustain their intensity.

'Be my wife, Ravina,' faltered he. 'Be my wife. You are safe enough from all pursuit here, and if that does not suit you I can easily convert my estate into a large sum of money, and we can fly to other lands, where you can have nothing to fear from the Russian police.'

'And does Paul Sergevitch actually mean to offer his hand to a woman whose name he does not even know, and of whose feelings towards him he is entirely ignorant?' asked the woman, with her customary mocking laugh.

'What do I care for name or birth,' returned he, hotly, 'I have enough for both, and as for love, my passion would soon kindle some sparks of it in your breast, cold and frozen as it may now be.'

'Let me think a little,' said Ravina; and throwing herself into an armchair she buried her face in her hands and seemed plunged in deep reflection, whilst Paul paced impatiently up and down the room like a prisoner awaiting the verdict that would restore him to life or doom him to a shameful death.

At length Ravina removed her hands from her face and spoke.

'Listen,' said she. 'I have thought over your proposal seriously, and upon certain conditions, I will consent to become your wife.'

'They are granted in advance,' broke in Paul, eagerly.

'Make no bargains blindfold,' answered she, 'but listen. At the present moment I have no inclination for you, but on the other hand I feel no repugnance for you. I will remain here for a month, and during that time I shall remain in a suite of apartments which you will have prepared for me. Every evening I will visit you here, and upon your making yourself agreeable my ultimate decision will depend.'

'And suppose that decision should be an unfavourable one?' asked Paul.

'Then,' answered Ravina, with a ringing laugh, 'I shall, as you say, leave this house and take your heart with me.'

'These are hard conditions,' remarked Paul. 'Why not shorten the time of probation?'

'My conditions are unalterable,' answered Ravina, with a little stamp of the foot. 'Do you agree to them or not?'

'I have no alternative,' answered he, sullenly; 'but remember that I am to see you every evening.'

'For two hours,' said the woman, 'so you must try and make yourself as agreeable as you can in that time; and now, if you will give orders regarding my rooms, I will settle myself in them with as little delay as possible.'

Paul obeyed her, and in a couple of hours three handsome chambers were got ready for their fair occupant in a distant part of the great rambling house.

The awakening of the wolf

The days slipped slowly and wearily away, but Ravina showed no signs of relenting. Every evening, according to her bond, she spent two hours with Paul and made herself most agreeable, listening to his far-fetched compliments and asseverations of love and tenderness either with a cold smile or with one of her mocking laughs. She refused to allow Paul to visit her in her own apartments, and the only intruder she permitted there, save the servants, was little Katrina, who had taken a strange fancy to the fair woman. Alexis, on the contrary, avoided her as much as he possibly could, and the pair hardly ever met. Paul, to while away the time, wandered about the farm and the village, the inhabitants of which had recovered from their panic as the white wolf appeared to have entirely desisted from her murderous attacks upon belated peasants.

The shades of evening had closed in as Paul was one day returning from his customary round, rejoiced with the idea that the hour for

Ravina's visit was drawing near, when he was startled by a gentle touch upon the shoulder, and turning round, saw the old man Michal standing just behind him. The intendant's face was perfectly livid, his eyes gleamed with the lustre of terror, and his fingers kept convulsively clasping and unclasping.

'My lord,' exclaimed he, in faltering accents; 'oh, my lord, listen to me, for I have terrible news to narrate to you.'

'What is the matter?' asked Paul, more impressed than he would have liked to confess by the old man's evident terror.

'The wolf, the white wolf! I have seen it again,' whispered Michal.

'You are dreaming,' retorted his master, angrily. 'You have got the creature on the brain, and have mistaken a white calf or one of the dogs for it.'

'I am not mistaken,' answered the old man, firmly. 'And oh, my lord, do not go into the house, for she is there.'

'She – who – what do you mean?' cried Paul.

'The white wolf, my lord. I saw her go in. You know the strange lady's apartments are on the ground floor on the west side of the house. I saw the monster cantering across the lawn, and, as if it knew its way perfectly well, make for the centre window of the reception room; it yielded to a touch of the fore paw, and the beast sprang through. Oh, my lord, do not go in; I tell you that it will never harm the strange woman. Ah! let me – '

But Paul cast off the detaining arm with a force that made the old man reel and fall, and then, catching up an axe, dashed into the house, calling upon the servants to follow him to the strange lady's rooms. He tried the handle, but the door was securely fastened, and then, in all the frenzy of terror, he attacked the panels with heavy blows of his axe. For a few seconds no sound was heard save the ring of metal and the shivering of panels, but then the clear tones of Ravina were heard asking the reason for this outrageous disturbance.

'The wolf, the white wolf,' shouted half a dozen voices.

'Stand back and I will open the door,' answered the fair woman. 'You must be mad, for there is no wolf here.'

The door flew open and the crowd rushed tumultuously in; every nook and corner were searched, but no signs of the intruder could be discovered, and with many shamefaced glances Paul and his servants were about to return, when the voice of Ravina arrested their steps.'

'Paul Sergevitch,' sad she, coldly, 'explain the meaning of this daring intrusion on my privacy.'

She looked very beautiful as she stood before them, her right arm extended and her bosom heaving violently, but this was doubtless caused by her anger at the unlooked-for invasion.

Paul briefly repeated what he had heard from the old serf, and Ravina's scorn was intense.

'And so,' cried she, fiercely, 'it is to the crotchets of this old dotard that I am indebted for this. Paul, if you ever hope to succeed in winning me, forbid that man ever to enter the house again.'

Paul would have sacrificed all his serfs for a whim of the haughty beauty, and Michal was deprived of the office of intendant and exiled to a cabin in the village, with orders never to show his face again near the house. The separation from the children almost broke the old man's heart, but he ventured on no remonstrance and meekly obeyed the mandate which drove him away from all he loved and cherished.

Meanwhile, curious rumours began to be circulated regarding the strange proceedings of the lady who occupied the suite of apartments which had formerly belonged to the wife of the owner of Kostopchin. The servants declared that the food sent up, though hacked about and cut up, was never tasted, but that the raw meat in the larder was frequently missing. Strange sounds were often heard to issue from the rooms as the panic-stricken serfs hurried past the corridor upon which the doors opened, and dwellers in the house were frequently disturbed by the howlings of wolves, the footprints of which were distinctly visible the next morning, and, curiously enough, invariably in the gardens facing the west side of the house in which the lady dwelt. Little Alexis, who found no encouragement to sit with his father, was naturally thrown a great deal amongst the serfs, and heard the subject discussed with many exaggerations. Weird old tales of folklore were often narrated as the servants discussed their evening meal, and the boy's hair would bristle as he listened to the wild and fanciful narratives of wolves, witches, and white ladies with which the superstitious serfs filled his ears. One of his most treasured possessions was an old brass-mounted cavalry pistol, a present from Michal; this he had learned to load, and by using both hands to the cumbrous weapon could contrive to fire it off, as many an ill-starred sparrow could attest. With his mind constantly dwelling upon the terrible tales he had so greedily listened to, this pistol became his daily companion, whether he was wandering about the long echoing corridors of the house or wandering through the neglected shrubberies of the garden.

For a fortnight matters went on in this manner, Paul becoming more and more infatuated by the charms of his strange guest, and she every now and then letting drop occasional crumbs of hope which led the unhappy man further and further upon the dangerous course that he was pursuing. A mad, soul-absorbing passion for the fair woman and the deep draughts of brandy with which he consoled himself during her hours of absence were telling upon the brain of the master of Kostopchin, and except during the brief space of Ravina's visit, he would relapse into moods of silent sullenness from which he would occasionally break out into furious bursts of passion for no assignable cause. A shadow seemed to be closing over the house of Kostopchin; it became the abode of grim whispers and undeveloped fears; the men and maidservants went about their work glancing nervously over their shoulders, as though they were apprehensive that some hideous thing was following at their heels.

After three days of exile, poor old Michal could endure the state of suspense regarding the safety of Alexis and Katrina no longer; and, casting aside his superstitious fears, he took to wandering by night about the exterior of the great white house, and peering curiously into such windows as had been left unshuttered. At first he was in continual dread of meeting the terrible white wolf; but his love for the children and his confidence in the crucifix he wore prevailed, and he continued his nocturnal wanderings about Kostopchin and its environs. He kept near the western front of the house, urged on to do so from some vague feeling which he could in no wise account for. One evening as he was making his accustomed tour of inspection, the wail of a child struck upon his ear. He bent down his head and eagerly listened; again he heard the same faint sounds, and in them he fancied he recognised the accents of his dear little Katrina. Hurrying up to one of the ground-floor windows, from which a dim light streamed, he pressed his face against the pane, and looked steadily in. A horrible sight presented itself to his gaze. By the faint light of a shaded lamp, he saw Katrina stretched upon the ground; but her wailing had now ceased, for a shawl had been tied across her little mouth. Over her was bending a hideous shape, which seemed to be clothed in some white and shaggy covering. Katrina lay perfectly motionless, and the hands of the figure were engaged in hastily removing the garments from the child's breast. The task was soon effected; then there was a bright gleam of steel, and the head of the thing bent closely down to the child's bosom.

With a yell of apprehension, the old man dashed in the window frame, and, drawing the cross from his breast, sprang boldly into the room. The creature sprang to its feet, and the white fur cloak falling from its had and shoulders disclosed the pallid features of Ravina, a short, broad knife in her hand, and her lips discoloured with blood.

'Vile sorceress!' cried Michal, dashing forward and raising Katrina in his arms. 'What hellish work are you about?'

Ravina's eyes gleamed fiercely upon the old man, who had interfered between her and her prey. She raised her dagger, and was about to spring in upon him, when she caught sight of the cross in his extended hand. With a low cry, she dropped the knife, and, staggering back a few paces, wailed out: 'I could not help it; I liked the child well enough, but I was so hungry.'

Michal paid but little heed to her words, for he was busily engaged in examining the fainting child, whose head was resting helplessly on his shoulder. There was a wound over the left breast, from which the blood was flowing; but the injury appeared slight, and not likely to prove fatal. As soon as he had satisfied himself on this point, he turned to the woman, who was crouching before the cross as a wild beast shrinks before the whip of the tamer.

'I am going to remove the child,' said he, slowly. 'Dare you to mention a word of what I have done or whither she has gone, and I will arouse the village. Do you know what will happen then? Why, every peasant in the place will hurry here with a lighted brand in his hand to consume this accursed house and the unnatural dwellers in it. Keep silence, and I leave you to your unhallowed work. I will no longer seek to preserve Paul Sergevitch, who has given himself over to the powers of darkness by taking a demon to his bosom.'

Ravina listened to him as if she scarcely comprehended him; but, as the old man retreated to the window with his helpless burden, she followed him step by step; and as he turned to cast one last glance at the shattered window, he saw the woman's pale face and bloodstained lips glued against an unbroken pane, with a wild look of unsatiated appetite in her eyes.

Next morning the house of Kostopchin was filled with terror and surprise, for Katrina, the idol of her father's heart, had disappeared, and no signs of her could be discovered. Every effort was made, the woods and fields in the neighbourhood were thoroughly searched; but it was at last concluded that robbers had carried off the child for the sake of the ransom that they might be able to extract from the father. This seemed the more likely as one of the windows in the fair stranger's room bore marks of violence, and she declared that, being alarmed by the sound of crashing glass, she had risen and confronted a man who was endeavouring to enter her apartment, but who, on perceiving her, turned and fled away with the utmost precipitation.

Paul Sergevitch did not display as much anxiety as might have been expected from him, considering the devotion which he had ever evinced for the lost Katrina, for his whole soul was wrapped up in one mad, absorbing passion for the fair woman who had so strangely crossed his life. He certainly directed the search, and gave all the necessary orders; but he did so in a listless and half-hearted manner, and hastened back to Kostopchin as speedily as he could as though fearing to be absent for any length of time from the casket in which his new treasure was enshrined. Not so Alexis; he was almost frantic at the loss of his sister, and accompanied the searchers daily until his little legs grew weary, and he had to be carried on the shoulders of a sturdy moujik. His treasured brass-mounted pistol was now more than ever his constant companion; and when he met the fair woman who had cast a spell upon his father, his face would flush, and he would grind his teeth in impotent rage.

The day upon which all search had ceased, Ravina glided into the room where she knew that she would find Paul awaiting her. She was fully an hour before her usual time, and the lord of Kostopchin started to his feet in surprise.

'You are surprised to see me,' said she; 'but I have only come to pay you a visit for a few minutes. I am convinced that you love me, and could I but relieve a few of the objections that my heart continues to raise, I might be yours.'

'Tell me what these scruples are,' cried Paul, springing towards her, and seizing her hands in his; 'and be sure that I will find means to overcome them.'

Even in the midst of all the glow and fervour of anticipated triumph, he could not avoid noticing how icily cold were the fingers that rested in his palm, and how utterly passionless was the pressure with which she slightly returned his enraptured clasp.

'Listen,' said she, as she withdrew her hand; 'I will take two more hours for consideration. By that time the whole of the house of Kostopchin will be cradled in slumber; then meet me at the old sundial near the yew tree at the bottom of the garden, and I will give you my reply. Nay, not a word,' she added, as he seemed about to remonstrate, 'for I tell you that I think it will be a favourable one.'

'But why not come back here?' urged he; 'there is a hard frost tonight, and – '

'Are you so cold a lover,' broke in Ravina, with her accustomed laugh, 'to dread the changes of the weather? But not another word; I have spoken.'

She glided from the room, but uttered a low cry of rage. She had almost fallen over Alexis in the corridor.

'Why is that brat not in his bed? ' cried she, angrily; 'he gave me quite a turn.'

'Go to your room, boy,' exclaimed his father, harshly; and with a malignant glance at his enemy, the child slunk away.

Paul Sergevitch paced up and down the room for the two hours that he had to pass before the hour of meeting. His heart was very heavy, and a vague feeling of disquietude began to creep over him. Twenty times he made up his mind not to keep his appointment, and as often the fascination of the fair woman compelled him to rescind his resolution. He remember that he had from childhood disliked that spot by the yew tree, and had always looked upon it as a dreary, uncanny place; and he even now disliked the idea of finding himself here after dark, even with such fair companionship as he had been promised. Counting the minutes, he paced backwards and forwards, as though moved by some concealed machinery. Now and again he glanced at the clock, and at last its deep metallic sound, as it struck the quarter, warned him that he had but little time to lose, if he intended to keep his appointment. Throwing on a heavily furred coat and pulling a travelling cap down over his ears, he opened a side door and sallied out into the grounds. The moon was at its full, and shone coldly down upon the leafless trees, which looked white and ghostlike in its beams. The paths and unkept lawns were now covered with hoar frost, and a keen wind every now and then swept by, which, in spite of his wraps, chilled Paul's blood in his veins. The dark shape of the yew tree soon rose up before him, and in another moment he stood beside its dusky boughs. The old grey sundial stood only a few paces off, and by its side was standing a slender figure, wrapped in a white, fleecy-looking cloak. It was perfectly motionless, and again a terror of undefined dread passed through every nerve and muscle of Paul Sergevitch's body.

'Ravina!' said he, in faltering accents. 'Ravina!'

'Did you take me for a ghost?' answered the fair woman, with her shrill laugh; 'no, no, I have not come to that yet. Well, Paul Serge-vitch, I have come to give you my answer; are you anxious about it?'

'How can you ask me such a question?' returned he; 'do you not know that my whole soul has been aglow with anticipations of what your reply might be? Do not keep me any longer in suspense. Is it yes, or no?'

'Paul Sergevitch,' answered the young woman, coming up to him and laying her hands upon his shoulders, and fixing her eyes upon his with that strange weird expression before which he always quailed; 'do you really love me, Paul Sergevitch?' asked she.

'Love you!' repeated the lord of Kostopchin; 'have I not told you a thousand times how much my whole soul flows out towards you, how I only live and breathe in your presence, and how death at your feet would be more welcome than life without you?'

'People often talk of death, and yet little know how near it is to them,' answered the fair lady, a grim smile appearing upon her face; 'but say, do you give me your whole heart?'

'All I have is yours, Ravina,' returned Paul, 'name, wealth, and the devoted love of a lifetime.'

'But your heart,' persisted she; 'it is your heart that I want; tell me, Paul, that it is mine and mine only.'

'Yes, my heart is yours, dearest Ravina,' answered Paul, endeavouring to embrace the fair form in his impassioned grasp; but she glided from him, and then with a quick bound sprang upon him and glared in his face with a look that was absolutely appalling. Her eyes gleamed with a lurid fire, her lips were drawn back, showing her sharp, white teeth, whilst her breath came in sharp, quick gasps.

'I am hungry,' she murmured, 'oh, so hungry; but now, Paul Sergevitch, your heart is mine.'

Her movement was so sudden and unexpected that he stumbled and fell heavily to the ground, the fair woman clinging to him and falling upon his breast. It was then that the full horror of his position came upon Paul Sergevitch, and he saw his fate clearly before him; but a terrible numbness prevented him from using his hands to free himself from the hideous embrace which was paralysing all his muscles. The face that was glaring into his seemed to be undergoing some fearful change, and the features to be losing their semblance of humanity. With a sudden, quick movement, she tore open his garments, and in another moment she had perforated his left breast with a ghastly wound, and, plunging in her delicate hands, tore out his heart and bit at it ravenously. Intent upon her hideous banquet she heeded not the convulsive struggles which agitated the dying form of the lord of Kostopchin. She was too much occupied to notice a diminutive form approaching, sheltering itself behind every tree and bush until it had arrived within ten paces of the scene of the terrible tragedy. Then the moonbeams glistened upon the long shining barrel of a pistol, which a boy was levelling with both hands at the murderess. Then quick and sharp rang out the report, and with a wild shriek, in which there was something beastlike, Ravina leaped from the body of the dead man and staggered away to a thick clump of bushes some ten paces distant. The boy Alexis had heard the appointment that had been made, and dogged his father's footsteps to the trysting place. After firing the fatal shot his courage deserted him, and he fled backwards to the house, uttering loud shrieks for help. The startled servants were soon in the presence of their slaughtered master, but aid was of no avail, for the lord of Kostopchin had passed away. With fear and trembling the superstitious peasants searched the clump of bushes, and started back in horror as they perceived a huge white wolf, lying stark and dead, with a half-devoured human heart clasped between its forepaws.

* * *

No signs of the fair lady who had occupied the apartments in the western side of the house were ever again seen. She had passed away from Kostopchin like an ugly dream, and as the moujiks of the village sat around their stoves at night they whispered strange stories regarding the fair woman of the forest and the white wolf of Kostopchin. By order of the Tsar a surtee was placed in charge of the estate of Kostopchin, and Alexis was ordered to be sent to a military school until he should be old enough to join the army. The meeting between the boy and his sister, whom the faithful Michal, when all danger was at an end, had produced from his hiding place, was most affecting; but it was not until Katrina had been for some time resident at the house of a distant relative at Vitepak, that she ceased to wake at night and cry out in terror as she again dreamed that she was in the clutches of the white wolf.

The Other Side

[a Breton legend]

COUNT STENBOCK

A la joyeuse Messe noire

'Not that I like it, but one does feel so much better after it – oh, thank you, Mère Yvonne, yes just a little drop more.' So the old crones fell to drinking their hot brandy and water (although of course they only took it medicinally, as a remedy for their rheumatics), all seated round the big fire, and Mère Pinquèle continued her story.

'Oh, yes, then when they get to the top of the hill, there is an altar with six candles quite black and a sort of something in between, that nobody sees quite clearly, and the old black ram with the man's face and long horns begins to say Mass in a sort of gibberish nobody understands, and two black strange things like monkeys glide about with the book and the cruets – and there's music too, such music. There are things the top half like black cats, and the bottom part like men only their legs are all covered with close black hair, and they play on the bag-pipes, and when they come to the elevation, then – '

Amid the old crones there was lying on the hearth-rug, before the fire, a boy whose large lovely eyes dilated and whose limbs quivered in the very ecstasy of terror.

'Is that all true, Mère Pinquèle?' he said.

'Oh, quite true, and not only that, the best part is yet to come; for they take a child and – ' here Mère Pinquèle showed her fang-like teeth.

'Oh! Mère Pinquèle, are you a witch too?'

'Silence, Gabriel,' said Mère Yvonne, 'how can you say anything so wicked? Why, bless me, the boy ought to have been in bed ages ago.'

Just then all shuddered, and all made the sign of the cross except Mère Pinquèle, for they heard that most dreadful of dreadful sounds – the howl of a wolf, which begins with three sharp barks and then lifts itself up in a long protracted wail of commingled cruelty and despair, and at last subsides into a whispered growl fraught with eternal malice.

There was a forest and a village and a brook; the village was on one side of the brook, none had dared to cross to the other side. Where the village was, all was green and glad and fertile and fruit- ful; on the other side the trees never put forth green leaves, and a dark shadow hung over it even at noon-day, and in the night-time one could hear the wolves howling – the werewolves and the wolf- men and the men-wolves, and those very wicked men who for nine days in every year are turned into wolves; but on the green side no wolf was ever seen, and only one little running brook like a silver streak flowed between.

It was spring now and the old crones sat no longer by the fire but before their cottages sunning themselves, and everyone felt so happy that they ceased to tell stories of the 'other side'. But Gabriel wan- dered by the brook as he was wont to wander, drawn thither by some strange attraction mingled with intense horror.

His schoolfellows did not like Gabriel; all laughed and jeered at him, because he was less cruel and more gentle of nature than the rest; and even as a rare and beautiful bird escaped from a cage is hacked to death by the common sparrows, so was Gabriel among his fellows. Everyone wondered how Mère Yvonne, that buxom and worthy matron, could have produced a son like this, with strange dreamy eyes, who was as they said '*pas comme les autres gamins*'. His only friends were the Abbé Félicien whose Mass he served each morning, and one little girl called Carmeille, who loved him, no-one could make out why.

The sun had already set. Gabriel still wandered by the brook, filled with vague terror and irresistible fascination. The sun set and the moon rose, the full moon, very large and very clear, and the moonlight flooded the forest both this side and the 'other side', and just on the 'other side' of the brook, hanging over, Gabriel saw a large deep blue flower, whose strange intoxicating perfume reached him and fascinated him even where he stood.

'If I could only make one step across,' he thought, 'nothing could harm me if I only plucked that one flower, and nobody would know I had been over at all,' for the villagers looked with hatred and suspicion on anyone who was said to have crossed to the 'other side', so summing up courage he leapt lightly to the other side of the brook. Then the moon breaking from a cloud shone with unusual brilliance, and he saw, stretching before him, long reaches of the same strange blue flowers, each one lovelier than the last, till, not being able to make up his mind which one flower to take or whether to take several, he went on and on, and the moon shone very brightly and a strange unseen bird, somewhat like a nightingale, but louder and lovelier, sang, and his heart was filled with longing for he knew not what, and the moon shone and the nightingale sang. But on a sudden a black cloud covered the moon entirely, and all was black, utter darkness, and through the darkness he heard wolves howling and shrieking in the hideous ardour of the chase, and there passed before him a horrible procession of wolves (black wolves with red fiery eyes), and with them men that had the heads of wolves and wolves that had the heads of men, and above them flew owls (black owls with red fiery eyes) and bats and long serpentine black things, and last of all seated on an enormous black ram with hideous human face the wolf-keeper on whose face was eternal shadow; but they continued their horrid chase and passed him by, and when they had passed the moon shone out more beautiful than ever, and the strange nightingale sang again, and the strange intense blue flowers were in long reaches in front to the right and to the left. But one thing was there which had not been before; among the deep blue flowers walked one with long gleaming golden hair, and she turned once round and her eyes were of the same colour as the strange blue flowers, and she walked on and Gabriel could not choose but follow. But when a cloud passed over the moon he saw no beautiful woman but a wolf, so in utter terror he turned and fled, plucking one of the strange blue flowers on the way, and leapt again over the brook and ran home.

When he got home Gabriel could not resist showing his treasure to his mother, though he knew she would not appreciate it; but when she saw the strange blue flower, Mère Yvonne turned pale and said, 'Why child, where hast thou been? Sure it is the witch flower'; and so saying she snatched it from him and cast it into the corner, and immediately all its beauty and strange fragrance faded from it and it looked charred as though it had been burnt. So Gabriel sat down silently and rather sulkily, and having eaten no supper went up to bed, but he did got sleep but waited and waited till all was quiet within the house. Then he crept downstairs in his long white night-shirt and bare feet on the square cold stones and picked hurriedly up the charred and faded flower and put it in his warm bosom next his heart, and immediately the flower bloomed again lovelier than ever, and he fell into a deep sleep, but through his sleep he seemed to hear a soft low voice singing underneath his window in a strange language (in which the subtle sounds melted into one another), but he could distinguish no word except his own name.

When he went forth in the morning to serve Mass, he still kept the flower with him next his heart. Now when the priest began Mass and said 'Intrabo ad altare Dei', then said Gabriel 'Qui nequiquam laetificavit juventutem meam'. And the Abbé Félicien turned round on hearing this strange response, and he saw the boy's face deadly pale, his eyes fixed and his limbs rigid, and as the priest looked on him Gabriel fell fainting to the floor, so the sacristan had to carry him home and seek another acolyte for the Abbé Félicien.

Now when the Abbé Félicien came to see after him, Gabriel felt strangely reluctant to say anything about the blue flower and for the first time he deceived the priest.

In the afternoon as sunset drew nigh he felt better and Carmeille came to see him and begged him to go out with her into the fresh air. So they went out hand in hand, the dark haired, gazelle-eyed boy, and the fair wavy-haired girl, and something, he knew not what, led his steps (half knowingly and yet not so, for he could not but walk thither) to the brook, and they sat down together on the bank.

Gabriel thought at least he might tell his secret to Carmeille, so he took out the flower from his bosom and said, 'Look here, Carmeille, hast thou seen ever so lovely a flower as this?' but Carmeille turned pale and faint and said, 'Oh, Gabriel what is this flower? I but touched it and I felt something strange come over me. No, no, I don't like its perfume, no there's something not quite right about it, oh, dear Gabriel, do let me throw it away,' and before he had time to answer, she cast it from her, and again all its beauty and fragrance went from it and it looked charred as though it had been burnt. But suddenly where the flower had been thrown on this side of the brook, there appeared a wolf, which stood and looked at the children.

Carmeille said, 'What shall we do?' and clung to Gabriel, but the wolf looked at them very steadfastly and Gabriel recognised in the eyes of the wolf the strange deep intense blue eyes of the wolf-woman he had seen on the 'other side', so he said, 'Stay here, dear Carmeille, see she is looking gently at us and will not hurt us.'

'But it is a wolf,' said Carmeille, and quivered all over with fear, but again Gabriel said languidly, 'She will not hurt us.' Then Carmeille seized Gabriel's hand in an agony of terror and dragged him along with her till they reached the village, where she gave the alarm and all the lads of the village gathered together. They had never seen a wolf on this side of the brook, so they excited themselves greatly and arranged a grand wolf-hunt for the morrow, but Gabriel sat silently apart and said no word.

That night Gabriel could not sleep at all nor could he bring himself to say his prayers; but he sat in his little room by the window with his shirt open at the throat and the strange blue flower at his heart and again this night he heard a voice singing beneath his window in the same soft, subtle, liquid language as before –

> Ma zála liral va jé
> Cwamûlo zhajéla je
> Cárma urádi el javé
> Járma, symai, – carmé –
> Zhála javály thra je
> Al vú al vlaûle va azré
> Safralje vairálje va já?
> Cárma serâja
> Lâja lâja
> Luzhà!

and as he looked he could see the silvern shadows slide on the glimmering light of golden hair, and the strange eyes gleaming dark blue through the night and it seemed to him that he could not but follow; so he walked half clad and bare foot as he was with eyes fixed as in a dream silently down the stairs and out into the night.

And ever and again she turned to look on him with her strange blue eyes full of tenderness and passion and sadness beyond the sadness of things human – and as he foreknew, his steps led him to the brink of the brook. Then she, taking his hand, familiarly said, 'Won't you help me over, Gabriel?'

Then it seemed to him as though he had known her all his life – so he went with her to the 'other side' but he saw no-one by him; and looking again, beside him there were two wolves. In a frenzy of terror, he (who had never thought to kill any living thing before) seized a log of wood lying by and smote one of the wolves on the head.

Immediately he saw the wolf-woman again at his side with blood streaming from her forehead, staining her wonderful golden hair, and with eyes looking at him with infinite reproach, she said – 'Who did this?'

Then she whispered a few words to the other wolf, which leapt over the brook and made its way towards the village, and turning again towards him she said, 'Oh Gabriel, how could you strike me, who would have loved you so long and so well.' Then it seemed to him again as though he had known her all his life but he felt dazed and said nothing – but she gathered a dark green strangely shaped leaf and holding it to her forehead, she said – 'Gabriel, kiss the place all will be well again.' So he kissed as she had bidden him and he felt the salt taste of blood in his mouth and then he knew no more.

Again he saw the wolf-keeper with his horrible troupe around him, but this time not engaged in the chase but sitting in strange conclave in a circle and the black owls sat in the trees and the black bats hung downwards from the branches. Gabriel stood alone in the middle with a hundred wicked eyes fixed on him. They seemed to deliberate about what should be done with him, speaking in that same strange tongue which he had heard in the songs beneath his window. Suddenly he felt a hand pressing in his and saw the mysterious wolf-woman by his side. Then began what seemed a kind of incantation where human or half human creatures seemed to howl, and beasts to speak with human speech but in the unknown tongue. Then the wolf-keeper whose face was ever veiled in shadow spake some words in a voice that seemed to come from afar off, but all he could distinguish was his own name Gabriel and her name Lilith. Then he felt arms enlacing him.

Gabriel awoke – in his own room – so it was a dream after all – but what a dreadful dream. Yes, but was it his own room? Of course there was his coat hanging over the chair – yes but – the Crucifix – where was the Crucifix and the benetier and the consecrated palm branch and the antique image of Our Lady *perpetuae salutis*, with the little ever-burning lamp before it, before which he placed every day the flowers he had gathered, yet had not dared to place the blue flower.

Every morning he lifted his still dream-laden eyes to it and said *Ave Maria* and made the sign of the cross, which bringeth peace to the soul – but how horrible, how maddening, it was not there, not at all. No surely he could not be awake, at least not *quite* awake, he would make the benedictive sign and he would be freed from this fearful illusion – yes but the sign, he would make the sign – oh, but what was the sign? Had he forgotten? Or was his arm paralysed? No he could not move. Then he had forgotten – and the prayer – he must remember that. *A – vae – nunc – mortis – fructus.* No surely it did not run thus – but something like it surely – yes, he was awake, he could move at any rate – he would reassure himself – he would get up – he would see the grey old church with the exquisitely pointed gables bathed in the light of dawn, and presently the deep solemn bell would toll and he would run down and don his red cassock and lace-worked cotta and light the tall candles on the altar and wait reverently to vest the good and gracious Abbé Félicien, kissing each vestment as he lifted it with reverent hands.

But surely this was not the light of dawn; it was like sunset! He leapt from his small white bed, and a vague terror came over him, he trembled and had to hold on to the chair before he reached the window. No, the solemn spires of the grey church were not to be seen – he was in the depths of the forest, but in a part he had never seen before – but surely he had explored every part, it must be the 'other side'. To terror succeeded a languor and lassitude not without charm – passivity, acquiescence, indulgence – he felt, as it were, the strong caress of another will flowing over him like water and clothing him with invisible hands in an impalpable garment; so he dressed himself almost mechanically and walked downstairs, the same stairs it seemed to him down which it was his wont to run and spring. The broad square stones seemed singularly beautiful and iridescent with many strange colours – how was it he had never noticed this before – but he was gradually losing the power of wondering – he entered the room below – the wonted coffee and bread-rolls were on the table.

'Why Gabriel, how late you are today.' The voice was very sweet but the intonation strange – and there sat Lilith, the mysterious wolf-woman, her glittering gold hair tied in a loose knot; an embroidery whereon she was tracing strange serpentine patterns, lay over the lap of her maize-coloured garment – and she looked at Gabriel steadfastly with her wonderful dark blue eyes and said, 'Why, Gabriel, you are late today,' and Gabriel answered, 'I was tired yesterday, give me some coffee.'

A dream within a dream – yes, he had known her all his life, and they dwelt together; had they not always done so? And she would take him through the glades of the forest and gather for him flowers, such as he had never seen before, and tell him stories in her strange, low deep voice, which seemed ever to be accompanied by the faint vibration of strings, looking at him fixedly the while with her marvellous blue eyes.

Little by little the flame of vitality which burned within him seemed to grow fainter and fainter, and his lithe lissom limbs waxed languorous and luxurious – yet was he ever filled with a languid content and a will not his own perpetually overshadowed him.

One day in their wanderings he saw a strange dark blue flower like unto the eyes of Lilith, and a sudden half remembrance flashed through his mind.

'What is this blue flower?' he said, and Lilith shuddered and said nothing; but as they went a little further there was a brook – *the* brook he thought, and felt his fetters falling off him, and he prepared to spring over the brook; but Lilith seized him by the arm and held him back with all her strength, and trembling all over she said, 'Promise me Gabriel that you will not cross over.'

But he said, 'Tell me what is this blue flower, and why you will not tell me?'

And she said, 'Look Gabriel at the brook.' And he looked and saw that though it was just like the brook of separation it was not the same, the waters did not flow.

As Gabriel looked steadfastly into the still waters it seemed to him as though he saw voices – some impression of the Vespers for the Dead. '*Hei mihi quia incolatus sum*', and again '*De profundis clamavi ad te*' – oh, that veil, that overshadowing veil! Why could he not hear properly and see, and why did he only remember as one looking through a threefold semi-transparent curtain. Yes they were praying for him – but who were they? He heard again the voice of Lilith in whispered anguish, 'Come away!'

Then he said, this time in monotone, 'What is this blue flower, and what is its use?'

And the low thrilling voice answered, 'it is called "lûli uzhûri", two drops pressed upon the face of the sleeper and he will *sleep*.'

He was as a child in her hand and suffered himself to be led from thence, nevertheless he plucked listlessly one of the blue flowers, holding it downwards in his hand. What did she mean? Would the sleeper wake? Would the blue flower leave any stain? Could that stain be wiped off?

But as he lay asleep at early dawn he heard voices from afar off praying for him – the Abbé Félicien, Carmeille, his mother too, then some familiar words struck his ear: '*Libera mea porta inferi.*' Mass was being said for the repose of his soul, he knew this. No, he could not stay, he would leap over the brook, he knew the way – he had forgotten that the brook did not flow. Ah, but Lilith would know – what should he do? The blue flower – there it lay close by his bedside – he understood now; so he crept very silently to where Lilith lay asleep, her long hair glistening gold, shining like a glory round about her. He pressed two drops on her forehead, she sighed once, and a shade of preternatural anguish passed over her beautiful face. He fled – terror, remorse, and hope tearing his soul and making fleet his feet. He came to the brook – he did not see that the water did not flow – of course it was the brook for separation; one bound, he should be with things human again. He leapt over and –

A change had come over him – what was it? He could not tell – did he walk on all fours? Yes surely. He looked into the brook, whose still waters were fixed as a mirror, and there, horror, he beheld himself; or was it himself? His head and face, yes; but his body transformed to that of a wolf. Even as he looked he heard a sound of hideous mocking laughter behind him. He turned round – there, in a gleam of red lurid light, he saw one whose body was human, but whose head was that of a wolf, with eyes of infinite malice; and, while this hideous being laughed with a loud human laugh, he, essaying to speak, could only utter the prolonged howl of a wolf.

But we will transfer our thoughts from the alien things on the 'other side' to the simple human village where Gabriel used to dwell. Mère Yvonne was not much surprised when Gabriel did not turn up to breakfast – he often did not, so absent-minded was he; this time she said, 'I suppose he has gone with the others to the wolf-hunt.' Not that Gabriel was given to hunting, but, as she sagely said, 'there was no knowing what he might do next.' The boys said, 'Of course that muff Gabriel is skulking and hiding himself, he's afraid to join the wolf-hunt; why, he wouldn't even kill a cat,' for their one notion of excellence was slaughter – so the greater the game the greater the glory. They were chiefly now confined to cats and sparrows, but they all hoped in after time to become generals of armies.

Yet these children had been taught all their life through with the gentle words of Christ – but alas, nearly all the seed falls by the wayside, where it could not bear flower or fruit; how little these know the suffering and bitter anguish or realise the full meaning of the words to those of whom it is written, 'Some fell among thorns.'

The wolf hunt was so far a success that they did actually see a wolf, but not a success, as they did not kill it before it leapt over the brook to the 'other side', where, of course, they were afraid to pursue it. No emotion is more inrooted and intense in the minds of common people than hatred and fear of anything 'strange'.

Days passed by but Gabriel was nowhere seen – and Mère Yvonne began to see clearly at last how deeply she loved her only son, who was so unlike her that she had thought herself an object of pity to other mothers – the goose and the swan's egg. People searched and pretended to search, they even went to the length of dragging the ponds, which the boys thought very amusing, as it enabled them to kill a great number of water rats, and Carmeille sat in a corner and cried all day long. Mère Pinquèle also sat in a corner and chuckled and said that she had always said Gabriel would come to no good. The Abbé Félicien looked pale and anxious, but said very little, save to God and those that dwelt with God.

At last, as Gabriel was not there, they supposed he must be no-where – that is *dead* (their knowledge of other localities being so limited, that it did not even occur to them to suppose he might be living elsewhere than in the village). So it was agreed that an empty catafalque should be put up in the church with tall candles round it, and Mère Yvonne said all the prayers that were in her prayer book, beginning at the beginning and ending at the end, regardless of their appropriateness – not even omitting the instructions of the rubrics. And Carmeille sat in the corner of the little side chapel and cried, and cried. And the Abbé Félicien caused the boys to sing the Vespers for the Dead (this did not amuse them so much as dragging the pond), and on the following morning, in the silence of early dawn, said the Dirge and the Requiem – *and this Gabriel heard*.

Then the Abbé Félicien received a message to bring the Holy Viaticum to one sick. So they set forth in solemn procession with great torches, and their way lay along the brook of separation.

Essaying to speak he could only utter the prolonged howl of a wolf – the most fearful of all bestial sounds. He howled and howled again – perhaps Lilith would hear him! Perhaps she could rescue him? Then he remembered the blue flower – the beginning and end of all his woe. His cries aroused all the denizens of the forest – the wolves, the wolf-men, and the men-wolves. He fled before them in an agony of terror – behind him, seated on the black ram with human face, was the wolf-keeper, whose face was veiled in eternal shadow. Only once he turned to look behind – for among the shrieks and howls of bestial chase he heard one thrilling voice moan with pain. And there among them he beheld Lilith, her body too was that of a wolf, almost hidden in the masses of her glittering golden hair, on her forehead was a stain of blue, like in colour to her mysterious eyes, now veiled with tears she could not shed.

The way of the Most Holy Viaticum lay along the brook of separation. They heard the fearful howlings afar off, the torch bearers turned pale and trembled – but the Abbé Félicien, holding aloft the Ciborium, said 'They cannot harm us.'

Suddenly the whole horrid chase came in sight. Gabriel sprang over the brook, the Abbé Félicien held the most Blessed Sacrament before him, and his shape was restored to him and he fell down prostrate in adoration. But the Abbé Félicien still held aloft the Sacred Ciborium, and the people fell on their knees in the agony of fear, but the face of the priest seemed to shine with divine effulgence. Then the wolf-keeper held up in his hands the shape of something horrible and inconceivable – a monstrance to the Sacrament of Hell, and three times he raised it, in mockery of the blessed rite of Benediction. And on the third time streams of fire went forth from his fingers, and all the 'other side' of the forest took fire, and great darkness was over all.

All who were there and saw and heard it have kept the impress thereof for the rest of their lives – nor till in their death hour was the remembrance thereof absent from their minds. Shrieks, horrible beyond conception, were heard till nightfall – then the rain rained.

The 'other side' is harmless now – charred ashes only; but none dares to cross but Gabriel alone – for once a year for nine days a strange madness comes over him.

The Terror in the Snow

B. FLETCHER ROBINSON

Hendry, my servant, saw to it that I should not forget Inspector Addington Peace. Shortly after the adventure which I have already narrated, I left London for a round of country visits. And if a paragraph concerning that eminent detective chanced to appear in a newspaper, the substance of it was brought to me with my shaving-water in the morning.

'I see as 'e 'as bin up to 'is games again, sir,' was Hendry's usual overture. 'My word, but 'e's a sly one, by all accounts,' was the customary conclusion.

I believe that Hendry often gained considerable notoriety in the servants' hall by a boasted friendship with Peace. To this I attribute the fact of his being consulted by Mr Heavitree's butler on the occasion of the burglary that took place while I was staying at Crandon. Hendry's ludicrous fiasco, which resulted in a lawsuit for false imprisonment, need not be narrated here, though it was considered a remarkably good joke against me at the time.

Towards the end of December, I returned to London for a few days, and on the third night after my arrival I decided to visit the inspector. Hendry had discovered that he was a bachelor, and lived in two little rooms on the third floor. The floors that separated us were let out as offices, so that Peace at the top and I at the bottom had the old house to ourselves after seven o'clock. The little man was at home, and seemed pleased to see me. With his sparrow-like agility he hopped about, producing glasses and a bottle of whisky. Finally, with our pipes in full blast, we sat facing each other across the fire, and soon dropped into a conversation which to me, at least, was of unusual interest. A very curious knowledge of London and its peoples, had Inspector Addington Peace.

An hour quickly slipped by, and when I rose to go I asked him if he would dine with me on my return from Cloudsham in Norfolk, where I was spending Christmas. He would be pleased, he told me;

and then, as he stooped to light a spill in the coals – 'You stay with the Baron Steen, I suppose?' he asked.

'Yes.'

'And why?'

'Why?' I echoed in some surprise.

'You have relatives or other friends?'

'My nearest relative is a sour old uncle in Bradford, who calls me hard names for using the gifts Providence gave me instead of adding up figures in a smoky office. As for friends – well, I am a fairly rich man, Inspector, and, as such, have many friends. What is there against the Baron Steen?'

'Oh, nothing,' he said, puffing at his pipe, so that he spoke as from a cloud, mistily.

'I know that he has played a bold game on the Stock Exchange,' I continued, 'and there may be a few outwitted financiers growling at his heels. But it would be hard to find a more thoughtful host. Yes, I am going to Cloudsham tomorrow.'

We shook hands warmly on parting, and as I descended the stairs he leant over the rail, smiling down upon me.

'Remember your dinner engagement,' I called up to him. 'I shall see you after the New Year.'

'Yes, if not before,' he said; and I seemed to catch the faint echo of a laugh as I turned the corner.

It was on the afternoon of December 24th that I stepped from the train at the little station of Cloudsham. Fresh snow had fallen, and the wind came bitterly over the frozen levels of the fen country. A distant clock was striking four as the carriage passed into the crested entrance-gates and tugged up a rising slope of parkland dotted with ragged oaks and storm-bowed spinneys, which showed as black stains upon its snow-clad undulations. At the summit the road bent sharply, and I saw below me the old manor of Cloudsham, beyond which – a sombre plain, losing itself in the evening mists that swathed the horizon – stretched the restless waters of the North Sea.

The house lay in a broad depression, in shape as the hollow of a hand, save only on the seaward side, where the line of cliff bit into it like the grip of a giant's teeth. The grey front looked up, across a slope of grass land, to a semicircle of forest that swept away in dark shadings of fir and oak. From the long oblong of the main buildings were thrust back two wings, flanked on the nearer side by a chapel.

From the back of the house to the edge of the sea cliffs, a distance of some quarter of a mile, ran an irregular avenue of firs with clipped yew walks and laurel-edged flower gardens on either hand.

A dozen men sweeping the paths and a telegraph boy on a pony mounting the hill towards me showed as black pygmies against the drifts of snow.

My bachelor host was absent when I was ushered into the great central hall where the house-party were met together for their tea. I am by nature shy of strangers, taken in large doses, and it was with relief that I recognised Jack Talman, the grizzled cynic of an Academician, sitting in a corner seat well out of reach of draughts and female conversation.

'Hello, Phillips,' he welcomed me. 'And what financial gale brings you here?'

'What do you mean?'

'Don't put on frills with me. I've come to paint old Steen's picture, if he will give me the fifteen hundred that I'm asking for it. Lord Tommy Retford yonder is here to unload some of his old furniture – you know Tommy's rooms in Piccadilly, don't you? Furnished by a dealer in Bond Street, and twenty-five per cent. commission to Tommy on everything he can sell out of them. That's Mrs Talbot Slingsly talking to him. Pretty woman, got into trouble in New York, was cut by all America, and captured Slingsly and London Society at one blow. Scandal never does cross the Atlantic somehow – all the dirty linen gets washed in the herring-pond. That's old Lord Blane by the fire; very respectable, and lends money on the sly. "Private gentleman will make advances on note of hand" – you know. Fine woman Mrs Billy Blades – that's she on the sofa. She's been making desperate love to Steen, but no go. The gay old dog's too clever for her. That long chap's her husband. Watch him prowling round, looking to see if he can pouch a silver ashtray or something, I expect. By Jove, Phillips, but it's as good as a play, ain't it?'

'And this is London Society?' I exclaimed.

'No,' he cackled, shaking with vast amusement. 'No, man; no. It's the Smart Set, that advertised, criticised, glorious, needy brigade of rogues and vagabonds – the Smart Set. Bless 'em all, say I; they're the best of company, but it's as well to lock up your valuables before you become too intimate with them.'

I finished off my tea while old Talman sucked at his cigarette in great entertainment.

'You'd like to see the house,' he commenced again. 'Come along, I'll show you round – I want a walk before dinner.'

It was a most interesting ramble. We passed from room to room admiring the carved oak, the splendid pictures, the Sheraton furniture, the cabinets of old china, the armour, and the tapestry. For the manor was filled with the heirlooms of the de Launes, from whom the Baron Steen rented it. And though the present peer, a broken-down old drunkard, was living in a little villa at Eastbourne on eight hund.ed pounds a year, the family had been a great and glorious one, finding mention on many a page in English history.

At the end of the great dining-room, set in the black-oak wainscot above the fire, was the portrait of a boy. It was a Reynolds, and a worthy effort of that master hand. The lad could have been no more than fifteen years of age, but in his eyes was that grave, distracted expression that usually comes with the painful wisdom of later years. In more closely examining the picture, I noticed that a large portion of it at the bottom right-hand corner had been repaired or painted out. I called Talman's attention to this misfortune, asking if he knew the cause.

'They painted out the wolf,' he said, 'and with good enough reason, too.'

'A wolf?' I said.

'If old de Laune were to hear me gossiping about it he'd kick me out of the place – he would, by Jove! But with Steen in possession it's safe enough. Mind you, though, you mustn't mention it to the ladies – on your word, now.'

'Yes, yes,' I said eagerly; 'go on.'

'Such things frighten the women,' he explained. 'Well, it was in this way. Phillip, and he was the sixth earl, was our ambassador at St Petersburg somewhere about the year 1790. Once when he was out hunting he shot an old she-wolf that was peering from the mouth of a cave, and inside they found a thriving family of four cubs. One of them was white, an albino, I suspect. He saved it from the dogs and took it home. When he came back to Cloudsham the next year, he brought it along with his wife and his boy – an only son. They say it was a great pet at first, but it grew sulky with age, and finally was kept chained in the stables.

'One Christmas Eve, just as dusk was closing in, de Laune was trotting down the drive – he had been hunting at a distant meeting – when he heard a fearful screaming from the lower gardens towards the cliff. He put spurs to his horse, and in two minutes was galloping through the shadows of the fir avenue towards the sea. All of a sudden his horse pulled up dead, threw him, and bolted. When he got to his feet – he wasn't hurt, luckily – what did he see but the body of his son, lying with his throat torn out, and the white wolf standing over him, the broken chain dangling at its neck.

'They say he was a giant, this Philip de Laune, and of a very wild and passionate temper. Anyway, he went straight for the beast, and, though he was dreadfully mauled, he killed it – Heaven knows how – with his bare hands. That's why the present branch of the family came by the place. Pretty gruesome, isn't it?'

'A strange story,' I told him; 'but why must it be kept a secret from the ladies?'

'Because the beast walks, man. There's not a labourer in Norfolk who would go into the lower gardens on any night of the year, much less on Christmas Eve.'

'My good Talman, do you mean to say you believe this?'

'I don't know – but I wouldn't go into the lower gardens tonight, if I could walk round. Think of it, Phillips, the white shape with the bloody jaws lurking in the shadows! Ugh – let's go and get a cocktail before – '

'I beg your pardon, sir, but the Baron is looking for you.'

He was a tall, hatchet-faced fellow, with that mixture of respect and dignity that marks the well-trained British manservant. Upon the soft pile of the rugs we had not heard his footsteps.

'He asked me to find you, sir,' he continued, addressing himself to me with a slight bow. 'He is waiting in his room.'

As he preceded us thither, Talman whispered that Henderson – meaning thereby our conductor – was Steen's valet, and a very clever follow by all accounts.

The Baron, fat, high-coloured, and hearty, welcomed me with an open sincerity of pleasure well calculated to place a guest at his ease. A remarkable old boy was the Baron Steen. He always seemed to carry with him a jovial atmosphere of his own, in which those to whom he spoke were lost and blinded out of their better judgment. He was kind enough to pay me some compliments upon my water-colour work. Whatever else can be brought against him, no-one can deny that he was a sound judge of art. The dinner passed pleasantly enough that night, with free and witty conversation. Our bachelor host was in his most humorous mood, keeping those about him in shouts of laughter. Facing him, at the extremity of the long table, was his secretary, a thin, melancholy youth of about four-and-twenty.

My fair neighbour told me that Terry, as he was named, had been intended for the Church, but that his father, having ruined himself on the Stock Exchange, had persuaded the Baron to give him work. He was devoted to his patron, which, she smiled, was not surprising, seeing that he must be well on his way to rebuilding the fortune his father had lost.

I am not an ardent gambler, and when I do play I admit a preference for games in which brains are of some account. The roulette-table soon bored me, and after I had seen the last of a few pounds, I contented myself by watching the changing fortunes of the rest of the party. Just before eleven the Baron, who had parted with considerable sums of money in perfect good humour, excused himself, and before the rest had settled down to the table again, I slipped away to my bedroom, where a selection of novels and a favourite pipe offered more congenial attractions.

The room was of considerable size and majestically furnished. It was on the first floor at the extremity of the right-hand wing, and looked out over the gardens on the cliff. A branch road from the main drive ran beneath the windows to an entrance at the back of the house.

They had steam heat on the upper floors, and the high temperature of my room had drawn stale and heavy odours from the tapestry on the walls and the ancient hangings that fringed the huge four-post bedstead. It was the atmosphere of an old clothes shop on a July day. I pulled back the curtains, opened the window and thrust out my head for a mouthful of fresh air.

It was a quiet, moonless night, lit by the stars that blinked in their thousand constellations. Though the snow lay deep, the air struck mildly. Indeed, if it were freezing, it could not have been by more than two degrees. Upon the edge of the distant cliffs robes of confusing mist curled in veils as thin as moonlight; but in the foreground the yew walks and aisles of ancient laurel showed clearly upon the white carpet. About the central avenue of firs which carved the gardens into two the darkness lay in impenetrable pools of shadow. As I waited, the silence was startled by a bell. It rang the four quarters in a tinkling measure, followed by eleven musical strokes. I knew that the sound must come from the little church that lay to my right; but, though I leant from my window, the angle of the wing in which I was hid the building from me.

I feel that the story which I have now to tell may well turn me into an object for ridicule. I can only describe that which I saw; as for the conclusions at which I arrived there are many more practical people in the world than myself who would have judged no differently. At best it was a ghastly business.

I had returned to the dressing-table and was changing my dress-coat for a comfortable smoking-jacket when I heard it – a faint and distant cry, yet a cry which was crowded with such terror that I clung to a chair with my white face and goggling eyes staring back at me from the mirror on the table. Again it sounded, and again; then silence fell like the shutter of a camera. I rushed to the window, peering out into the night.

The great gardens lay sleeping in the dusky shadows. There was nothing to be heard; nothing moved save the curling wreaths of mist that came creeping up over the cliffs like the ghosts of drowned sailormen from their burial sands below. Could it have been some trick of the imagination? Could it – and the suggestion which I despised thrust itself upon me – could it bear reference to that grim tragedy that had been played in the old fir avenue so many years ago?

And then I first saw the THING that came towards me.

It was moving up a narrow path, hedged with yew, that led from the gardens and passed to the right of the wing in which I stood. The yew had been clipped into walls some five feet high, but the eastern gales had beaten out gaps and ragged indentations in the lines of greenery, so that in my sideways view of it the path itself was here and there exposed. It was through one of these breaches in the walls that I noticed a sign of movement. I waited, straining my eyes. Yes, there it showed again, a something, moving swiftly towards the house with a clumsy rolling stride.

It was never nearer to me than fifty yards, and the stars gave a shifty light. Yet it left me with an impression that it was about four feet in height and of a dull white colour. I remember that its body contrasted plainly with the dark hedges, but melted into uncertainty against a patch of snow. Once it stopped and half raised itself on its hind legs as if listening. Then again it tumbled forward in its shambling, ungainly fashion – now hidden by the yew wall, now thrust into momentary sight by a ragged gap until it disappeared round the angle of the house. Doubtless it would turn to the left, round the old chapel, across the snow-bound park, and so to the woods – where a wolf should be!

I was still staring from the window in the blank fear of the unknown, when I heard the swift tap of feet upon the road beneath me. Round the corner of the wing came a man, running with a patter of little strides, while a dozen yards behind him were a pair of less active followers. What they wanted I did not consider; for at that moment the sight of my own kind was joy enough for me. The electric lamps in the room behind me threw a broad golden patch upon the snow, and as the leader reached it he stopped, glancing up at where I stood. The light struck him fairly in the face. It was Addington Peace!

'Did you hear that cry?' he panted; and then, with a sudden nod of recognition: 'I see who it is. Mr Phillips – well, and did you hear it?'

'It came from over there – in the fir avenue,' said I, pointing with a trembling finger. 'I don't understand it, Inspector; I don't indeed. There was something that came up that yew walk behind you about a minute afterwards. I should have thought it would have passed you.'

'No, I saw nothing. What was it like?'

'A sort of a dog,' I stammered; for under his steady eye I had not nerve enough to tell him of my private imaginings.

'A dog – that's curious. Are all the rest of you in bed?'

'No; they're gambling!'

'Very good. I see there is a door at the back there. Will you come down and let me in, after I've had l look round the gardens?'

'Certainly.'

'If you meet any of your friends, you need not mention that I have arrived. Do you understand?'

I nodded, and he hopped away across the lawn with his two companions at his heels.

I slipped on an overcoat and made my way quietly down the stairs. From the roulette-room, as I passed it, came the chink of money and the murmur of merry voices. They would not disturb us, that was certain. I reached the garden doors in the centre of the main building, turned the key, and walked out into the gloom of a great square porch.

As I have said, the temperature was scarcely below freezing-point, and if I shivered in my fur-lined overcoat it was more from excitement than any great chill in the air. For a good twenty minutes I waited listening and peering into the night. It was not a pleasant time, for my nerves were jangled, and I searched the shadows with timorous eyes, half fearing, half expecting, Heaven knows what hideous apparition. It was with a start which set my heart thumping that I saw Peace turn the corner of the right-hand wing and come trotting down the drive towards me. There was something in his aspect that told a story of calamity.

'What is it?' I asked him, as he panted up.

'I want you – come along,' he whispered, and started back by the way he had come.

We passed round the right-hand wing, under my bedroom window, and stopped where the yew walk ended. To right and left of the entrance two stone fauns leered upon us under the starlight.

'This thing you call a dog – could you see it as far as this?'

'No; the angle of the wing prevented me.'

'You saw it pass in this direction. Are you certain it did not go back the way it came?'

'Yes. I am quite certain.'

'Then it must either have turned up the road, in which case I should have met it; or down the road, where you would have seen it as it passed under your windows; or else have run straight on. If we take these facts as proved, it must have run straight on.'

'That is so.'

We had our backs to the laughing fauns. Before us lay a broad triangle of even snow, with the chapel and wing of the house for its sides, and for its base the carriage-drive on which we stood. There was no shrub or tree in any part of it that might conceal a fugitive. Close to the wall of the house ran a path ending in a small side door. The chapel, which was joined to the mansion, had no entrance on the garden side.

'If it entered this triangle and disappeared – for I am certain it was not here when I ran by – we may conclude that it found its way into the house. It had no other method of escape. Kindly stay here, Mr Phillips. This snow is fortunate, but I wish the sweepers had not been so conscientious about their work on the paths.'

He drew a little electric lantern from his coat, touched the spring, and with an eye of light moving before him, turned into the path under the wall. He walked slowly, bending double as he swept the brilliant circle now on the exposed ground, now on the snow ridges to right and left. The sills of the ground-floor window were carefully examined, and when he reached the door he searched the single step before it with minute attention. A curious spectacle he made, this little atom of a man, as he peeped and peered his way like some slow-hunting beast on a cold scent.

It was not until he left the path for the snow-covered grass-plot that I saw him give any sign of success. He dropped on his knees with a little chirrup of satisfaction like the note of a bird. Then he rose again, shaking his head and staring up at the windows above him in a cautious, suspicions manner. Finally he came slowly back to me, with his head on one side, staring at the ground before him.

'You thought it was a dog?' he asked. 'Why a dog?'

'It looked to me like a big dog – or a wolf,' I told him boldly.

'Whether it be beast or man, or both, I believe the thing that killed him is in the house now.'

I jumped back, staring at him with a sudden exclamation. 'Who has been killed?' I stammered out.

'Baron Steen. We found him on the cliffs yonder. He was badly cut about.'

'It's impossible, Inspector,' I cried. 'He left the roulette-table not a quarter of an hour before you came.'

'Ah – he was a cool hand, Mr Phillips. It was like him to put off bolting till the last minute. The warrant against him for company frauds is in my pocket now. But someone gave the game away to him, for his yacht is lying off the beach there, with a boat from her waiting at the foot of the cliff. But we've no time to lose – come along.'

Before the big garden porch the inspector's two companions were waiting. He drew them aside for a minute's whispered conversation before they separated, and disappeared into the night. What had they done with the body? I had not the courage to inquire.

We entered the house, moving very softly. In the hall Peace took me by the arm.

'You're a bit shaken, Mr Phillips, and I'm not surprised. But I want your assistance badly. Can you pull yourself together and help me to see this through?'

'I'll do what I can.'

'Take me up to your room, then.'

We were in luck, for we tiptoed up the great stairs and down the long passages without meeting a guest or servant. Once in my room, the inspector walked across and pushed the electric bell. Three, four minutes went by before the summons was answered, and then it was by a flushed and disordered footman who bounced into the room and halted, staring openmouthed from me to my companion.

'Sorry to disturb your dance,' said Peace, beaming upon him.

'Beg pardon, sir, but you startled me – yes, we was 'aving a little dance in the servants' 'all; but it's of no consequence, sir.'

'A slippery floor, eh, with so much French chalk on it?'

The young man glanced at the powder on his shoes and grinned.

'So you are all dancing in the servants' hall, are you?'

'I believe so, sir, barring Edward, who is waiting on the party, and Mr Henderson.'

'And where is Mr Henderson?'

'He is the baron's man, sir. I should not presume to inquire where he was. Beg pardon, sir, but are you staying here tonight?'

'This is a friend of mine,' I interposed. 'He will stay the night; but you need not trouble about that now.'

'A smart fellow like you can keep his mouth shut,' continued the inspector, sweetly. 'You wouldn't go shouting all over the house if you were let into a secret – now, would you?'

'Oh no, sir; on my word I wouldn't.'

And so Peace told him of the projected arrest, of the murder, and of his own identity. The colour faded from the young man's cheeks, but he stood stiff and silent, never taking his eyes from the little detective's face.

'And what can I do, sir?' he asked, when the tale was over. 'He was a good master to us, sir; whatever there was against him, he was good to us. You can trust me to help catch the scoundrel who killed him if I can.'

'I see this room is warmed by steam heat. Is that the case with all the bedrooms and passages?'

'Yes, sir. The only open fires are in the reception-rooms. When the baron made the alterations last year, they left the grates for the sake of appearance; but they are never lighted, save on the ground floor.'

'And in what reception-rooms are there fires at the present moment?'

'The dining-room fire has died out by now,' said the young man, ticking off the numbers on his fingers. 'But there is one in the big hall, one in the library where the party is playing, one in the little drawing-room, and one in the baron's room.'

'And the kitchen?'

'Of course, sir, one in the kitchen and one in the servants' hall.'

'That is all. Are you certain?'

'Quite certain, sir.'

'Good; and now for the bath-rooms.'

'The bath-rooms, sir?'

'Exactly.'

'There are two bath-rooms in each wing; some of the gentlemen have tubs in their own rooms besides.'

'Now, I think we know where we are,' said the inspector, briskly. 'No chance of the roulette party breaking up, is there?'

'Oh no, sir; not for another two hours, at least.'

'I want you to return, Mr Phillips, and try your luck at the tables for a spell,' he said, with a quick glance at me. 'It is now eleven thirty; be back in this room at twelve fifteen. I am going to take a walk round the house with our young friend here in the meanwhile. The baron had a secretary, I believe?'

'Yes, a man called Terry.'

'Bring him up with you when you come. I shall want a talk with him. Is all quite plain?'

'Yes,' I told him; and so we parted.

When I stepped into the roulette-room I stood for a moment blinking at the players like a yokel at a pantomime. The scene was to me something unreal, a clever piece of stage effect, with its flushed and covetous faces, its frocks and its diamonds, its piles of sparkling gold, and the cry of the banker as he twirled the wheel. How could they be doing this with that bloodstained patch on the cliff edge, with that unknown horror slinking through the snow – how could they be doing this if they were not acting a part! An odd figure I must have looked, if there had been anyone to notice me. But they were too eager in the game to hear the opening of the door, or to see who went and came. I walked over to the fireplace, lit a cigarette, and watched them, my nerves growing steadier in the merry chatter of tongues. They were all there, the men and women of that careless house-party, all there – save one who lay silent wherever they had laid him.

Half an hour had slipped by, until, at last, with an effort, I walked to the table and threw down two sovereigns on the red.

It won, and I laughed at the melancholy omen; not, perhaps, without an odd note in my voice, for the man over whose shoulder I leaned to gather my winnings glanced up with a startled expression. It was young Terry, the secretary; the very person I wanted to see.

'Anything the matter, Mr Phillips?' he asked. 'You're not looking very well.'

'Don't worry about me,' I told him. 'But I want a word with you in private.'

'Certainly – just one moment.'

He had been winning heavily, and it took him some time to crowd the banknotes into his pockets. A sovereign slipped from his fingers and rolled under the table as he rose; but he paid no attention to it.

'I have something to tell you. Can you come up to my room?' I asked him.

He hesitated, looking regretfully at the table, where Fortune had been so kind to him.

'It happens to be rather important,' I said.

He followed me without another word. I did not attempt to explain until we had passed up the stairs and through the corridors to my room. He seated himself on the great bed with a shiver of cold, drawing the heavy curtains about his shoulders. And there I told him the story from the beginning to the end, hiding nothing, not even my belief in the supernatural nature of the thing which I had seen.

He never moved, but his face grew so pale and drawn that towards the end it seemed as if it were a powdered mask that stared at me from the shadows of the curtains. 'My God,' he cried, and fell back upon the bed in a passion of hysterical tears.

I tried to help him, but he thrust me fiercely away, so I thought it best to let him get over it himself. He was still lying on the thick quilt, sobbing and shivering, when the door opened and Peace stepped into the room. I explained the situation in a hurried whisper; but when I turned again Terry had got to his feet and was watching us, clinging to the bed-post.

'This is Inspector Addington Peace,' I told him. 'Perhaps you can give him some information?'

'Not tonight,' he cried, 'don't ask me tonight, gentlemen. You cannot tell what this means to me; tomorrow, perhaps – '

He dropped down upon the bed, covering his face with his hands. He seemed a helpless sort of creature, and my heart went out to him in his calamity.

'A night's rest is what you want,' I said, patting him on the shoulder. 'Come, let me give you an arm.'

He took it at once, with a grateful glance, and I led him down the corridor, with Peace in sympathetic attendance. Fortunately, his room was in the same wing, so we had not far to go. When we reached it, he thanked us for our care of him. And so we left him, returning to my bedroom in silence, for, indeed, the scene had been a painful one.

'Peace,' I said, when the door had closed behind us, 'what was the thing I saw in the yew walk?'

He had seated himself in an easy-chair, and was polishing the bowl of a well-stained meerschaum pipe, with a silk pocket-handkerchief.

'I think you already have an explanation,' he answered cheerfully.

'If it amuses you to sneer at my superstition – '

'You refer to the legend of the de Launes. I have heard the story before, Mr Phillips; nor am I surprised that you believed it to be the ghost wolf.'

'I did – but now I want you to disprove it.'

'On the contrary, all my evidence supports your theory.'

I stared at him, with a creeping horror in my blood. I was beginning to be afraid – seriously afraid. Peace leant back in his chair, with his eyes, vacant in expression, fixed on the wall. He seemed rather to be arguing with himself than addressing a listener.

'Baron Steen,' he said, 'met with his death on an open path between a shallow duck-pond and a little pavilion. He had fought hard for life, had rolled and struggled with his enemy. There were four or five punctured wounds in his throat and neck, from which he had bled profusely. And now for the thing that killed him – whatever it was. It could not have fled down the cliff path, for the boat's crew waiting below had heard the screams, and had come running up by that way. They were with him when we arrived, and assured me they had seen nothing. It could not have turned to the right or left, for, though the paths had been swept clean – doubtless by the baron's orders, for he would not desire his way of escape to be easily traced – the snow on either side lay in unbroken levels. It could only have retired by the yew avenue, and it did not break through the hedge. That, again, the snow proved clearly. So we may take it that whatever the thing may have been which you saw – it killed Baron Steen; further, it escaped into the house – this, you will remember, we decided in the garden. Let us imagine it was a man – that you were deceived by the uncertain light. His clothes must of necessity have been drenched in blood. He could not have struggled so fiercely with his victim and escaped those fatal signs. Yet, he cannot have burned his clothes, for the fires are downstairs where people were passing. Nor can he have washed them, for neither the bathrooms nor the bedroom basins have been recently used. I have spent some time in searching boxes and wardrobes with no result. Stranger still, as far as my limited information goes, everyone in the house can prove an alibi – save two.'

'And who are they?' I asked eagerly.

'Mr Henderson, the baron's valet – and yourself.'

'Inspector Peace – ' I began angrily.

'Tut, tut, my dear Mr Phillips. I was merely stating the facts. Mr Henderson's case, however, presents an interesting feature, for he has run away.'

'Run away,' I said. 'Then that settles it.'

'Not altogether, I'm afraid. I think it is more a matter of theft than murder with Mr Henderson.'

I stared at him in silence as he sat there, with his little hands clasped upon his lap, a picture of irritating composure.

'Peace,' I said, struggling to control my voice. 'What are you hiding from me? It is something inhuman, unnatural that has done this dreadful thing.'

The little detective stretched himself, yawned, and then rose to his feet. 'I have no opinion except that I think you had better get to bed. Don't lock your door, for I may find time for an hour's sleep on your sofa before morning.'

The news was out after breakfast – the news that led to mild hysterics and scurrying lady's-maids to the packing of boxes, and the chastened sorrow of those gentlemen who owed the baron money. Through all the turmoil of the morning moved the little detective, the most sympathetic of men. It was he who apologised so humbly for the locked doors of the bathrooms; he who superintended the lighting of fires, and the making of the beds, and the packing of trunks for the station so closely that the housemaids were convinced that he entertained a secret passion for each one of them; it was he who announced Henderson's robbery of the gold plate, following it by information as to the culprit's arrest. The establishment had by this time become convinced that Henderson was the murderer, and breathed relief at the news.

They had brought the body of Baron Steen to the house early in the morning – it had been laid in the garden pavilion on its first discovery.

With death in so strange a form present amongst us, I was disgusted by the noise and bustle, the gossip and chatter amongst the guests of the dead man. I wandered off in search of the one person who had seemed sincerely affected by the news, the young secretary, Maurice Terry. He was nowhere to be found. A servant of whom I inquired told me that the secretary had kept to his bed, being greatly un-nerved by the tragedy, and I strolled up the stairs again on an errand of consolation. The door was locked, and there came no answer to my continued tapping.

'Terry,' I called through the keyhole. 'It is I, Phillips; won't you let me in?'

'I have a key that will fit, if you will kindly stand aside,' suggested a modest voice.

I rose from my knees to find the inspector at my elbow.

'It would be a gross intrusion,' I told him. 'If he wishes to be alone with his sorrow, we have no right to disturb him.'

'He is seriously ill.'

'How did you discover that?'

'By borrowing a gardener's ladder and looking through his window. He is unconscious, or was ten minutes ago.'

A skilful twist or two with a bit of wire and the key was pushed from the lock. The duplicate opened the door. Peace walked into the room, and I followed at his heels.

On his bed, fully dressed, lay poor Terry, with a face paler than his pillows. His breath came and went in short, painful gasps. One hand strayed continuously about his throat, groping and plucking at his collar with feverish unrest. It was a very painful spectacle.

'I will send for a doctor at once,' I whispered, stepping to the bell. But Peace held up a warning hand.

'Come here,' he said, 'I have something to show you.'

With movements as tender as a woman's he unfastened the man's collar and slipped out the stud. Then he paused. The eyes that watched me had turned cold and hard.

'If it is as I suspect, you may be called as a witness. Do you object?'

'Yes; but I shall not leave you on that account?'

'Very well,' he said, as he opened the shirt and the vest beneath it. Smeared and patched in dark etching upon the white skin was a broad stain of blood, of dried and clotted blood, the life's blood of a man.

'He is wounded, Peace,' I cried. 'Poor fellow, he must have nearly bled to death.'

'Do not alarm yourself,' said the inspector, drily. 'It is the blood of Baron Steen.'

* * *

A week had gone by, and I was sitting alone in my Keble Street rooms, when Peace walked in, with a heavy travelling-coat over his arm. 'Thank Heaven, you have come at last,' I cried. 'How is Maurice Terry?'

'Dead – poor fellow,' he said, with an honest sorrow in his voice. 'Yet, after all, Mr Phillips, it was the best that could have happened to him.'

'And his story – the causes – the method?' I demanded.

'It has taken some hard work, but the bits of the puzzle are fitted together at last. You wish to hear it, I suppose?'

'According to your promise,' I reminded him.

'It is a case of unusual interest,' he said. 'Though it bears a certain similarity to the Gottstein trial at Kiel in '89.'

He paused to light his big pipe, and then sat back in his chair, with his eyes fixed in abstract contemplation.

'I was convinced that the murderer was in the house; and that he had entered by the side door, towards which you had seen him pass. When studying the spot I made a discovery of some importance. Steen had left by the same exit. Also he had reason to fear some person in that wing, for he had turned from the path and made a circuit over the grass. I had already noted his broad-toed boots when examining his body – and the footprints in the snow were unmistakable. Who was his enemy in that wing? It was a problem to be solved.

'I discovered no stained clothing, and no signs of its cleansing or destruction. From what information I could gather, all the house party had been in the roulette-room save you yourself; and all the servants had been at the dance save Henderson and a man waiting on the guests. But in the course of my search the footman who accompanied me discovered that a quantity of gold plate was missing. It was reasonable to imagine that Henderson was the thief. Probably the confidential valet had learnt of the Baron's projected flight and of the warrant for his arrest. It was a moment for judicious robbery, the traces of which would be covered by the confusion of the news. But was Henderson also a murderer? I did not think so. The death of his master was the one thing which would wreck his scheme. In the early morning I interviewed the farmer on whose cart he had driven into Norbridge. He told me that, acting on orders he had received from Henderson, he met that person at the corner of the stables at eleven o'clock precisely – five minutes before the murder occurred. That finally eliminated the valet from the list.

'On my return from the farm I examined the gardens again with great minuteness. At the corner of the little pavilion, about fifteen feet from where the body had lain, there was a patch of bloody snow. This puzzled me a good deal, until the solution offered itself that the murderer had tried to wash his hands in the snow, the water of the pond being frozen hard. Yet his clothing would also bear the stain. What had he worn that showed so white to you in the starlight? Could it have been that he wore no clothes at all?'

A naked man! The suggestion was full of possibilities.

'It was fortunate that I had brought assistants to help me in Steen's capture. Their presence gave me a wider scope, for they were both good men. I left them to search the pavilion and laurels for the clothing, which the murderer might have concealed when he realised how fatal was its evidence. As I walked back to the house I began to understand the situation more clearly. The main drive, curving down the slope of the park, was in view of a tall man coming up by the yew walk. The murderer might have noticed our approach. What more natural than that he should have bent double as he ran, thus obtaining the cover of the left-hand hedge, which was not more than four to five feet high? Did not this answer to your description of the thing you had seen? It would have been cold work for him. I made a note to be on the lookout for chills.

'For a couple of hours I devoted myself to speeding those guests who caught the eleven-thirty train. I do not think a trunk left for the station of which I have not a complete inventory. Indeed, the baron's creditors have to thank me for the return of several trifles of value, which were included, accidentally, no doubt, in the ladies' dressing-bags.

'After the carriages had started I went in search of Terry, and discovered that he had not left his room. Equally to the point, his windows looked down upon the spot where the baron made his detour over the grass while escaping.

I became interested in this young man. The score was creeping up against him. A ladder from an obliging gardener allowed me to observe him from the window. A visit to the housekeeper gave me a duplicate hey to his door. What happened in the room you know, Mr Phillips.'

'But, the motive – why did he kill his patron?' I asked him eagerly.

'I doubt if we shall ever learn the truth on that point,' he said. 'As far as I can make out, Steen was directly responsible for the ruin and disgrace of Terry's father. Probably the son did not fully realise this when the baron, with a pity most unusual in the man, gave him the secretaryship. But of all participation in the flight he was certainly innocent, for he was in bed at the time.'

'In bed!' I cried.

'Don't interrupt, if you please. What happened I take to be as follows: Terry was in bed when the old man tried to creep past his window. Somehow he heard him, and, looking out, understood what was up. Perhaps that rascal Henderson had told him the truth about his father; perhaps Steen had promised him compensation – he had a mother and sister dependent on him – which promise the financier meant to avoid, along with many more serious obligations, by running away. At any rate, passion, revenge, the sense of injustice – call it what you like – took hold of the lad. He caught up the first handy weapon, it chanced to be a dagger paper-knife – dangerous things, I hate them – and rushed down a back staircase and through the side door in pursuit of his enemy.

'When that had happened which happened, the fear that comes to all amateurs in crime took him by the throat. He wiped his hands in the snow; he tore off his sleeping suit – that is how I know he had been in bed – and thrust it, with its terrible evidences of murder, into the thatch of the little pavilion. We found it there a day later. Then he started back to the house as naked as a baby.

'He saw us running down the hill, and made for the side door, bending double behind the hedge. Who were we? Had we noticed him? Believe me, Mr Phillips, whether he had held the murder righteous or no, it was only the rope he saw dangling before him. Might not the alarm be given at any moment? He dared not wash himself, and the stains had dried upon him. He hurried on his clothes, shivering in the chill that had struck home, and so to the safest place he could find – the roulette-table.'

'It is well that he died,' I said simply.

'It saved the law some trouble,' remarked the inspector, with a grim little nod at the wall.

A Werewolf of the Campagna

MRS HUGH FRASER

Santiago is rich in gruesome things, but the most terrifying that I ever saw there was when I was leaning out of the drawing-room window one night, just before I went to bed. It was late, and there was a bright moon shining that threw the whole of the Alameda into vivid relief. I had been absorbed in my thoughts for some time, trying to dream myself back into Italy, and see, in the stucco *palatios*, the real palaces of Rome – wondering what all the dear people there were doing (one has to snatch at the tricks of childhood sometimes in the ends of the earth, to help quiet the *Heimweh*), when, suddenly, from far up the street, I heard the howl of a wolf. There was no mistaking it. It was not a dog; no dog had ever lived that could imitate it. Staring down in the direction from which it came, I saw the figure of a man lurch out of the trees into the full light of the moon – a man dressed in evening clothes – I could see the white shirt-front clearly. On he came, staggering from side to side, and bumping his head crazily against the trees, as though trying to break them down – and not by accident, for I saw him, three or four times, lower his head and run at them. And all the time he howled – that awful howl of a wolf!

The street was quite deserted, not even a policeman being in sight, and I had a full view of him as he passed beneath the window. His eyes were shut, his lips were drawn back in a grin that showed his teeth, and his mouth was wide open. I could not leave the window, though my own teeth were chattering like castanets, and I was trembling all over. Down the street I watched him go, weaving from side to side in the moonlight, and rushing, head-on, against the trees, howling, until at last he disappeared in the distance. But the screeching came back to me for two or three minutes after he had vanished himself.

What was it? The good God who made him only knows. He was not drunk, for no drunken man could have thrown himself at the trees in that fashion – and no sober man, either, that I have ever seen or heard of. The howl, at least, was not that of any human being, whatever the body might have been. It was that of a famished wolf and not anything else. Does that sound like superstition? Well, superstition it may be. But which is the worst offender – he who, having seen much and experienced many strange adventures, prefers to think all things possible in the creation of an omnipotent God, or he who fastens that word 'superstition' over the entrance to every avenue of knowledge that pertains to the Twilight Kingdom?

I am reminded of an article I read some time ago on the subject of miracles by a divine of one of the free churches, whose name I forget. Having set forth his belief in an almighty and all-powerful Providence, the writer set himself the task of attempting to prove the miracles could not happen in our day – and this is how he went about it. Compelled by the incontrovertible evidence of the Gospel, he acknowledged that our Lord performed many in His time, and that His followers performed many more. But, he went on to say, such things then were obviously needed to convert the heathen and give the church a start. Leaving it to be understood that no such necessity existed nowadays, there being, presumably, no more heathen to convert, he let fall the astounding observation that, should an all-just, all-seeing, all-understanding God, in His infinite wisdom, do such a thing in our time – and fly in the face of the writer's personal opinions on the subject – he would cease ('cease!' the Eternal would 'cease!' that was his word) to be a just God, thereby, of course, ceasing to be God at all! Put into plainer words, the Almighty might continue to sit on His throne as long as He behaved Himself in accordance with the reverend gentleman's idea of how a God should behave – but not a moment longer. And the writer was – will you believe it? – a Professor of Theology at a nonconformist seminary!

It is a strange attitude of mind that acknowledges omnipotence in one breath and sets rigid limits to it in the next. But to go back to the man-wolf.

One of our old Italian servants used to tell a fearful story – and she spoke of it as though it were of common knowledge. It was about a certain hunter who lived far out in the Campagna by himself, in a small stone house. One evening, just as he was preparing to go to bed, he heard someone knocking at the door and, opening it, saw a man and a woman of the better class standing outside. They were well dressed, although the woman was dusty and tired, and they begged him to let them stay the night, the man saying that they had gone for a walk earlier in the day, taking some food with them, and intending to return to Rome in the evening. After eating, he had taken a little nap, and when he woke up, found that his wife had disappeared. She had wandered away to pick some flowers, from her own account, and had lost herself – a simple enough thing to do thereabouts. They were ready to pay handsomely, they said, for the night's lodging, and he, glad enough to earn money so easily, led them in and, having given them something to eat and drink, led them upstairs and left them there. The next morning, as he was leaving the house, the husband called out to him that he would be very glad to buy from him any game that he might get, and added that he was going back to bed again – for he was singularly sleepy.

The man started off – cheerfully, as one may understand – and the other went back to bed, where he slept until the early afternoon. On awakening, he saw that his wife was sitting by one of the windows, wrapped in a shawl. She was cold, she said, and anxious to start for home again as soon as possible. He assured her that he would not keep her waiting for long, dressed himself, and went downstairs, leaving her by the window.

Having refreshed himself, he sat down by the door, borrowing his host's pipe and tobacco, and waited for the latter's return. After some time had sped he left the house and walked a little way in the direction which the hunter had taken in the morning, but he had not proceeded far before he met him. The man was evidently labouring under some great excitement, and he also seemed to be very dizzy, for he staggered as he came up, and sat down abruptly. His game-bag was empty, but the other noticed a smear of blood on his coat, and, thinking him to have met with some accident, stooped down. But the hunter waved him back. He could not speak for a minute or two, and only after he had recovered himself somewhat he told his story.

A mile or so from the house he had sat down to rest and look about for the signs of any game. The day was very still, and he had been listening and watching intently, when, without an instant's warning, a heavy body leaped on him from behind, threw him over, and held him in a pair of mighty jaws by the coat-collar, face downward. So stunned was he with fright and astonishment that, at first, he lay still. But presently, as the teeth began to work upwards towards his neck he wriggled his head around and saw, a few inches away, the paw of an enormous wolf. Wolves there were, as he said, and wolves, but nothing like this one had he ever heard of. In proof of which, he showed the barrel of his gun which had been slung on his back, bitten almost in two. His hands had been free, and he had managed to get out his knife, hardly knowing what to do with it, till his eyes fell once more on the great paw by his head. In desperation, he slashed at it, and the long, razor-edged blade went through bone and flesh; when, with a howl, the wolf jumped away from him, and he fainted.

How long he lay there he had no idea, but when he came to himself, and got to his feet, the paw was beside him. So saying, he produced it – and it bore out his story, for it was larger than a man's hand. Together they returned to the house, where, after making sure that the hunter was none the worse for his experience, the visitor asked if he might look at the paw again. In the hasty glance he had had of it by the side of the road, he had not had time to satisfy his curiosity. Such a thing was not to be seen twice in a lifetime. The hunter agreed with him, and put his hand into his leather game-bag – only to withdraw it with a scream. 'Do not go near it!' he begged as the other approached. 'As you value your soul, do not touch it!'

But the visitor was made of sterner stuff, and, despite his host's pleadings, dived into the game-bag and brought out – a human hand!

Dropping it on the floor, he sprang away, but his eyes were drawn back to the gruesome thing in spite of him, and he saw the glitter of a ring. There was something diabolically familiar about the hand. He looked again and closer. There was something familiar about the ring, too. He had seen it elsewhere and very lately. He left his host in the chair where he had collapsed, ran upstairs, and burst in on his wife. She was still sitting by the window, and when she heard his voice she turned and looked at him. Her face was changed almost out of recognition, and the hate of the other world was in her eyes, but he seized the shawl she had wrapped around her, though she bit and struggled. At last he tore it off, and a glance showed him the rough bandages over one arm where the hand should have been. It was her hand that he had taken out of the game-bag! The end of the story (which I can only tell as it was told to me) is that the woman was burnt as a witch.

The White Wolf

ANDREW LANG

Once upon a time there was a king who had three daughters; they were all beautiful, but the youngest was the fairest of the three. Now it happened that one day their father had to travel to a distant part of his kingdom. Before he left, his youngest daughter made him promise to bring her back a wreath of wild flowers. When the king was ready to return to his palace, he bethought himself that he would like to take home presents to each of his three daughters; so he went into a jeweller's shop and bought a beautiful necklace for the eldest princess; then he went to a rich merchant's and bought a dress embroidered in gold and silver thread for the second princess, but in none of the flower shops nor in the market could he find the wreath of wild flowers that his youngest daughter had set her heart on.

So he had to set out on his homeward way without it. Now his journey led him through a thick forest. While he was still about four miles distant from his palace, he noticed a white wolf squatting on the roadside, and, behold, on the head of the wolf there was a wreath of wild flowers.

Then the king called to the coachman, and ordered him to get down from his seat and fetch him the wreath from the wolf's head. But the wolf heard the order and said, 'My lord and king, I will let you have the wreath, but I must have something in return.'

'What do you want?' answered the king. 'I will gladly give you rich treasure in exchange for it.'

'I do not want rich treasure,' replied the wolf. 'Only promise to give me the first thing that meets you on your way to your castle. In three days I shall come and fetch it.'

And the king said to himself, 'I am still a good long way from home, I am sure to meet a wild animal or a bird on the road, it will be quite safe to promise.' So he consented, and carried the wreath away with him. But all along the road he met no living creature till he turned into the palace gates, where his youngest daughter was waiting to welcome him home.

That evening the king was very sad, remembering his promise, and when he told the queen what had happened, she too shed bitter tears. The youngest princess asked them why they both looked so sad and why they wept. Then her father told her what a price he would have to pay for the wreath of wild flowers he had brought home to her, for in three days a white wolf would come and claim her and carry her away, and they would never see her again. But the queen thought and thought, and at last she hit upon a plan.

There was in the palace a servant maid the same age and the same height as the princess, and the queen dressed her up in a beautiful dress belonging to her daughter, and determined to give her to the white wolf, who would never know the difference.

On the third day the wolf strode into the palace yard and up the great stairs, to the room where the king and queen were seated.

'I have come to claim your promise,' he said. 'Give me your youngest daughter.'

Then they led the servant maid up to him, and he said to her, 'You must mount on my back and I will take you to my castle.' With these words he swung her on to his back and left the palace.

When they reached the place where he had met the king and given him the wreath of wild flowers, he stopped, and told her to dismount that they might rest a little.

So they sat down by the roadside.

'I wonder,' said the wolf, 'what your father would do if this forest belonged to him?'

And the girl answered, 'My father is a poor man, so he would cut down the trees and saw them into planks. He would sell the planks and we should never be poor again, but always have enough to eat.'

Then the wolf knew that he had not been given the real princess, and he swung the servant maid on to his back and carried her to the castle. He strode angrily into the king's chamber, and spoke.

'Give me the real princess at once. If you deceive me again I will cause such a storm to burst over your palace that the walls will fall in, and you will all be buried in the ruins.'

Then the king and the queen wept but they saw there was no escape. So they sent for their youngest daughter, and the king said to her: 'Dearest child, you must go with the white wolf, for I promised you to him and I must keep my word.'

So the princess prepared to leave her home; but first she went to her room to fetch her wreath of wild flowers, which she took with her. Then the white wolf swung her on his back and bore her away. But when they came to the place where he had rested with the servant maid, he told her to dismount that they might rest for a little at the roadside.

Then he turned to her and said, 'I wonder what your father would do if this forest belonged to him?'

And the princess answered, 'My father would cut down the trees and turn it into a beautiful park and gardens, and he and his courtiers would come and wander among the glades in the summer time.'

'This is the real princess,' said the wolf to himself. But aloud he said, 'Mount once more on my back and I will bear you to my castle.'

And when she was seated on his back he set out through the woods, and he ran and ran and ran, till at last he stopped in front of a stately courtyard, with massive gates.

'This is a beautiful castle,' said the princess, as the gates swung back and she stepped inside. 'If only I were not so far away from my father and my mother!'

But the wolf answered, 'At the end of a year we will pay a visit to your father and mother.'

And at these words the white furry skin slipped from his back, and the princess saw that he was not a wolf at all, but a beautiful youth, tall and stately. He gave her his hand and led her up the castle stairs.

One day, at the end of half a year, he came into her room and said, 'My dear one, you must get ready for a wedding. Your eldest sister is going to be married, and I will take you to your father's palace. When the wedding is over, I shall come and fetch you home. I will whistle outside the gate, and when you hear me, pay no heed to what your father or mother say, leave your dancing and feasting, and come to me at once, for if I have to leave without you, you will never find your way back alone through the forests.'

When the princess was ready to start, she found that he had put on his white-fur skin, and was changed back into the wolf. He swung her on to his back and set out with her to her father's palace, where he left her, while he himself returned home alone. But, in the evening, he went back to fetch her and, standing outside the palace gate, he gave a long, loud whistle. In the midst of her dancing the princess heard the sound, and at once she went to him, and he swung her on his back and bore her away to his castle.

Again, at the end of half a year, the prince came into her room, as the white wolf, and said, 'Dear heart, you must prepare for the wedding of your second sister. I will take you to your father's palace today, and we will remain there together till tomorrow morning.'

So they went together to the wedding. In the evening, when the two were alone together, he dropped his fur skin and, ceasing to be a wolf, became a prince again. Now they did not know that the princess's mother was hidden in the room. When she saw the white skin lying on the floor, she crept out of the room, and sent a servant to fetch the skin and to burn it in the kitchen fire. The moment the flames touched the skin there was a fearful clap of thunder heard, and the prince disappeared out of the palace gate in a whirlwind and returned to his palace alone.

But the princess was heartbroken and spent the night weeping bitterly. Next morning she set out to find her way back to the castle, but she wandered through woods and forests and could find no path or track to guide her. For fourteen days she roamed in the forest, sleeping under the trees, living upon wild berries and roots, and at last she reached a little house. She opened the door and went in, and found the wind seated in the room all by himself, and she spoke to the wind and said: 'Wind; have you seen the white wolf?'

And the wind answered, 'All day and all night I have been blowing round the world, and I have only just come home, but I have not seen him.'

But he gave her a pair of shoes, in which, he told her, she would be able to walk a hundred miles with every step. Then she walked through the air till she reached a star, and she said, 'Tell me, star, have you seen the white wolf?'

And the star answered, 'I have been shining all night and I have not seen him.'

But the star gave her a pair of shoes, and told her that if she put them on she would be able to walk two hundred miles at a stride. So the princess drew them on and walked to the moon, and she said, 'Dear moon, have you not seen the white wolf?'

But the moon answered, 'All night long I have been sailing through the heavens, and I have only just come home, but I did not see him.'

But he gave her a pair of shoes, in which she would be able to cover four hundred miles with every stride. So she went to the sun, and said, 'Dear sun, have you seen the white wolf?'

And the sun answered, 'Yes, I have seen him and he has chosen another bride, for he thought you had left him and would never return. He is preparing for the wedding. But I will help you. Here is a pair of shoes. If you put these on you will be able to walk on glass or ice and to climb the steepest places. And here is a spinning wheel, with which you will be able to spin moss into silk. When you leave me you will reach a glass mountain. Put on the shoes that I have given you and with them you will be able to climb it quite easily. At the summit you will find the palace of the white wolf.'

Then the princess set out and before long reached the glass mountain. At the summit she found the white wolf's palace, as the sun had said.

But no-one recognised her, as she had disguised herself as an old woman and had wound a shawl round her head. Great preparations were going on in the palace for the wedding, which was to take place the next day. Then the princess, still disguised as an old woman, took out her spinning wheel, and began to spin moss into silk. And as she spun the new bride passed by and, seeing the moss turn into silk, she said to the old woman: 'Little mother, I wish you would give me that spinning wheel.'

And the princess answered, 'I will give it to you if you will allow me to sleep tonight on the mat outside the prince's door: And the bride replied, 'Yes, you may sleep on the mat outside the door.'

So the princess gave her the spinning wheel. And that night, winding the shawl all round her, so that no-one could recognise her, she lay down on the mat outside the white wolf's door. And when everyone in the palace was asleep she began to tell the whole of her story. She told how she had been one of three sisters, that she had been the youngest and the fairest of the three, and that her father had betrothed her to a white wolf. And she told how she had gone first to the wedding of one sister, and then with her husband to the wedding of the other sister, and how her mother had ordered the servant to throw the white-fur skin into the kitchen fire. Then she told of her wanderings through the forest and of how she had sought the white wolf weeping; and how the wind and star and moon and sun had befriended her and had helped her to reach his palace. And when the white wolf heard all the story, he knew that it was his wife, who had sought him and had found him, after such great dangers and difficulties.

He said nothing. Instead he waited till the next day, when many guests-kings and princes from far countries were coming to his wedding. Then, when all the guests were assembled in the banqueting hall, he spoke to them and said: 'Hearken to me, ye kings and princes, for I have something to tell you. I had lost the key of my treasure casket, so I ordered a new one to be made; but I have since found the old one. Now, which of these keys is the better?'

Then all the kings and royal guests answered, 'Certainly the old key is better than the new one.'

'Then,' said the wolf, 'if that is so, my former bride is better than my new one.'

And he sent for the new bride and he gave her in marriage to one of the princes who was present. Then he turned to his guests, and said, 'And here is my former bride' – and the beautiful princess was led into the room and seated beside him on his throne.

'I thought she had forgotten me and that she would never return. But she has sought me everywhere, and now we are together once more, we shall never part again.'

The Boy and the Wolves, or The Broken Promise

ANDREW LANG

Once upon a time an Indian hunter built himself a house in the middle of a great forest, far away from all his tribe; for his heart was gentle and kind; and he was weary of the treachery and cruel deeds of those who had been his friends. So he left them, and took his wife and three children, and they journeyed on until they found a spot near to a clear stream, where they began to cut down trees, and to make ready their wigwam. For many years they lived peacefully and happily in this sheltered place, never leaving it except to hunt the wild animals, which served them both for food and clothes. At last, however, the strong man felt sick, and before long he knew he must die.

So he gathered his family round him, and said his last words to them. 'You, my wife, the companion of my days, will follow me ere many moons have waned to the island of the blest. But for you, O my children, whose lives are but newly begun, the wickedness, unkindness, and ingratitude from which I fled are before you. Yet I shall go hence in peace, my children, if you will promise always to love each other, and never to forsake your youngest brother.'

'Never!' they replied, holding out their hands. And the hunter died content.

Scarcely eight moons had passed when, just as he had said, the wife went forth, and followed her husband; but before leaving her children she bade the two elder ones think of their promise never to forget the younger, for he was a child, and weak. And while the snow lay thick upon the ground, they tended him and cherished him; but when the earth showed green again, the heart of the young man stirred within him, and he longed to see the wigwams in the village where his father's youth. was spent.

Therefore he opened all his heart to his sister, who answered: 'My brother, I understand your longing for our fellow-men, whom here we cannot see. But remember our father's words. Shall we not seek our own pleasures, and forget the little one?'

But he would not listen, and, making no reply, he took his bow and arrows and left the hut. The snows fell and melted, yet he never returned; and at last the heart of the girl grew cold and hard, and her little boy became a burden in her eyes, till one day she spoke thus to him: 'See, there is food for many days to come. Stay here within the shelter of the hut. I go to seek our brother, and when I have found him I shall return hither.'

But when, after hard journeying, she reached the village where her brother dwelt, and saw that he had a wife and was happy, and when she, too, was sought by a young brave, then she also forgot the boy alone in the forest, and thought only of her husband.

Now, soon the little boy had eaten all the food which his sister had left him, so he went out into the woods, and gathered berries and roots, and while the sun shone he was contented and had his fill. But when the snows began and the wind howled, then his stomach felt empty and his limbs cold, and he hid in trees all the night, and only crept out to eat what the wolves had left behind. And by-and-by, having no other friends, he sought their company, and sat by while they devoured their prey, and they grew to know him, and gave him food. And without them he would have died, in the snow.

But at last the snows melted, and the ice upon the great lake, and as the wolves went down to the shore, the boy went after them. And it happened one day that his big brother was fishing in his canoe near the shore, and he heard the voice of a child singing in the Indian tone, 'My brother, my brother! I am becoming a wolf, I am becoming a wolf!'

And when he had so sung he howled as wolves howl.

Then the heart of the elder sunk, and he hastened towards him, crying, 'Brother, little brother, come to me'; but he, being half a wolf, only continued his song. And the louder the elder called him, 'Brother, little brother, come to me', the swifter he fled after his brothers the wolves, and the heavier grew his skin; till, with a long howl, he vanished into the depths of the forest.

So, with sorrow and anguish in his soul, the elder brother went back to his village, and, with his sister, mourned the little boy and the broken promise till the end of his life.

William and the Werewolf

F. J. HARVEY DARTON

I

William the cowherd

In the old days there lived in Apulia a King named Embrons, with his wife Felice. He ruled prosperously and well, and under him all men were content.

Embrons and Felice had one son, whom they christened William. This child would one day be King of Apulia, for he was the King's sole heir; and great care was taken to keep him in health, and to bring him up as became a young prince. But a brother of Embrons, being next in succession to the throne after William, plotted many times to take his life, and perchance would have succeeded, but for what came to pass when the child was four years old.

King Embrons and all his court at a certain season of the year went to Palermo (for Sicily also was part of his dominions), where they feasted and made merry. There was near the royal palace a large, fair orchard, where often the King and his company took their pleasure. As they walked there one day, William was playing on the grass beside them, and gathering flowers, when suddenly a huge wolf leapt among the folk. His jaws were agape, his eyes glaring, and he sprang forward like a whirlwind. Before anyone could stop him, he had seized William in his mouth, and sprang away as silently and swiftly as he had come.

(Now this wolf, you must know, was a werewolf, with a man's soul under his wolf's hide. He was of noble birth, being no less than Alfonso, the King of Spain's son. When he was yet young, his mother died, and the King his father before long married again. His second wife was Braunden, daughter of the King of Portugal. She was very skilled in magic and the black art, and when she saw that her stepson was so dear to his father that he would be King after him, rather than her own son, she cast about to do hurt to him. She made an ointment of great strength, full of enchantments, and anointed her stepson therewith. Immediately he was turned into a wolf, with all his man's wits the same as before, but clad outwardly with shaggy hair. He knew that the change came through his stepmother, and sprang at her, and well nigh strangled her; but help came speedily to her, and the werewolf was driven forth. Fast away he fled into far-off lands, and journeyed many days till he came to Apulia, where on a sudden he was moved to carry off William, as we have seen.)

Embrons made a great hue and cry after the werewolf, and men pursued the beast for many leagues.

But he ran with exceeding swiftness, despite the weight of the child in his mouth, and speedily outdistanced them all. On and on he went, till he reached the Straits of Messina; he plunged boldly into the sea and swam across the Straits, and came safely to the mainland. Still he ran on, without pausing to eat, on and on till he came to a great forest near Rome. There he laid the child down, and made as it were a burrow for it: in a little bank overhung by trees he scraped away the earth with his paws, until he had dug a long cave or passage, wherein he put ferns and grass to make a soft bed for his captive. In it he set the child, and there they tarried for many days. The werewolf lay close to William, and cuddled him tenderly, and brought him food, doing him no hurt.

In that forest where the werewolf had made his den, there dwelt an old churl, a cowherd, who for many winters had kept men's kine there. It chanced that one day he led his herd to pasture close to the den. With him came his hound, who was wont to marshal the herd for him; and while the kine fed the cowherd sat contentedly on the green sward, clouting his shoes, the dog beside him, scarce a furlong away from where William lay.

The werewolf had gone forth to seek prey, whereon to feed himself and William. The child, already grown stout and strong for his age, sat near the mouth of the den. Outside all was green shade and sunlight; the trees were in full leaf, birds sang merrily, and many a fair flower shone in the grass. Presently William came a little way out of the burrow, and picked the flowers, and sat listening to the birds' song.

Suddenly he looked up and saw the cowherd's dog close to him. At the same moment the dog saw him, and began to bark and bay loudly. William set up a great crying, and the noise of the two brought the cowherd running to the spot. There before him, as he came up, he saw his hound barking furiously at a little child clad only in a shirt of fine linen, sitting at the mouth of what seemed the burrow of some wild animal.

The cowherd called his hound off angrily, and holding it in, came towards William with friendly looks and gentle words. Soon he overcame the child's fears, and took him in his arms and kissed him. Then he set out straightway for his home with William, the dog running beside them.

'Wife,' said the cowherd when he came to his cottage, 'I have found this child in the forest, in a wild beast's den. Let us take him in, and care for him as if he were our own.'

'Gladly, goodman,' she answered, and turned to the child; 'what is your name, dear child?' she asked.

'William,' answered he.

'Then, William,' said she, 'you shall be our child, for we have none, and we will keep you in all love.'

So the cowherd and his wife brought William up in their cottage. He grew into a strong lad, fair to look on, active and hardy through his life in the fields with the poor cowherd. He learnt to run and leap, and to shoot well with the bow; and many a coney and hare, many a fieldfare and pheasant did he catch in snares when he went out to tend the cattle in the forest. He was beloved by all who knew him (for there were other herdsmen and peasants and farmers dwelling near the forest), and grew up full of manly courage and spirits.

But the werewolf, when he came back to his den on the day when the cowherd found William, was sad and sorrowful to see it empty. He roared aloud in his grief, and rent his hide. But soon he cast about to find where William had gone, and he came upon the cowherd's tracks. He followed them away from the den to the cottage, and he guessed that the man had carried off William. All round the cottage he looked, but saw nought, until he found a crevice in the wall. He peered through, and saw inside the cowherd's wife fondling and petting the child. Then he was blithe and gay for the child's sake, for he knew that all was well with it; and he went away with a glad heart, purposing only to watch over William from a distance, for he loved the child, and would fain keep him always from harm.

When William was well-nigh full grown, it came to pass that the Emperor of Rome hunted in the forest; and as he chased a great boar, he became separated from his men, and at last missed his way altogether. He rode along seeking to find a path out of the forest. Suddenly he saw before him a werewolf, which was pursuing a hart that ran on far ahead. At that sight the Emperor was filled anew with desire for the chase, and he in turn pursued the werewolf. Onwards they raced, the Emperor neither gaining nor losing ground; ever and anon the werewolf looked back, as if he knew he was followed. The hart was often out of sight, and indeed it seemed to the Emperor as though there were but one chase – his chase of the werewolf, who led him, as it were, whithersoever it pleased to go.

Suddenly the werewolf sprang aside and vanished into a thicket; and when the Emperor came to the spot, there was no trace of the beast to be seen. He cast his eyes all round, and in a moment he was aware of a lad coming towards him through the forest, as though this were a place where the werewolf knew they would meet.

The Emperor looked at the youth. He was well-built and comely, and bore himself with such grace that he seemed almost of fairy lineage, so fair was he. 'Greeting, my lord,' said he courteously.

'Greeting,' said the Emperor. 'I am lost in this forest. Tell me your name, I pray you, and your parentage.'

'I will tell you, sir, since you ask it,' said the lad. 'I am called William. A cowherd of this country is my kind father, and my mother is his wife. They have fostered me and fed me well all my days, and I keep the kine here for them. No more of my kindred do I know than that.'

When the Emperor heard those words, he marvelled that so comely a lad should be a cowherd's son. 'Go, call this cowherd,' he said. 'I would speak with him.'

'Nay, sir,' said William, 'you are a great lord, and may perchance mean him some evil. No hurt shall come to him through me.'

'Bring him hither, I say,' said the Emperor; 'no harm shall come to him, but rather advantage.'

'I trust your word, sir,' answered William. 'I will go.'

He went speedily and found the cowherd. 'My father,' he said, 'a great lord is yonder, and would fain speak with you. I pray you go to him, lest he be angered.'

'What, son,' said the cowherd, 'did you tell him I was here, nearby?' For he feared lest some hard service might be asked of him, on pain of punishment.

'Yes, certes,' answered William. 'But he vowed that he meant you no harm.'

The cowherd grumbled, but went with William to the Emperor.

'This is my father, my lord,' said William; and the cowherd did a reverence humbly.

'Cowherd,' said the Emperor, 'have you ever seen the Emperor of Rome?'

'Nay, my lord, never in my life.'

'Know then that I am he. I would fain ask you certain questions; I conjure you, answer me truly. Tell me whether this lad is your child, or does he come of other kin?'

The cowherd knew not the reason of the question, he began to tremble, and fear exceedingly, lest he should perchance be charged with having stolen William from his parents, whoever they might be.

'I will tell you truly, sire,' he said at length. 'The boy is not my son.' And he rehearsed how he had found William in the forest many years before, clad only in a little shirt of fine linen.

'I thank you for telling me the truth,' said the Emperor, when he had heard all the tale. 'You shall not suffer for it. Now hear me. My heart is very fain to have this boy at Rome; he shall go with me, and dwell at my court.'

Sad and sorry was the cowherd when he heard that word, for he loved William dearly. But he must not refuse, for William was not his son, and he had no power to keep him.

When William heard that the cowherd was not his father, and that he would be taken from him, he began to weep and lament. 'Alas, I know nought of my birth,' he said; 'I am no man's son, and have no kin. I am much beholden to this cowherd and his wife, who have cared for me; and I love them truly. But I cannot repay their kindness, for I have neither kith nor kin. I am nothing in the world.'

'Be still, boy,' quoth the Emperor; 'cease your sorrow. At Rome you shall be treated well, and will come into honour and esteem, so that you can requite your friends. Now, cowherd, help him to mount my horse in front of me, and we will ride to Rome.'

'Farewell, dear father,' cried William to the good cowherd. 'Greet well my dear foster-mother, and may you both live happily and long.'

Then the Emperor rode away, and the cowherd went home sorrowfully.

Before they had ridden far, William and the Emperor came upon some of the huntsmen. All the Emperor's company marvelled at the comeliness of the lad, and when they rode back to Rome, the whole court was amazed at his fairness.

The Emperor had a daughter named Melior, of the same age as William, and full lovely to look upon. To her he gave William for a page, telling her the whole story of his birth, and bidding her care for him well, for it was likely that he was of good birth, from his seemly manners and his lusty frame; and Melior gladly took William for a page, and clad him richly, and treated him with all honour and courtesy.

2

The Emperor's daughter and the page

William busied himself in serving Melior well and truly. He soon learnt all that behoves a page, and began to have a great skill in arms and at jousting, until before long there were none at the Emperor's court so free and debonair as he. Often did Melior cast her eyes upon him and admire him; and at last she found that she was deep in love with him. When she perceived this, and remembered that, for all his comeliness, William was but a page in her father's service, she fell in great sorrow, and began to pine and grow ill. Many an hour did she spend lamenting her love in secret, and weeping and wondering whether she should not tell William, until she hecame so pale and wan that Alexandrine, her cousin and favourite handmaid, asked her what ailed her.

'Tell me the cause of your illness, dear lady,' said Alexandrine. 'What is your grief? I am your cousin, and you know full well that you can trust me with your secrets.'

'Dear cousin,' answered Melior, 'I thank you for your comfort. I, will tell you the truth. I love William, and think upon him so often that every man who speaks to me seems to be he. Give me good counsel, dear Alexandrine, how shall I quell this love? '

Alexandrine marvelled greatly, but she gave her friend comfort. 'I will find you a certain herb which will cure you,' she said. 'You will like well the sweetness of it.'

'Get me this herb, dear cousin, as quickly as may be.'

Alexandrine went from her, and racked her brain to find a plan to bring her wile to pass; for she knew no healing herb save William himself, whom she purposed to tell of Melior's love. She was skilled in weaving spells and enchantments, and before long she gained her end in this wise. By magic arts she caused William to dream that Melior came to him and said, 'Dear William, I love you truly; kiss me'; and so real did this dream seem to William that he woke to find himself kissing his pillow as if it had been Melior herself.

'What is this? 'he said to himself when he was fully awake. 'I could have been sure that my lady Melior was here. How fair she seemed! How sweetly did she look upon me! I vow I love her more than any lady in the world.'

The more he thought of this dream, the more deeply he came to love Melior, until at length he became as love-sick as she was. Yet he durst say nothing to her, for she was a princess; and he but a page whose birth no man knew. Often he pondered his fate, and grieved that he could not even tell Melior of his love. The image of Melior was ever before his eyes, and he would go and sit in a garden beneath her chamber window, under an apple tree, for hours, watching the window and thinking only of his love. Every day he was to be found there, gazing up, saying nought.

It chanced that Alexandrine learnt of this custom of his, and was minded to make use of it. She watched him there daily, though he saw her not; and at last she obtained her desire, for William fell asleep in the garden, weary with long watching.

'Dear lady,' she said to Melior, 'let us go into the garden. There we shall see many fair flowers, and hear the merry song of birds, and have much comfort. Perchance I may find there that herb of which I spoke to you.'

They went with other maidens into the fair garden, wherein grew all manner of lovely flowers, and birds sang sweetly for joy in the spring; but nought could make Melior glad. She sat down under a sycamore tree, heavy at heart, and thought of her love for William.

Alexandrine wandered a little from her. But anon she came running back, as if in great surprise and wonder. 'Madame, there is a man asleep here,' she cried. 'Whether he be knight or squire I know not, for I cannot see his face; but he is a comely body to look on. Come hither and see him.'

Melior rose and went towards the apple tree, under which William lay sleeping. She saw in a moment who he was, and she would fain have kissed him, but durst not, for fear someone should see her and spread a tale about her.

As she looked, Alexandrine, by her enchantment, caused William to dream again; and he dreamed that Melior herself brought him a fair rose, and he took it readily, and in a trice was healed of his lovesickness.

Thus he dreamed; and in the midst of it he awoke and saw Melior herself standing at his side, and speaking words which she deemed unheard.

'Sweet love,' he heard her saying, 'Heaven give you joy.'

'Dear Lady Melior,' he said, starting up, 'was it I whom you called sweet love?'

'Even so, William,' she answered, seeing that her love was no longer hidden from him.

'Said I not, Lady Melior,' said Alexandrine, 'that in this garden you would find the herb to cure your sickness? '

'You said it,' answered Melior; 'All is cured.' There and then William and Melior plighted their troth; but they agreed to keep their love secret until William could win high rank for himself by deeds of valour, for they knew that the Emperor would be wroth if he heard that William, a foundling, dared to love his daughter.

Before long there came a chance for William to win fame in arms. The Duke of Saxony marched against Rome with a great host of men, and the Emperor was forced to summon all his vassals to defend his city. When William heard of the war, he was blithe and glad, and went to the Emperor and besought him to dub him knight, that he right do battle against Rome's enemies. The Emperor granted his boon, and William bore arms against the Saxons. Many feats of might did he do, and often did his courage turn a doubtful battle, and at last he took the Duke of Saxony prisoner with his own hand; so that, when the wars were ended, and the Saxons were driven from the lands of Rome, William was fain to tell the Emperor of his love for Melior, who had heard of his doughty deeds with joy and gladness.

But ere he could say or do aught, an ill chance turned all their plans to nothing. After the war against the Saxons, the Emperor held a great feast, to which all his nobles and knights came, William among them. As they made merry, the doors of the hall were suddenly thrown open, and thirty men bravely apparelled in cloth of gold and fine linen were ushered in; they greeted the Emperor, and when he had asked their business, a certain lord among them, Roachas by name, spoke in answer.

'Lord Emperor,' he said, 'the good Emperor of Greece sends you greeting and friendship by us his messengers. He says to you that he has a dear son, a man well tried in all doughty deeds, who will be Emperor after him. He has often heard tell of your fair daughter the lady Melior, and would fain ask her hand in marriage for his son. If you will give her, she shall have in Greece more gold than you have silver, and more proud cities and seemly castles than you have small towns or mean houses. What is your will, sire? All your lords are here with you, and you can take counsel with them, and give us an answer speedily.'

Thus they spoke; and, to be short, the Emperor consented to give Melior to the Prince of Greece. The marriage was to be held at Midsummer, it being then Easter-tide; and at Midsummer the Emperor of Greece and his son would come to Rome for the wedding.

When Melior and William heard these tidings they were utterly downcast; all their plans had failed, and it seemed that Melior would be forced to go to Greece. No device could they think of to escape this wedding, until at last, when the Emperor of Greece was already come to Rome, and the streets were strewn with roses, and the city echoed with mirth and minstrelsy, they besought Alexandrine to help them.

'I know no plan,' said she at first, weeping sore for their sad plight. 'You cannot escape from Rome or the country round, for when they found that you were gone, they would raise a hue and cry; each bridge and pass would be closely guarded, so that neither clerk, nor knight, nor country churl would escape unseen.'

But in a little while she spoke again. 'There is one way, as it seems to me. The men in the Emperor's kitchen here every day flay many beasts – hinds and harts, bucks and bears, for meat. Now if you were to wear two of the skins they cast aside, and creep away in them as secretly as may be, perchance you might be taken for beasts, and so escape. Of all beasts, bears seem to me the best for the purpose, for they are grisly and terrible, and men shrink from the sight of them, and do not look too closely at them. If we could by craft obtain two bears' skins, then might your purpose be fulfilled.'

Melior and William were filled with joy at this plan, and begged Alexandrine to procure the bearskins for them. But that was no easy matter, and she could only get them by disguising herself as a kitchen-boy, and doing menial work in the Emperor's kitchen, . . . and stealing thence the skins of two white bears.

She brought the skins to Melior and William, and dressed them in them, sewing them over their clothes.

'How like you me now?' asked Melior, when her bearskin was cunningly fitted on. 'Am I not a fine bear? '

'Yes, madame, you are as grisly a sight as man could wish to see. You are a very wild bear to look on.'

And when William was sewn into his skin, even Melior could scarce look on him without terror, so like a bear did he seem.

That evening, as it grew dusk, the two bears crept quietly out of the Emperor's palace into a garden, and Alexandrine, having bidden them farewell and wished them god-speed, let them out at a little postern gate. Away they ran, on two legs when they were alone, on four whensoever they came near other folk; and so they fled out into the night together, away from Rome.

But they were not unseen, though they knew not that anyone was watching them. A certain Greek chanced to be resting in the garden, hidden by the shady trees. Suddenly he saw two white bears steal hurriedly across the grass, and disappear in the direction of the garden wall. Half out of his wits with fear, he fled into the palace, and when he found some of his comrades, told them what he had seen. But they only laughed at his story, and did not believe him. They said that he had fallen asleep, and had dreamed about two bears; and seeing that no-one put faith in his words, he himself came to think that it was a dream, until later he had cause to change his mind.

3

The two bears

Melior and William hastened away, and journeyed all night. By morn they had come to a great forest, and finding in it a little cave, they rested there, for they did not wish to travel by day, lest they should be seen. They were very weary, but thankful to have escaped, though before long hunger made them forget all else.

'Would that we knew how to get food, dear love,' said William. 'If we do not, I fear we may die of hunger,'

'Nay, by your leave, William,' answered Melior, 'I think we can live well on love alone, if God help us to find a few berries; bullaces and blackberries, hips and haws, acorns, hazel-nuts, and other fruits grow on the trees in this forest, and with them and our love to sweeten them, we may well be content.'

'Nay, dear, you have never known hardship. You must fare better than that. I will go forth, and see if I can find any wayfarer, some churl, or perchance a chapman coming from market or fair; from him, if he have any, I will take meat and drink. Else shall we both lose our lives through hunger.'

'Go not forth, William, I pray you. If you took aught from any man, he would raise a hue and cry, and carry the news to Rome, and we should come to harm. It is better for us to abide here and live on whatever fruits we can find in the forest.'

So they picked berries and fruits, and abode there in the forest, in dire straits, but well content with one another's love.

But help was nigh, though they knew it not. The werewolf had long remained near Rome, hearing tidings of William from passers-by; and he had seen William and Melior steal away, clad in bearskins. He had followed them to the forest, and overheard all their talk; and when he saw their sorry plight, he hastened away to find them food.

It was not long before he came upon what he wanted. A man passed near carrying bread and beef in a great wallet. With a loud roar the werewolf sprang out at him, and made as if to tear him to pieces. The man dropped his wallet and fled for his life, never doubting that he would be caught and devoured in a trice. But the good werewolf cared nothing for the man; he only had need of his wallet, which he seized and carried off in his mouth.

William and Melior were eating their poor meal of nuts and berries when they heard a pattering and rustling in the forest near them. They looked and saw coming towards them a great wolf, bearing in its mouth a wallet.

Melior clung to William in terror; hut William saw that the wolf was gentle and meant no harm to them. He said no word as the animal drew near. It came right up to them and laid the wallet at their feet; then it turned and bounded out of sight again.

William wondered much at this strange hap. He picked up the wallet and opened it: in it he saw the bread and beef.

'Lo, dear love,' he said gaily, 'see what great grace God has showed us. He has sent us meat to succour us in our sore need. Never saw I such a wonder as that a wolf should bring food to us.'

They fell to gladly, and ate the meat with no sauce but hunger. Suddenly the werewolf appeared again, carrying in his mouth two flagons of fine wine, which he had taken from a serving-man who was bearing them to a rich burgess of that country. He laid them before the two lovers, and again disappeared. But he did not go far off; that day and for many days more he remained near them, and brought them food for their needs each day. William had well-nigh forgotten the wolf in whose den he formerly lived, and he marvelled greatly at this strange companion: but he felt no fear of him.

Gay and blithe were William and Melior as they made merry over what the werewolf had brought them. When they had feasted well, they rested till nightfall, and then set forth on their journey again, the werewolf following close behind, yet unseen.

Meanwhile at Rome the preparations for the wedding of Melior to the Prince of Greece went forward apace. The wedding-day itself (it was the day after William and Melior had fled) came, and all Rome was full of mirth and minstrelsy. But when the appointed hour drew nigh, Melior had not yet appeared. The Emperor sent a baron to bid her come, and he went to her chamber, but found no-one there. Then the Emperor himself came. But Melior was not to be seen. He questioned Alexandrine straitly. But Alexandrine said that she had not seen Melior since midnight; she knew that the Princess was loth to wed the Prince of of Greece, and that she loved William in her heart; but more than that she could not say.

Search was made everywhere, but they found no sign of Melior, nor could William be discovered. It was clear that they had fled together.

'Alas, that traitrous foundling has betrayed me,' said the Emperor. 'I brought him up and cared for him as well as any in the land, and now he is false to me. The Greeks will make war on me if Melior does not wed their Prince. I am utterly undone.'

He held a great council straightway. His lords advised him to tell the Emperor of Greece all that had befallen, and ask his grace and pardon; and the Emperor did so with great sorrow and humility.

The Emperor of Greece was wroth, but restrained his anger. He counselled that proclamation should be made throughout the dominions of Rome that every man should immediately search for William and Melior. Every pass and bridge and road was to be guarded; if any man were slothful or careless in his watch he should be hanged, while whosoever found William and Melior should receive great rewards.

It was done as he said. But all the search was in vain, until, hearing the proclamation, the Greek who had seen the two bears in the Castle garden told of what he had seen The skins in the Emperor's kitchen were counted; two white bearskins were found to be missing. It was plain that William and Melior had fled in them.

There was a great hue and cry set on foot. Huntsmen and hounds went forth as if in search of real bears. All the land was scoured high and low for William and Melior.

But the werewolf did not desert his charge. The hunt came nigh the two bears, and was close upon their heels; but the werewolf left them and faced the hounds and huntsmen, so that they turned aside to pursue him. Over hill and dale and marsh they ran after him, and always he kept ever so little ahead of them. Far away did he lead them from William and Melior, who pushed on their road with all speed and came at length into Apulia, where they rested. Anon the Greeks and Romans, wearied with pursuing the werewolf in vain, gave up the chase and returned to Rome, to wait for tidings of the white bears. The werewolf, as soon as they were gone, hasted across country in the track of William and Melior, and came up with them near the strong walled city of Benevento; and all three lay hid in a cave in a quarry nearby under a high hill, the werewolf under a crag at the entrance, ever alert to watch for danger.

Hardly had they rested a few hours when certain workmen came to the quarry to dig stone. One of them wandered nigh the cave, and peering in from a little distance saw therein two seemly white bears. Straightway he called to mind the cry that had been sent through all the country concerning two white bears; and he ran swiftly to his comrades.

'Hearken now, friends,' he said, 'you are mindful of the cry about two bears, and the reward that was to be given to him who found them?'

'We know it full well,' said they; 'what of it?'

'I will tell you how to win that reward,' he answered. 'I know where the two white bears are.'

'Tell us straightway,' they cried. 'We are not afraid of two bears. Where are they?'

'In yonder cave they lie. Now hark you; we will do this all in order, lest we fail to catch the bears and to win the reward. I will go to the Provost of Benevento and tell him all, so that he may come hither with officers and a host of men, lest the bears escape. Do you abide here and watch the cave, that they go not forth.'

'Be it so,' they said. 'See that you lose no time in going to Benevento.'

The man hastened to Benevento and called the Provost; and the Provost, mindful of the Emperor's proclamation, summoned all the men of the city, a great host, well nigh two thousand strong. They set out for the quarry in high hope of capturing the bears. With them went the women and children of Benevento, to watch what befell; and among the children was the little son of the Provost, a fair boy well known and loved by all the citizens.

William and Melior were resting in the cave. Suddenly the werewolf pricked up his ears. A confused noise sounded outside. They looked out, and beheld the Provost of Benevento and a host of men surrounding the cave.

'Alas! our end is come,' said William. 'Woe is me that I have brought you to this pass, dear Melior. But I will take on me all the harm. Do you take off your bearskin, and show them that you are a woman; then will they do you no hurt. I will abide their anger as I am, and perchance when they have taken me and slain me their wrath will be turned aside. Ah, if I had a horse and armour I would not yield easily!'

'What, William, do you think I would live if you were dead?' answered Melior. 'Whatsoever fate befalls you, that also will I readily suffer.'

The Provost and his men began to draw near the mouth of the cave. But the werewolf was on the watch. Suddenly he rushed forth with a loud roar, William and the werewolf scattering those who were nearest; in a trice he had leapt upon the Provost's little son, playing idly with the other children, and run off with him before the men knew what had come to pass.

'Help, good men,' cried the Provost, as he saw his son borne away in the mouth of the fierce wolf, who roared savagely as he darted swiftly away. 'After him, ere he can gain his den, or my son is lost!'

Thereat the citizens turned from the cave's mouth, and set themselves to hunt the werewolf with hound and horn and great clamour. The werewolf led them afar to the mountains, ever keeping beyond their reach: if they fell too far behind, he waited until they grew closer, and then led them on as before. All day he ran, doing no hurt to the child; and they pursued till every thought of the bears was almost forgotten.

When William and Melior saw that the folk were all gone from outside the cave, they knew that the werewolf had saved them again; and they fell on their knees and prayed to God to keep him safe. Then they set about fleeing again themselves. They were sure now that their bearskins were known to all men as a disguise, and it seemed best to cast them off, and go thence in their own clothes.

They stripped off the skins, and stood upright in their own clothes, blithe and gay to see one another in a true guise. Then they set forth a-wandering once more, taking with them the bearskins in case they should need them again. For many miles they fled, until, weary and hungry, they lay down to rest in a great forest.

Meanwhile the werewolf, having led the Provost and his men a sorry dance all day, perceived that he had gone far enough. About sunset he ran well ahead of his pursuers, and laid the child carefully down, unharmed, on the ground. Then he darted off, freed of his burden, and was gone in a trice.

When the Provost came up, he found the child unhurt, and gave thanks to Heaven. Then, seeing that it was vain to pursue the wolf further, he bade his tired men go home. That night, sore wearied, they rested in Benevento. On the morrow they rose betimes, and went to the quarry to see if they could catch the white bears. But they found the bears gone, and there was no trace of them to be seen: no man had spied a white skin anywhere. So the men of Benevento, having made one more great search in all the country round, gave up the attempt to find the white bears.

Melior and William were sitting in the forest, on the morning after their flight from the quarry, when the werewolf suddenly appeared, hastening on their track of the day before, as if eager to come up with them. In his mouth he bore great store of meat and drink for them. But when he had laid his burden before them, he departed again.

'In truth, Melior,' said William, 'this is no common wolf. He has man's nature; a man's wits are in him. See what he suffers to bring us out of harm; never does he fail to aid us, though it be at the peril of his life.'

'I trow he must be a man in wolf's guise,' answered Melior.

As they spoke they heard voices coming close to them. They crouched down in the long grass and bracken till they were quite hidden.

The voices drew nearer. The came from some charcoal-burners working not far away.

'Would that those white bears were here now,' said one. 'All the men in the world should not save them from us if they were. They are no bears, but the Emperor's daughter and some knight who is fleeing with her. A wolf saved them yesterday when the Provost of Benevento thought to take them; but if they were here now, not fourscore wolves should save them.'

Melior was nigh mad with fear at those words; but she lay still, and they were not yet seen.

'Bah, friend,' said another charcoal-burner, 'go you about your appointed work. What if the bears were here? What good would it do to take them? Many a hard hap have they escaped; may they come free out of many another. Say, let us to work, and do our own business, and win some money for ourselves thereby, instead of looking for white bears.'

They passed on, and Melior and William were out of peril again: But they saw from the first man's words that they were known for the princess and a knight, so that even without the bearskins they would be recognised.

'I know not what we must do,' said Melior. 'We shall be known however we are clad.'

Even as she spoke a huge hart, with a hind in its train, burst through the forest in a panic. Hard on the heels of the beasts flew the werewolf, and, almost as they passed before William and Melior, he caught them up and in a trice slew them. He stood over the dead bodies for a minute, looking steadfastly at his friends, as if he would tell them something. Then he turned, and trotted a little way into the forest.

'Never saw any man a wolf like this,' said William. 'What would he have us do with this hart and this hind that he has slain before our very eyes?'

'I know not,' answered Melior.

'Perchance they are for another disguise,' said William, when he had pondered the strange chance. 'If I were to flay these beasts, we could wrap ourselves in their skins, and so be unknown once more.'

'Dear William,' cried Melior, 'that is clearly the wolf's intent.'

William set to work and speedily flayed the dead beasts. Then he prepared the skins, and before long they two, who formerly had seemed to be bears, wore the guise of hart and hind.

When they were arrayed in their new garments, the werewolf came to them again; and going before them, he led them by devious ways through Apulia and Calabria, and sought to reach Sicily, whither, though the hue and cry once more began to grow hot behind them, no man durst follow them, for the island was at that time ravaged by a great war, that raged furiously and made all things unsafe.

But it was no easy matter to cross the Straits of Messina into Sicily, for they could not seek a ship openly. When they came to the port of Reggio, they lay hid near the haven till it was night and all men were asleep. Then they crept hastily down to the haven, and stealthily went to and fro, looking for a ship which should be made ready as if to sail at once. Soon they found one, loaded with great tuns of wine, and about to sail. The crew were all asleep or in the town enjoying themselves; and the werewolf led William and Melior on board without being seen. They went quietly down to the hold and hid themselves behind the great wine-barrels.

Presently the men came aboard, and, the wind being favourable, they set sail, and before long drew near the coast of Sicily.

But though they were well-nigh across the Straits in safety, the fugitives had yet to leave the ship without being seen.

The werewolf contrived a plan. As the ship neared land, he rushed out from their hiding-place, and sprang over the side. The men, in alarm at seeing the great beast in their midst, struck at him with oars and staves as he passed, and one of them hit him a shrewd blow; but he heeded it not, but leapt into the water and swam swiftly to land. The sailors hastily got out a little boat, and rowed after him; some in their eagerness jumped overboard and swam in pursuit. In a few moments all were gone but a little bare-legged boy.

William and Melior heard the noise on deck as the werewolf went away from them. Then came a great quiet. The ship seemed to be deserted. They crept out from behind the wine-tuns, and went stealthily up to the deck. There was only the boy there.

But the boy saw them, and in great terror seized a staff that lay by and swung it round wildly. It chanced to strike Melior as she was near the edge of the ship; and at the blow she lost her balance, and fell overboard.

William leapt after her in a trice, and came to her aid. She was not hurt, and together they swam to land, and, when they had reached the shore, ran swiftly inland, away from the ship.

The boy marvelled greatly at what he had seen. But he could do naught to catch the hart and the hind, for he might not leave the ship. Presently the crew came back, angry and weary, for they had pursued the werewolf a long way in vain. The boy told them what he had seen; but there was nothing which they could do now, for it was not safe for them to go far into Sicily, because of the great war. So they went to port with their cargo of wine, and sold it, and speedily forgot all about their strange passengers.

But William and Melior sped on their way as fast as might be, away from the Straits. Before long the werewolf found them, and led them through the deserted country (for it had been sorely handled by the fighting all over the island) till they came near Palermo. There he showed them a great park close under the city walls, and brought them food; and they rested in peace for a little, after their long flight.

4

The hart and the two hinds

William and Melior were now in the land of William's father, King Embrons, who formerly had reigned over Apulia and Calabria and Sicily itself. But Embrons was dead, and his Queen Felice reigned alone, since no sign of William had been seen since the werewolf had carried him off so long ago. With her dwelt her daughter Florence, as fair a maid as any man might wish to see. It was for the sake of Florence that war was being waged; for the King of Spain (the father of the werewolf, though none but the wicked Queen Braunden knew it) had sought her in marriage for his second son, Braundinis, and Queen Felice had refused to give her. Whereupon Spain made war, and laid Sicily waste from end to end, and pressed Felice so hard that she was besieged in the strong city of Palermo. The siege was very close and strict. It seemed certain that ere long the Spaniards must take the city. Certain of the Queen's captains were for yielding without more ado. But Felice was of a bold heart, and would never surrender while there were still men to fight. She bade them go about their business and quit themselves like men.

Herself she went to plead to God for help in her great straits. Long and earnestly did she pray, and at the end rose up comforted and went to rest.

As she lay asleep she dreamed. She seemed to see herself and Florence in the park that lay just outside the city walls; and they were girt about by an hundred thousand leopards and bears and all manner of beasts, in great peril of being devoured. On a sudden, just as the beasts would have fallen upon them, there appeared a werewolf and two white bears. As they drew near, the white bears changed into deer, and each of them had on his forehead a fair figure. On the greater of the two was the figure of such a knight as her own son William should have been; on the lesser, there was the figure of a fair maiden. Crowns were on their heads, of gold set with precious gems, bright and shining. With the werewolf they set upon the host of wild beasts, and tore and bit and drave them before them, taking the largest of them prisoner, and putting the rest of them to headlong flight far over dale and down.

The dream faded into another, wherein the Queen saw herself in her Castle: she went up to the highest tower of it, and looked all round, and stretched out her arms over the country that lay beneath;

and lo, one arm stretched till it was over Spain, and the other covered Rome; and at that she awoke.

She went to a learned man in her Castle, and told him all that she had dreamed.

'Madam, mourn no rnore,' he said; 'these visions are of good import. The beasts that beset you are those men who now besiege you. The hart and the bear signify certain knights who will come to your aid and deliver you. One shall capture the King of Spain and his son, and afterwards will be King of this realm; and one shall deliver the King of Spain, and through him you shall learn tidings of the son you have lost for so long: that son shall one day be King of Rome, and your daughter shall be given to the King of Spain's son, but not to that son who now wars against you.'

The Queen wept for joy at this good prophecy, and thanked the wise man. Then she went to her chamber and looked out from it over the park which she had seen in her dream. As she looked, her dream seemed to come true before her very eyes. There in the park, under a laurel tree in a green place, she saw the hart and the hind close together. She could hear nought of their talk; but she watched their loving gestures for a long time, and was filled with a new hope at seeing the help promised by her dream thus close at hand.

That night the Queen's knights came to her and begged her to yield to the Spaniards; the walls were battered down, they said, and the city must fall right soon if no help came. But Felice bade them be of good cheer, for succour had been promised to her in a dream; if it came not, then would be the time to talk of yielding, and they went away vowing to fight valiantly yet a little while longer.

The next day the Queen looked out on the park again. There were the hart and the hind still. But the heat of the sun had cracked the skins they wore, and their clothes showed plainly underneath.

The Queen summoned the wise man to look out.

'Be no more in dismay, liege lady,' he said, as soon as he saw the two deer. 'Here is your dream come true. You have heard of late of a great hue and cry concerning the Emperor of Rome's daughter and a knight who fled from Rome with her? These are they. That knight shall bring the war to an end, if you can but reach him and bring him hither.'

'They would flee from me, I trow,' said the Queen, 'if I so much as went near them. How if I also were to don a deerskin, and go forth to them? Perchance, if they thought me a deer, they would not be afraid; and if they saw that the skin was but a disguise, they might still have no fear, for they would know that it meant no harm, but rather friendliness to them. I will do it. Go you now, and get me a hind's skin, and I will put it on.'

It was done as she said, and before long she went forth to the park clad in the skin of a hind.

William and Melior held converse together, right glad to be no longer pursued; the werewolf had left them again, and they knew not where he was. Suddenly they saw coming towards them one arrayed like themselves in a deerskin. They knew not at first whether it were in truth a hind, or some mortal man in disguise.

'I think it must be indeed a hind,' said William. 'It shows no fear of us.'

'Nay, I have no fear of you,' said the Queen, for she heard his words; 'I know who you are, and I am not afraid.'

William marvelled at those words, and Melior trembled with fear. 'I conjure you,' said William, 'tell me without tarrying whether you, who say that you know who we are, are a good spirit or some fiend bent on evil.'

'I am a creature like yourselves,' answered the Queen full courteously: 'never, I hope, shall evil come on you of my making. I am come hither to beg your help, and pray you for charity's sake to deliver me out of sore straits. It has been shown me in a dream that you can aid me. If you will but give me your help, you shall be King here all your life, and this maid shall be your Queen.'

And she told them in what sorry case she lay because of the King of Spain and his men.

William was glad at heart when he heard that the Queen of that land was speaking to him: he knew that they would be safe with her, and that he might win honour in her service. Together all three went into the city, and doffed their deerskins. Then William chose for himself fair armour and stout arms from the Queen's armoury: on his shield he caused to be painted the device of a werewolf.

There was in the Queen's stable a horse of spirit and mettle, by name Saundbruel; formerly it had been King Embron's horse, but since he had died none had dared to mount it, or come nigh it, so fierce was its temper.

But when William came to the stable to choose himself a horse, Saundbruel broke all his fastenings for joy, and neighed marvellously, for he knew that William was his dear lord's son.

When William heard the neigh and saw how eager the horse was, he besought the Queen to give it to him.

'It was my lord King Embron's horse,' she answered. 'It is the best horse I have, if only any man could ride it. If you can ride it, it is yours.'

'Madam, I would fain have the horse,' said William; and having put on his armour ready for the fray, he went to the stable again. As soon as the horse saw him, it leaped and pranced; and when he came nigh, it knelt on the ground gently with its forefeet, to be saddled, and showed such joy as could not be exceeded.

William mounted Saundbruel, and rode forth. All through the ranks of Queen Felice's men he passed, exhorting them to be of good cheer, and bidding them make ready for a bold sally out against the enemy, who had begun to attack more furiously than ever. When he had spoken to them all, he chose four hundred picked men, and caused the great gates of Palermo to be thrown open, and rode out to meet the Spaniards.

The Spaniards were three thousand strong, led by the King's high steward; but William cared little for their numbers. He set his men in orderly array, himself at their head. Over against them were drawn up the Spanish host, the steward on a noble steed riding in front with his squires, a stark and terrible man of great might.

When they were close William set his spear in rest to charge the steward, and the steward on his side made ready. They rode together alone before their men, and William struck so strong and true that he drove the Spaniard clean out of his saddle to the ground, where he fell and lay as dead as a door-nail.

His squires bore the dead man away. Then the Queen's men and the Spaniards fell to with a will. Long and fiercely did they fight, and many a good warrior was struck down and rose no more. But William's might prevailed against the enemy, and when at last he slew the steward's nephew in single combat the Spaniards turned and fled. For five miles they were pursued, and many were taken prisoner; few escaped death or capture that day.

That evening a great feast was held in Palermo. After it the Queen sat talking with William and Melior in her chamber, looking over the park outside the city. As they held converse, they were aware of the werewolf in the park coming towards their window. When he was close beneath it, he looked up, and held up his forefeet together as if making some prayer; then he did them a reverence, and went thence swiftly.

The Queen marvelled greatly thereat. 'Sir William,' she said, 'saw you the doings of that noble wolf, how he lifted up his fore-paws as if in prayer? What meant he by that sign?'

'I know not exactly, madam,' answered William, 'save that when-ever this wolf appears he brings us good fortune.'

'When I look on that wolf,' said the Queen, 'a great sorrow which once befell me comes to my mind. Many years ago I had a dear son, fair and seemly to look on, named William, even as you are. When he was but four years old, he was playing yonder in the park, when suddenly a great wolf broke from the forest and carried him off before the very eyes of my lord the King and myself and all our court. Many miles was the wolf pursued, but he came to the Straits of Messina without being caught, and leapt therein, and was no more seen; and to this day we have heard naught of my son, save that two nights ago I dreamed a dream which a wise man has told me foretells the return of my son to me. But I think he must have been drowned when the wolf leapt into the sea with him.'

William thought of his own upbringing. The cowherd, he knew, was not his father, but had found him at the mouth of some wild beast's den. What if he were this lost son of Queen Felice? But the Queen thought her son was drowned. Perchance he might have been saved; and if so – but he knew that it was as yet idle to ponder such things, for there was no proof of his royal birth to be found.

'Dear lady,' he said gently to Felice,' I will be a son to you and stand by you at your need.' With that they talked no more of the matter, but supped with great mirth and comfort, and at nightfall went to bed much cheered by the victory over the Spaniards.

On the morrow the King of Spain vowed to avenge his steward's death. He set a great host in array, and put his own son, Braundinis, at its head, and bade him take William alive or dead.

William rode forth on Saundbruel, with six companies of picked men; and they dealt so mightily with the Spaniards that in a little time this second host also was put to flight and utterly defeated; and William took Braundinis prisoner with his own hand.

That evening again there was great rejoicing in Palermo. But as the Queen sat at her window with Melior and William she was very sorrowful. She looked on William, and as she looked she thought that never had she seen any man so like that comely knight, her dear lord, King Embrons. At that thought she began to weep.

'Why make you such sorrow, madam?' asked William, when he saw her tears. 'This is rather a day for rejoicing, since we have a second time defeated the Spaniards, and taken their King's son a prisoner.'

'You say true, Sir William,' answered Felice 'I do wrong to weep. But as I looked on you I called to mind my dear lord Embrons who is dead: you are like him in every part; you might almost be that son of ours who has so long been lost.'

William marvelled greatly at her words, and thought again of his strange upbringing. But he said naught of it. 'Madam, think no more of it,' he answered the Queen. 'King Embrons and his son without doubt are dead these many years past, and will never come back to you; make merry, therefore, over this present good fortune.'

But the Queen felt in her heart that her son was still alive, and that William was he; no longer did she think he had been drowned in the Straits of Messina.

As they sat there, they saw the werewolf coming again across the park. He ran up to the window, and knelt low before them as court-eously as might be; then he turned and went his way again.

'It is a vastly strange sight,' said the Queen, 'to see this comely wolf doing reverence to us. Would that we knew what he means thereby! I pray it may turn to good for us.'

'Truly it will bring good, though I know not what it means,' said William. 'Did not good fortune come to us today, as it always has after the werewolf has appeared? '

Then they went to meat, and after that to bed, with merry cheer and hope in their hearts.

On the next day another great battle was fought. The King of Spain was furious that his son was captured and his steward slain, and his men put to flight. But he fared no better than they. Long and fierce was the fight. Many deeds of valour were done on both sides. But in the end William and his men prevailed, and William took the King prisoner.

And now Palermo was freed of its enemies, for the Spaniards had little heart for fighting when their King and his son were captured. The siege was ended, and and Queen Felice's dominions were rid of war and strife. Great was the rejoicing in the city. For many days there was naught but mirth and feasting; and at the end of it all a great council was held to decide the terms of peace between Queen Felice and Spain.

5

The wolf prince

At the great council Queen Felice sat in the midst on a daïs; on one side of her was the King of Spain, and on the other William, with Melior beside him. All the lords and burgesses of Apulia and Sicily and Spain were there gathered together; and the Princess Florence sat at the King's side.

'Queen Felice,' said the King of Spain, when they were all assembled, 'I pray you grant that I may see my son.'

Braundinis was brought in. 'See, my son,' said his father, 'what sorrow have we come to by obeying the Queen Braunden, your mother. She would have me seek the Princess Florence in marriage for you, and naught has come of it but woe to us all.'

'We have done wrong, sire,' answered Braundinis. 'We must yield to the grace of Queen Felice, and let her do with us as seems good to her.'

The King sighed for their sorry case. 'Madam,' he said to Felice, 'let me make amends for the evil we have done in this war. I am ready to restore to you as much as any man may ordain to be right; all my power I will hold as from you, and be your vassal for the lands that are in my realm. If you like that not, I will be bound to you in any way that you will.'

The Queen and her councillors began to hold converse concerning his words. Suddenly there came boldly into the hall the werewolf. He heeded none of the great lords there, but ran straightway to the King of Spain, and knelt down at his feet and kissed them.

Then he saluted the Queen, and afterwards William and Melior, and turned and ran fast out of the hall. Many men there drew their swords at the sight of him; and when he went out, they would fain have hastened after him and slain him. But William started up.

'Hold! 'he cried. 'If any man hurt that wolf, whosoever he be, I will kill him myself.'

At those words none dared lift a hand to harm the wolf, for they were all in great dread of William's might.

But the King of Spain was sore troubled at the sight of the wolf, for there came to his mind a story he had heard concerning his lost son Alfonso, who Braunden had told him had been drowned by evil chance.

'Sir King,' said William to him when the wolf was gone, 'I conjure you to tell me why the wolf bowed himself before you and kissed your feet.'

The King sighed sore. 'Sir William,' he answered, 'this is the reason, I think, and sad I am at the thought. Many years ago I wedded a worshipful lady, a King's daughter; and she bore me a son, but alas, died at his birth. I had him nursed well, and he began to grow into a fair boy, strong and hardy; his name was Alfonso. But anon I married again, and Braunden, now my Queen, was my second wife. She bore Braundinis, this prince whom you have taken prisoner; and when Alfonso disappeared, being but three years of age, Braundinis became heir to my kingdom of Spain. Alfonso, it was said by Queen Braunden, was drowned by chance. But I have heard from certain true men in Spain another story, and this wolf called it to mind. They said that by enchantments and magic arts, wherein she was mightily skilled, Braunden turned my son Alfonso into a werewolf, being jealous of him for Braundinis' sake. Certainly a wolf was seen at my court once; it flew at the Queen in anger, and was driven out by my servants. But I put no faith in this story until this wolf came today and did obeisance to me. I pray that I have done no wrong, for truly this wolf bore himself strangely towards me.'

'Sire,' said William, 'this story may well be true. I know indeed that this wolf has a man's mind, a better mind, mayhap, than both of ours together. 'Many times had I been dead ere now had not this beast saved me. He must indeed be a werewolf, and I pray that he is your son. Lady Queen,' he said, turning to Felice, 'the king of Spain is my prisoner; I took him in fair fight. Grant me that I may make certain conditions with him.'

'I grant it,' answered the Queen.

'Hearken, sire,' continued William. 'You would be glad and blithe to see your lost son again, if, as I think, this werewolf be he. And you would be glad and blithe to be free once more. But I say to you that neither thing shall come to pass save upon one condition. Your Queen Braunden, if she be so skilled in witchcraft that she can change men into werewolves, as you say, can with her cunning and her quaint charms likewise change werewolves into men again. She shall change the werewolf into a man, and you shall command her straitly to come hither with all speed. Till she has come and tried her enchantments on the werewolf you shall never go free. Send a messenger and bid her come, and say that if she refuses, I will come to Spain with fire and sword and destruction, and hale her thence by force.'

The King of Spain chose certain of his lords to carry this message, and they set out at once. After many days' journey they came to the Queen in Spain, and gave her the King's commands. She made ready without tarrying, and in a little while they began the journey back to Palermo, and arrived there as speedily as might be.

They came into the great hall of Felice's palace, and Queen Braunden of Spain was led to a throne on the daïs. By her side sat the King and Prince Braundinis; and hard by were Felice, with William and Melior.

Meanwhile the werewolf had returned to Palermo, and abode in William's chamber till Braunden arrived. When all was ready he came into the hall. He passed among all the knights and barons, looking neither to the right nor to the left, and went to the foot of the daïs.

When he saw Braunden sitting by the King, he waxed wroth; all his bristles stood on end, and he opened his jaws wide and roared terribly with a noise grim to hear. In a moment he would have sprung upon her, if William had not caught him by the neck.

'Help me, dear lords,' cried Braunden in terror. 'I have done wrong, and deserve death; but spare me and take this wolf from me, and I will undo all the evil that I have wrought.'

'Trust me, dear beast, as your own brother,' said William to the werewolf, who growled fiercely and was fain to rend the Queen to pieces. 'I sent for her for your sake, to help you and bring you to your true form again. If she do not, then, by Him who made us, she shall be burnt to cold ashes, and her ashes scattered to the winds of heaven; and her husband and her son and all their nobles shall be put in prison for ever, to live their days dolefully till death takes them. Do her no harm, dear friend; she shall help you or die.'

At those words the werewolf was glad, and he crouched down at William's feet and kissed them. As soon as she saw that his wrath had passed, Braunden rose from her seat and came to him, and knelt beside him. 'Sweet Alfonso,' she said, 'you are truly my lord the King's son, my stepson. I have brought you to sorrow and done you great wrong, but if you will forgive me I will set right the evil that I have done.'

She turned to William and the other lords and begged them to spare her life. But they would not pardon her unless she would disenchant the werewolf; and that at last she vowed to do.

She took the werewolf into a chamber alone with her. Then she brought forth a rich and noble ring, with a stone in it of such value that no witchcraft could prevail over him who wore it. She bound the ring with a red silk thread round the werewolf's neck; and when she had done that she read for a long time enchantments out of a fair book which she took from a certain chest; and in a little while there stood before her no wolf, but a man as fairly shapen and as comely as could be.

Long and great were the rejoicings when the King of Spain and William and the rest found that Alfonso was a wolf no longer. But they rejoiced even more at what he said at a feast which they held straightway.

'This good knight, whose strength hath ended the war here,' he said, pointing to William, 'bore himself in true knightly fashion. None of you know who he is; but I will tell you. In helping Queen Felice, he helped his mother; he is her son, and Embrons was his father. I was the werewolf who stole him from Palermo many years ago; and I think I was sent by God Himself, for if I had not stolen William, he would have been foully done to death. Embrons' brother, that fell knight who, but for William, would have succeeded to the kingdom, bribed two nurses, and in a day or two they would have poisoned William, if I had not carried him off. I knew also that in time he would bring me back to my man's shape, and ever have I watched over him and delivered him out of danger.'

'Dear friend,' said William, embracing him, 'God reward you for your constancy and love, for I know not how to requite you.'

'It were not hard to requite me,' said Alfonso.

'In what manner?' asked William.

'Grant me one thing only,' answered Alfonso.

'I will give you all my realm, save only Melior;' said William.

'I care not for your realm, if you will but give me your sister the Princess Florence to wife.'

'Gladly will I, if she be willing;' and since Florence was ready enough to wed so comely a prince, Alfonso won his reward.

Then William was crowned King of Palermo; and when he was crowned he sent messengers to the Emperor of Rome, asking his pardon for carrying off his daughter, and begging him to come to Palermo and give her to him in marriage. He sent also other messengers to the good cowherd who had brought him up, and gave him for reward an earldom and a fair castle and great store of gold and silver.

Anon came the Emperor of Rome, and Melior was happily wedded to William, and Florence to Alfonso; and yet a third marriage was held, for Alexandrine came in the Emperor's train, and when Braundinis, the Prince of Spain, saw her, he fell so deeply in love with her that he must needs wed her on the instant.

Thus William and the werewolf came into happiness with their ladies. Long and prosperously did they reign in Apulia and Spain. When the Emperor of Rome died, William was chosen in his stead; and for many years he ruled justly and did good works, and ended his days in peace.

The Undying Thing

BARRY PAIN

I

Up and down the oak-panelled dining-hall of Mansteth the master of the house walked restlessly. At formal intervals down the long severe table were placed four silver candlesticks, but the light from these did not serve to illuminate the whole of the surroundings. It just touched the portrait of a fair-haired boy with a sad and wistful expression that hung at one end of the room; it sparkled on the lid of a silver tankard. As Sir Edric passed to and fro it lit up his face and figure. It was a bold and resolute face with a firm chin and passionate, dominant eyes. A bad past was written in the lines of it. And yet every now and then there came over it a strange look of very anxious gentleness that gave it some resemblance to the portrait of the fair-haired boy. Sir Edric paused a moment before the portrait and surveyed it carefully, his strong brown hands locked behind him, his gigantic shoulders thrust a little forward.

'Ah, what I was!' he murmured to himself – 'what I was!' Once more he commenced pacing up and down. The candles, mirrored in the polished wood of the table, had burnt low. For hours Sir Edric had been waiting, listening intently for some sound from the room above or from the broad staircase outside. There had been sounds – the wailing of a woman, a quick abrupt voice, the moving of rapid feet. But for the last hour he had heard nothing. Quite suddenly he stopped and dropped on his knees against the table.

'God, I have never thought of Thee. Thou knowest that – Thou knowest that by my devilish behaviour and cruelty I did veritably murder Alice, my first wife, albeit the physicians did maintain that she died of a decline – a wasting sickness. Thou knowest that all here in Mansteth do hate me, and that rightly. They say, too, that I am mad; but that they say not rightly, seeing that I know how wicked I am. I always knew it, but I never cared until I loved – oh, God, I never cared!'

His fierce eyes opened for a minute, glared round the room, and closed again tightly. He went on:

'God, for myself I ask nothing; I make no bargaining with Thee. Whatsoever punishment Thou givest me to bear I will bear it; whatsoever Thou givest me to do I will do it. Whether Thou killest Eve or whether Thou keepest her in life – and never have I loved but her – I will from this night be good. In due penitence will I receive the Holy Sacrament of Thy Body and Blood. And my son, the one child that I had by Alice, I will fetch back again from Challonsea, where I kept him in order that I might not look upon him, and I will be to him a father in deed and very truth. And in all things, so far as in me lieth, I will make restitution and atonement. Whether Thou hearest me or whether Thou hearest me not, these things shall be. And for my prayer, it is but this: of Thy loving kindness, most merciful God, be Thou with Eve and make her happy; and after these great pains and perils of childbirth send her Thy peace. Of Thy loving kindness, Thy merciful loving kindness, O God!'

Perhaps the prayer that is offered when the time for praying is over is more terribly pathetic than any other. Yet one might hesitate to say that this prayer was unanswered.

Sir Edric rose to his feet. Once more he paced the room. There was a strange simplicity about him, the simplicity that scorns an incongruity. He felt that his lips and throat were parched and dry. He lifted the heavy silver tankard from the table and raised the lid; there was still a good draught of mulled wine in it with the burnt toast, cut heartshaped, floating on the top.

'To the health of Eve and her child,' he said aloud, and drained it to the last drop.

Click, click! As he put the tankard down he heard distinctly two doors opened and shut quickly, one after the other. And then slowly down the stairs came a hesitating step. Sir Edric could bear the suspense no longer. He opened the dining-room door, and the dim light strayed out into the dark hall beyond.

'Dennison,' he said, in a low, sharp whisper, 'is that you?'

'Yes, yes. I am coming, Sir Edric.'

A moment afterwards Dr Dennison entered the room. He was very pale; perspiration streamed from his forehead; his cravat was disarranged. He was an old man, thin, with the air of proud humility. Sir Edric watched him narrowly.

'Then she is dead,' he said, with a quiet that Dr Dennison had not expected.

'Twenty physicians – a hundred physicians could not have saved her, Sir Edric. She was . . . ' he gave some details of medical interest.

'Dennison,' said Sir Edric, still speaking with calm and restraint, 'why do you seem thus indisposed and panic-stricken? You are a physician; have you never looked upon the face of death before? The soul of my wife is with God.'

'Yes,' murmured Dennison, 'a good woman, a perfect, saintly woman.'

'And,' Sir Edric went on, raising his eyes to the ceiling as though he could see through it, 'her body lies in great dignity and beauty upon the bed, and there is no horror in it. Why are you afraid?'

'I do not fear death, Sir Edric.'

'But your hands – they are not steady. You are evidently overcome. Does the child live?'

'Yes, it lives.'

'Another boy – a brother for young Edric, the child that Alice bore me?'

'There – there is something wrong. I do not know what to do. I want you to come upstairs. And, Sir Edric, I must tell you, you will need your self-command.'

'Dennison, the hand of God is heavy upon me; but from this time forth until the day of my death I am submissive to it, and God send that that day may come quickly! I will follow you and I will endure.'

He took one of the high silver candlesticks from the table and stepped towards the door. He strode quickly up the staircase, Dr Dennison following a little way behind him.

As Sir Edric waited at the top of the staircase he heard suddenly from the room before him a low cry. He put down the candlestick on the floor and leaned back against the wall listening. The cry came again, a vibrating monotone ending in a growl.

'Dennison, Dennison!'

His voice choked; he could not go on.

'Yes,' said the doctor, 'it is in there. I had the two women out of the room, and got it here. No-one but myself has seen it. But you must see it, too.'

He raised the candle and the two men entered the room – one of the spare bedrooms. On the bed there was something moving under cover of a blanket. Dr Dennison paused for a moment and then flung the blanket partially back.

They did not remain in the room for more than a few seconds. The moment they got outside, Dr Dennison began to speak.

'Sir Edric, I would fain suggest somewhat to you. There is no evil, as Sophocles hath it in his *Antigone*, for which man hath not found a remedy, except it be death, and here – '

Sir Edric interrupted him in a husky voice. 'Downstairs, Dennison. This is too near.'

It was, indeed, passing strange. When once the novelty of this – this occurrence had worn off, Dr Dennison seemed no longer frightened. He was calm, academic, interested in an unusual phenomenon. But Sir Edric, who was said in the village to fear nothing in earth, or heaven, or hell, was obviously much moved.

When they had got back to the dining-room, Sir Edric motioned the doctor to a seat.

'Now, then,' he said, 'I will hear you. Something must be done – and tonight.'

'Exceptional cases,' said Dr Dennison, 'demand exceptional remedies. Well, it lies there upstairs and is at our mercy. We can let it live, or, placing one hand over the mouth and nostrils, we can – '

'Stop,' said Sir Edric. 'This thing has so crushed and humiliated me that I can scarcely think. But I recall that while I waited for you I fell upon my knees and prayed that God would save Eve. And, as I confessed unto Him more than I will ever confess unto man, it seemed to me that it were ignoble to offer a price for His favour. And I said that whatsoever punishment I had to bear, I would bear it; and whatsoever He called upon me to do, I would do it; and I made no conditions.'

'Well?'

'Now my punishment is of two kinds. Firstly my wife, Eve, is dead. And this I bear more easily because I know that she is numbered with the company of God's saints, and with them her pure spirit finds happier communion than with me; I was not worthy of her. And yet she would call my roughness by gentle, pretty names. She gloried, Dennison, in the mere strength of my body, and in the greatness of my stature. And I am thankful that she never saw this – this shame that has come upon the house. For she was a proud woman, with all her gentleness, even as I was proud and bad until it pleased God this night to break me even to the dust. And for my second punishment, that, too, I must bear. This thing that lies upstairs, I will take and rear; it is bone of my bone and flesh of my flesh; only, if it be possible, I will hide my shame so that no man but you shall know of it.'

'This is not possible. You cannot keep a living being in this house unless it be known. Will not these women say, 'Where is the child?'

Sir Edric stood upright, his powerful hands linked before him, his face working in agony; but he was still resolute.

'Then if it must be known, it shall be known. The fault is mine. If I had but done sooner what Eve asked, this would not have happened. I will bear it.'

'Sir Edric, do not be angry with me, for if I did not say this, then I should be but an ill counsellor. And, firstly, do not use the word shame. The ways of nature are past all explaining; if a woman be frail and easily impressed, and other circumstances concur, then in some few rare cases a thing of this sort does happen. If there be shame, it is not upon you but upon nature – to whom one would not lightly impute shame. Yet it is true that common and uninformed people might think that this shame was yours. And herein lies the great trouble – the shame would rest also on her memory'

'Then,' said Sir Edric, in a low, unfaltering voice, 'this night for the sake of Eve I will break my word, and lose my own soul eternally.'

About an hour afterwards Sir Edric and Dr Dennison left the house together. The doctor carried a stable lantern in his hand. Sir Edric bore in his arms something wrapped in a blanket. They went through the long garden, out into the orchard that skirts the north side of the park, and then across a field to a small dark plantation known as Hal's Planting. In the very heart of Hal's Planting there are some curious caves: access to the innermost chamber of them is exceedingly difficult and dangerous, and only possible to a climber of exceptional skill and courage. As they returned from these caves, Sir Edric no longer carried his burden. The dawn was breaking and the birds began to sing.

'Could not they be quiet just for this morning?' said Sir Edric wearily.

There were but few people who were asked to attend the funeral of Lady Vanquerest and of the baby which, it was said, had only survived her by a few hours. There were but three people who knew that only one body – the body of Lady Vanquerest – was really interred on that occasion. These three were Sir Edric Vanquerest, Dr Dennison, and a nurse whom it had been found expedient to take into their confidence.

During the next six years Sir Edric lived, almost in solitude, a life of great sanctity, devoting much of his time to the education of the younger Edric, the child that he had by his first wife. In the course of this time some strange stories began to be told and believed in the neighbourhood with reference to Hal's Planting, and the place was generally avoided.

When Sir Edric lay on his deathbed the windows of the chamber were open, and suddenly through them came a low cry. The doctor in attendance hardly regarded it, supposing that it came from one of the owls in the trees outside. But Sir Edric, at the sound of it, rose right up in bed before anyone could stay him, and flinging up his arms cried, 'Wolves! wolves! wolves!' Then he fell forward on his face, dead. And four generations passed away.

2

Towards the latter end of the nineteenth century, John Marsh, who was the oldest man in the village of Mansteth, could be prevailed upon to state what he recollected. His two sons supported him in his old age; he never felt the pinch of poverty, and he always had money in his pocket; but it was a settled principle with him that he would not pay for the pint of beer which he drank occasionally in the parlour of The Stag. Sometimes Farmer Wynthwaite paid for the beer; sometimes it was Mr Spicer from the post office; sometimes the landlord of The Stag himself would finance the old man's evening dissipation. In return, John Marsh was prevailed upon to state what he recollected; this he would do with great heartiness and strict impartiality, recalling the intemperance of a former Wynthwaite and the dishonesty of some ancestral Spicer, while he drank the beer of their direct descendants. He would tell you, with two tough old fingers crooked round the handle of the pewter that you had provided, how your grandfather was a poor thing, 'fit for nowt but to brak steeans by ta rord-side'. He was so disrespectful that it was believed that he spoke truth. He was particularly disrespectful when he spoke of that most devilish family, the Vanquerests; and he never tired of recounting the stories that from generation to generation had grown up about them. It would be objected, sometimes, that the present Sir Edric, the last surviving member of the race, was a pleasant-spoken young man, with none of the family wildness and hot temper. It was for no sin of his that Hal's Planting was haunted – a thing which everyone in Mansteth, and many beyond it, most devoutly believed. John Marsh would hear no apology for him, nor for any of his ancestors; he recounted the prophecy that an old mad woman had made of the family before her strange death, and hoped, fervently, that he might live to see it fulfilled.

The third baronet, as has already been told, had lived the latter part of his life, after his second wife's death, in peace and quietness. Of him John Marsh remembered nothing, of course, and could only recall the few fragments of information that had been handed down to him. He had been told that this Sir Edric, who had travelled a good deal, at one time kept wolves, intending to train them to serve as dogs; these wolves were not kept under proper restraint, and became a kind of terror to the neighbourhood. Lady Vanquerest, his second wife, had asked him frequently to destroy these beasts, but Sir Edric although it was said that he loved his second wife even more than he hated the first, was obstinate when any of his whims were crossed, and put her off with promises. Then one day Lady Vanquerest herself was attacked by the wolves; she was not bitten, but she was badly frightened. That filled Sir Edric with remorse, and, when it was too late, he went out into the yard where the wolves were kept and shot them all. A few months afterwards Lady Vanquerest died in childbirth. It was a queer thing, John Marsh noted, that it was just at this time that Hal's Planting began to get such a bad name. The fourth baronet was, John Marsh considered, the worst of the race; it was to him that the old mad woman had made her prophecy, an incident that Marsh himself had witnessed in his childhood and still vividly remembered.

The baronet, in his old age, had been cast up by his vices on the shores of melancholy; heavy-eyed, grey-haired, bent, he seemed to pass through life as in a dream. Every day he would go out on horseback, always at a walking pace, as though he were following the funeral of his past self. One night he was riding up the village street as this old woman came down it. Her name was Ann Ruthers; she had a kind of reputation in the village, and although all said that she was mad, many of her utterances were remembered, and she was treated with respect. It was growing dark, and the village street was almost empty; but just at the lower end was the usual group of men by the door of The Stag, dimly illuminated by the light that came through the quaint windows of the old inn. They glanced at Sir Edric as he rode slowly past them, taking no notice of their respectful salutes. At the upper end of the street there were two persons. One was Ann Ruthers, a tall, gaunt old woman, her head wrapped in a shawl; the other was John Marsh. He was then a boy of eight, and he was feeling somewhat frightened. He had been on an expedition to a distant and foetid pond, and in the black mud and clay about its borders he had discovered live newts; he had three of them in his pocket, and this was to some extent a joy to him, but his joy was damped by his knowledge that he was coming home much too late, and would probably be chastised in consequence. He was unable to walk fast or to run, because Ann Ruthers was immediately in front of him, and he dared not pass her, especially at night. She walked on until she met Sir Edric, and then, standing still, she called him by name. He pulled in his horse and raised his heavy eyes to look at her. Then in loud clear tones she spoke to him, and John Marsh heard and remembered every word that she said; it was her prophecy of the end of the Vanquerests. Sir Edric never answered a word. When she had finished, he rode on, while she remained standing there, her eyes fixed on the stars above her. John Marsh dared not pass the mad woman; he turned round and walked back, keeping close to Sir Edric's horse. Quite suddenly, without a word of warning, as if in a moment of ungovernable irritation, Sir Edric wheeled his horse round and struck the boy across the face with his switch.

On the following morning John Marsh – or rather, his parents – received a handsome solatium in coin of the realm; but sixty-five years afterwards he had not forgiven that blow, and still spoke of the Vanquerests as a most devilish family, still hoped and prayed that he might see the prophecy fulfilled. He would relate, too, the death of Ann Ruthers, which occurred either later on the night of her prophecy or early on the following day. She would often roam about the country at night, and on this particular night she left the main road to wander over the Vanquerest lands, where trespassers, especially at night, were not welcomed. But no-one saw her, and it seemed that she had made her way to a part where no-one was likely to see her; for none of the keepers would have entered Hal's Planting by night. Her body was found there at noon on the following day, lying under the tall bracken, dead, but without any mark of violence upon it. It was considered that she had died in a fit. This naturally added to the ill-repute of Hal's Planting. The woman's death caused considerable sensation in the village. Sir Edric sent a messenger to the married sister with whom she had lived, saying that he wished to pay all the funeral expenses. This offer, as John Marsh recalled with satisfaction, was refused.

Of the last two baronets he had but little to tell. The fifth baronet was credited with the family temper, but he conducted himself in a perfectly conventional way, and did not seem in the least to belong to romance. He was a good man of business, and devoted himself to making up, as far as he could, for the very extravagant expenditure of his predecessors. His son, the present Sir Edric, was a fine young fellow and popular in the village. Even John Marsh could find nothing to say against him; other people in the village were interested in him. It was said that he had chosen a wife in London – a Miss Guerdon – and would shortly be back to see that Mansteth Hall was put in proper order for her before his marriage at the close of the season. Modernity kills ghostly romance. It was difficult to associate this modern and handsome Sir Edric, bright and spirited, a good sportsman and a good fellow, with the doom that had been foretold for the Vanquerest family. He himself knew the tradition and laughed at it. He wore clothes made by a London tailor, looked healthy, smiled cheerfully, and, in a vain attempt to shame his own head keeper, had himself spent a night alone in Hal's Planting. This last was used by Mr Spicer in argument, who would ask John Marsh what he made of it. John Marsh replied, contemptuously, that it was 'newt'. It was not so that the Vanquerest family was to end; but when the thing, whatever it was, that lived in Hal's Planting, left it and came up to the house, to Mansteth Hall itself, then one would see the end of the Vanquerests. So Ann Ruthers had prophesied. Sometimes Mr Spicer would ask the pertinent question, how did John Marsh know that there really was anything in Hal's Planting? This he asked, less because he disbelieved, than because he wished to draw forth an account of John's personal experiences. These were given in great detail, but they did not amount to very much. One night John Marsh had been taken by business – Sir Edric's keepers would have called the business by hard names – into the neighbourhood of Hal's Planting. He had been suddenly startled by a cry, and had run away as though he were running for his life. That was all he could tell about the cry – it was the kind of cry to make a man lose his head and run. And then it always happened that John Marsh was urged by his companions to enter Hal's Planting himself, and discover what was there. John pursed his thin lips together, and hinted that that also might be done one of these days. Whereupon Mr Spicer looked across his pipe to Farmer Wynthwaite, and smiled significantly.

Shortly before Sir Edric's return from London, the attention of Mansteth was once more directed to Hal's Planting, but not by any supernatural occurrence. Quite suddenly, on a calm day, two trees there fell with a crash; there were caves in the centre of the plantation, and it seemed as if the roof of some big chamber in these caves had given way. They talked it over one night in the parlour of The Stag. There was water in these caves, Farmer Wynthwaite knew it; and he expected a further subsidence. If the whole thing collapsed, what then?

'Ay,' said John Marsh. He rose from his chair, and pointed in the direction of the Hall with his thumb. 'What then?'

He walked across to the fire, looked at it meditatively for a moment, and then spat in it.

'A trewly wun'ful owd mon,' said Farmer Wynthwaite as he watched him.

3

In the smoking-room at Mansteth Hall sat Sir Edric with his friend and intended brother-in-law, Dr Andrew Guerdon. Both men were on the verge of middle-age; there was hardly a year's difference between them. Yet Guerdon looked much the older man; that was, perhaps, because he wore a short, black beard, while Sir Edric was clean-shaven. Guerdon was thought to be an enviable man. His father had made a fortune in the firm of Guerdon, Guerdon, and Bird; the old style was still retained at the bank, although there was no longer a Guerdon in the firm. Andrew Guerdon had a handsome allowance from his father, and had also inherited money through his mother. He had taken the degree of Doctor of Medicine; he did not practise, but he was still interested in science, especially in out-of-the-way science. He was unmarried, gifted with perpetually good health, interested in life, popular. His friendship with Sir Edric dated from their college days. It had for some years been almost certain that Sir Edric would marry his friend's sister, Ray Guerdon, although the actual betrothal had only been announced that season.

On a bureau in one corner of the room were spread a couple of plans and various slips of paper. Sir Edric was wrinkling his brows over them, dropping cigar-ash over them, and finally getting angry over them. He pushed back his chair irritably, and turned towards Guerdon.

'Look here, old man!' he said. 'I desire to curse the original architect of this house – to curse him in his down-sitting and his uprising.'

'Seeing that the original architect has gone to where beyond these voices there is peace, he won't be offended. Neither shall I. But why worry yourself? You've been rooted to that blessed bureau all day, and now, after dinner, when every self-respecting man chucks business, you return to it again – even as a sow returns to her wallowing in the mire.'

'Now, my good Andrew, do be reasonable. How on earth can I bring Ray to such a place as this? And it's built with such ingrained malice and vexatiousness that one can't live in it as it is, and can't alter it without having the whole shanty tumble down about one's ears. Look at this plan now. That thing's what they're pleased to call a morning room. If the window had been *here* there would have been an uninterrupted view of open country. So what does this forsaken fool of an architect do? He sticks it *there*, where you see it on the plan, looking straight on to a blank wall with a stable yard on the other side of it. But that's a trifle. Look here again.'

'I won't look any more. This place is all right. It was good enough for your father and mother and several generations before them until you arose to improve the world; it was good enough for you until you started to get married. It's a picturesque place, and if you begin to alter it you'll spoil it.'

Guerdon looked round the room critically. 'Upon my word,' he said, 'I don't know of any house where I like the smoking-room as well as I like this. It's not too big, and yet it's fairly lofty; it's got those comfortable-looking oak-panelled walls. That's the right kind of fireplace, too, and these corner cupboards are handy.'

'Of course this won't *remain* the smoking-room. It has the morning sun, and Ray likes that, so I shall make it into her boudoir. It is a nice room, as you say'

'That's it, Ted, my boy,' said Guerdon bitterly; 'take a room which is designed by nature and art to be a smoking-room and turn it into a boudoir. Turn it into the very deuce of a boudoir with the morning sun laid on for ever and ever. Waste the twelfth of August by getting married on it. Spend the winter in foreign parts, and write letters that you can breakfast out of doors, just as if you'd created the mildness of the climate yourself Come back in the spring and spend the London season in the country in order to avoid seeing anybody who wants to see you. That's the way to do it; that's the way to get yourself generally loved and admired!'

'That's chiefly imagination,' said Sir Edric. 'I'm blest if I can see why I should not make this house fit for Ray to live in.'

'It's a queer thing: Ray was a good girl, and you weren't a bad sort yourself. You prepare to go into partnership, and you both straight-away turn into despicable lunatics. I'll have a word or two with Ray.

But I'm serious about this house. Don't go tinkering with it; it's got a character of its own, and you'd better leave it. Turn half Tottenham Court Road and the culture thereof – Heaven help it! – into your town house if you like, but leave this alone.'

'Haven't got a town house – yet. Anyway I'm not going to be unsuitable; I'm not going to feel myself at the mercy of a big firm. I shall supervise the whole thing myself. I shall drive over to Challonsea tomorrow afternoon and see if I can't find some intelligent and fairly conscientious workmen.'

'That's all right; you supervise them and I'll supervise you. You'll be much too new if I don't look after you. You've got an old legend, I believe, that the family's coming to a bad end; you must be consistent with it. As you are bad, be beautiful. By the way, what do you yourself think of the legend?'

'It's nothing,' said Sir Edric, speaking, however, rather seriously. 'They say that Hal's Planting is haunted by something that will not die. Certainly an old woman, who for some godless reason of her own made her way there by night, was found there dead on the following morning; but her death could be, and was, accounted for by natural causes. Certainly, too, I haven't a man in my employ who'll go there by night now.'

'Why not?'

'How should I know? I fancy that a few of the villagers sit boozing at The Stag in the evening, and like to scare themselves by swopping lies about Hal's Planting. I've done my best to stop it. I once, as you know, took a rug, a revolver and a flask of whisky and spent the night there myself. But even that didn't convince them.'

'Yes, you told me. By the way, did you hear or see anything?' Sir Edric hesitated before he answered. Finally he said:

'Look here, old man, I wouldn't tell this to anyone but yourself. I did think that I heard something. About the middle of the night I was awakened by a cry; I can only say that it was the kind of cry that frightened me. I sat up, and at that moment I heard some great, heavy thing go swishing through the bracken behind me at a great rate. Then all was still; I looked about, but I could find nothing. At last I argued as I would argue now that a man who is just awake is only half awake, and that his powers of observation, by hearing or any other sense, are not to be trusted. I even persuaded myself to go to sleep again, and there was no more disturbance. However, there's a real danger there now. In the heart of the plantation there are some caves and a subterranean spring; lately there has been some slight subsidence there, and the same sort of thing will happen again in all probability. I wired today to an expert to come and look at the place; he has replied that he will come on Monday. The legend says that when the thing that lives in Hal's Planting comes up to the Hall, the Vanquerests will be ended.

'If I cut down the trees and then break up the place with a charge of dynamite I shouldn't wonder if I spoiled that legend.'

Guerdon smiled.

'I'm inclined to agree with you all through. It's absurd to trust the immediate impressions of a man just awakened; what you heard was probably a stray cow.'

'No cow,' said Sir Edric impartially. 'There's a low wall all round the place – not much of a wall, but too much for a cow.'

'Well, something else – some equally obvious explanation. In dealing with such questions, never forget that you're in the nineteenth century. By the way, your man's coming on Monday. That reminds me today's Friday, and as an indisputable consequence tomorrow's Saturday, therefore, if you want to find your intelligent workmen it will be of no use to go in the afternoon.'

'True,' said Sir Edric, 'I'll go in the morning.' He walked to a tray on a side table and poured a little whisky into a tumbler. 'They don't seem to have brought any seltzer water,' he remarked in a grumbling voice.

He rang the bell impatiently.

'Now why don't you use those corner cupboards for that kind of thing? If you kept a supply there, it would be handy in case of accidents.'

'They're full up already'

He opened one of them and showed that it was filled with old account books and yellow documents tied up in bundles.

The servant entered.

'Oh, I say, there isn't any seltzer. Bring it, please.'

He turned again to Guerdon.

'You might do me a favour when I'm away tomorrow, if there's nothing else that you want to do. I wish you'd look through all these papers for me. They're all old. Possibly some of them ought to go to my solicitor, and I know that a lot of them ought to be destroyed. Some few may be of family interest. It's not the kind of thing that I could ask a stranger or a servant to do for me, and I've so much on hand just now before my marriage.'

'But of course, my dear fellow, I'll do it with pleasure.'

'I'm ashamed to give you all this bother. However, you said that you were coming here to help me, and I take you at your word. By the way, I think you'd better not say anything to Ray about the Hal's Planting story'

'I may be some of the things that you take me for, but really I am not a common ass. Of course I shouldn't tell her.'

'I'll tell her myself, and I'd sooner do it when I've got the whole thing cleared up. Well, I'm really obliged to you.'

'I needn't remind you that I hope to receive as much again. I believe in compensation. Nature always gives it and always requires it. One finds it everywhere, in philology and onwards.'

'I could mention omissions.'

'They are few, and make a belief in a hereafter to supply them logical.'

'Lunatics, for instance?'

'Their delusions are often their compensation. They argue correctly from false premises. A lunatic believing himself to be a millionaire has as much delight as money can give.'

'How about deformities or monstrosities?'

'The principle is there, although I don't pretend that the compensation is always adequate. A man who is deprived of one sense generally has another developed with unusual acuteness. As for monstrosities of at all a human type one sees none; the things exhibited in fairs are, almost without exception, frauds. They occur rarely, and one does not know enough about them. A really good textbook on the subject would be interesting. Still, such stories as I have heard would bear out my theory – stories of their superhuman strength and cunning, and of the extraordinary prolongation of life that has been noted, or is said to have been noted, in them. But it is hardly fair to test my principle by exceptional cases. Besides, anyone can prove anything except that anything's worth proving.'

'That's a cheerful thing to say. I wouldn't like to swear that I could prove how the Hal's Planting legend started; but I fancy, do you know, that I could make a very good shot at it.'

'Well?'

'My great-grandfather kept wolves – I can't say why. Do you remember the portrait of him? – Not the one when he was a boy, the other. It hangs on the staircase. There's now a group of wolves in one corner of the picture. I was looking carefully at the picture one day and thought that I detected some over-painting in that corner; indeed, it was done so roughly that a child would have noticed it if the picture had been hung in a better light. I had the over-painting removed by a good man, and underneath there was a group of wolves depicted. Well, one of these wolves must have escaped, got into Hal's Planting, and scared an old woman or two; that would start a story, and human mendacity would do the rest!

'Yes,' said Guerdon meditatively, 'that doesn't sound improbable. But why did your great-grandfather have the wolves painted out?'

4

Saturday morning was fine, but very hot and sultry. After breakfast, when Sir Edric had driven off to Challonsea, Andrew Guerdon settled himself in a comfortable chair in the smoking-room. The contents of the corner cupboard were piled up on a table by his side. He lit his pipe and began to go through the papers and put them in order. He had been at work about a quarter of an hour when the butler entered rather abruptly, looking pale and disturbed.

'In Sir Edric's absence, sir, it was thought that I had better come to you for advice. There's been an awful thing happened.'

'Well?'

'They've found a corpse in Hal's Planting about half an hour ago. It's the body of an old man, John Marsh, who used to live in the village. He seems to have died in some kind of a fit. They were bringing it here, but I had it taken down to the village where his cottage is. Then I sent for the police and a doctor.'

There was a moment or two's silence before Guerdon answered. 'This is a terrible thing. I don't know of anything else that you could do. Stop; if the police want to see the spot where the body was found, I think that Sir Edric would like them to have every facility.'

'Quite so, sir.'

'And no-one else must be allowed there.'

'No, sir. Thank you.'

The butler withdrew.

Guerdon arose from his chair and began to pace up and down the room.

'What an impressive thing a coincidence is!' he thought to himself. 'Last night the whole of Hal's Planting story seemed to be not worth consideration. But this second death there – it can only be coincidence. What else could it be?'

The question would not leave him. What else could it be? Had that dead man seen something there and died in sheer terror of it?

Had Sir Edric really heard something when he spent that night there alone? He returned to his work, but he found that he got on with it but slowly. Every now and then his mind wandered back to the subject of Hal's Planting. His doubts annoyed him. It was unscientific and unmodern of him to feel any perplexity, because a natural and rational explanation was possible; he was annoyed with himself for being perplexed.

After luncheon he strolled round the grounds and smoked a cigar. He noticed that a thick bank of dark, slate-coloured clouds was gathering in the west. The air was very still. In a remote corner of the garden a big heap of weeds was burning; the smoke went up perfectly straight. On the top of the heap light flames danced; they were like the ghosts of flames in the strange light. A few big drops of rain fell. The small shower did not last for five seconds. Guerdon glanced at his watch. Sir Edric would be back in an hour, and he wanted to finish his work with the papers before Sir Edric's return, so he went back into the house once more.

He picked up the first document that came to hand. As he did so, another, smaller, and written on parchment, which had been folded in with it, dropped out. He began to read the parchment; it was written in faded ink, and the parchment itself was yellow and in many places stained. It was the confession of the third baronet – he could tell that by the date upon it. It told the story of that night when he and Dr Dennison went together carrying a burden through the long garden out into the orchard that skirts the north side of the park, and then across a field to a small, dark plantation. It told how he made a vow to God and did not keep it. These were the last words of the confession:

Already upon me has the punishment fallen, and the devil's wolves do seem to hunt me in my sleep nightly. But I know that there is worse to come. The thing that I took to Hal's Planting is dead. Yet it will come back again to the Hall, and then will the Vanquerests be at an end. This writing I have committed to chance, neither showing it nor hiding it, and leaving it to chance if any man shall read it.

Underneath there was a line written in darker ink, and in quite a different handwriting. It was dated fifteen years later, and the initials R. D. were appended to it:

It is not dead. I do not think that it will ever die.

When Andrew Guerdon had finished reading this document, he looked slowly round the room. The subject had got on his nerves, and he was almost expecting to see something. Then he did his best to pull himself together. The first question he put to himself was this: 'Has Ted ever seen this?' Obviously he had not. If he had he could not have taken the tradition of Hal's Planting so lightly, nor have spoken of it so freely. Besides, he would either have mentioned the document to Guerdon, or he would have kept it carefully concealed. He would not have allowed him to come across it casually in that way. 'Ted must never see it,' thought Guerdon to himself. He then remembered the pile of weeds he had seen burning in the garden. He put the parchment in his pocket, and hurried out. There was no-one about. He spread the parchment on the top of the pile, and waited until it was entirely consumed. Then he went back to the smoking-room; he felt easier now.

'Yes,' thought Guerdon, 'if Ted had first of all heard of the finding of that body, and then had read that document, I believe that he would have gone mad. Things that come near us affect us deeply.'

Guerdon himself was much moved. He clung steadily to reason; he felt himself able to give a natural explanation all through, and yet he was nervous. The net of coincidence had closed in around him; the mention in Sir Edric's confession of the prophecy which had subsequently become traditional in the village alarmed him. And what did that last line mean? He supposed that R. D. must be the initials of Dr Dennison. What did he mean by saying that the thing was not dead? Did he mean that it had not really been killed, that it had been gifted with some preternatural strength and vitality and had survived, though Sir Edric did not know it? He recalled what he had said about the prolongation of the lives of such things. If it still survived, why had it never been seen? Had it joined to the wild hardiness of the beast a cunning that was human – or more than human? How could it have lived? There was water in the caves, he reflected, and food could have been secured – a wild beast's food. Or did Dr Dennison mean that though the thing itself was dead, its wraith survived and haunted the place? He wondered how the doctor had found Sir Edric's confession, and why he had written that line at the end of it. As he sat thinking, a low rumble of thunder in the distance startled him. He felt a touch of panic – a sudden impulse to leave Mansteth at once and, if possible, to take Ted with him. Ray could never live there. He went over the whole thing in his mind again and again, at one time calm and argumentative about it, and at another shaken by blind horror.

Sir Edric, on his return from Challonsea a few minutes afterwards, came straight to the smoking-room where Guerdon was. He looked tired and depressed. He began to speak at once.

You needn't tell me about it – about John Marsh. I heard about it in the village.'

'Did you? It's a painful occurrence, although, of course – '

'Stop. Don't go into it. Anything can be explained – I know that.'

'I went through those papers and account books while you were away. Most of them may just as well be destroyed; but there are a few – I put them aside there – which might be kept. There was nothing of any interest.'

'Thanks; I'm much obliged to you.'

'Oh, and look here, I've got an idea. I've been examining the plans of the house, and I'm coming round to your opinion. There are some alterations which should be made, and yet I'm afraid that they'd make the place look patched and renovated. It wouldn't be a bad thing to know what Ray thought about it.'

'That's impossible. The workmen come on Monday, and we can't consult her before then. Besides, I have a general notion what she would like.'

'We could catch the night express to town at Challonsea.'

Sir Edric rose from his seat angrily and hit the table.

'Good God! don't sit there hunting up excuses to cover my cowardice, and making it easy for me to bolt. What do you suppose the villagers would say, and what would my own servants say, if I ran away tonight? I am a coward – I know it. I'm horribly afraid. But I'm not going to act like a coward if I can help it.'

'Now, my dear chap, don't excite yourself. If you are going to care at all – to care as much as the conventional damn – for what people say, you'll have no peace in life. And I don't believe you're afraid. What are you afraid of?'

Sir Edric paced once or twice up and down the room, and then sat down again before replying.

'Look here, Andrew, I'll make a clean breast of it. I've always laughed at the tradition; I forced myself, as it seemed at least, to disprove it by spending a night in Hal's Planting; I took the pains even to make a theory which would account for its origin. All the time I had a sneaking, stifled belief in it. With the help of my reason I crushed that; but now my reason has thrown up the job, and I'm afraid. I'm afraid of the Undying Thing that is in Hal's Planting. I heard it that night. John Marsh saw it last night – they took me to see the body, and the face was awful; and I believe that one day it will come from Hal's Planting.'

'Yes,' interrupted Guerdon, 'I know. And at present I believe as much. Last night we laughed at the whole thing, and we shall live to laugh at it again, and be ashamed of ourselves for a couple of super-stitious old women. I fancy that beliefs are affected by weather – there's thunder in the air.'

'No,' said Sir Edric, 'my belief has come to stay.'

'And what are you going to do?'

'I'm going to test it. On Monday I can begin to get to work, and then I'll blow up Hal's Planting with dynamite. After that we shan't need to believe – we shall *know*. And now let's dismiss the subject. Come down into the billiard-room and have a game. Until Monday I won't think of the thing again.'

Long before dinner, Sir Edric's depression seemed to have com-pletely vanished. At dinner he was boisterous and amused. Afterwards he told stories and was interesting.

It was late at night; the terrific storm that was raging outside had awoke Guerdon from sleep. Hopeless of getting to sleep again, he had risen and dressed, and now sat in the window-seat watching the storm. He had never seen anything like it before; and every now and then the sky seemed to be torn across as if by hands of white fire. Suddenly he heard a tap at his door, and looked round. Sir Edric had already entered; he also had dressed. He spoke in a curious, subdued voice.

'I thought you wouldn't be able to sleep through this. Do you remember that I shut and fastened the dining-room window?'

'Yes, I remember it.'

'Well, come in here.'

Sir Edric led the way to his room, which was immediately over the dining-room. By leaning out of the window they could see that the dining-room window was open wide.

'Burglar,' said Guerdon meditatively.

'No,' Sir Edric answered, still speaking in a hushed voice. 'It is the Undying Thing – it has come for me.'

He snatched up the candle, and made towards the staircase; Guer-don caught up the loaded revolver which always lay on the table beside Sir Edric's bed and followed him. Both men ran down the staircase as though there were not another moment to lose. Sir Edric rushed at the dining-room door, opened it a little, and looked in. Then he turned to Guerdon, who was just behind him.

'Go back to your room,' he said authoritatively.

'I won't,' said Guerdon. 'Why? What is it?'

Suddenly the corners of Sir Edric's mouth shot outward into the hideous grin of terror.

'It's there! It's there!' he gasped.

'Then I come in with you.'

'Go back!'

With a sudden movement, Sir Edric thrust Guerdon away from the door, and then, quick as light, darted in, and locked the door behind him.

Guerdon bent down and listened. He heard Sir Edric say in a firm voice: 'Who are you? What are you?'

Then followed a heavy, snorting breathing, a low, vibrating growl, nn awful cry, a scuffle.

Then Guerdon flung himself at the door. He kicked at the lock, but it would not give way. At last he fired his revolver at it. Then he managed to force his way into the room. It was perfectly empty. Overhead he could hear footsteps; the noise had awakened the servants; they were standing, tremulous, on the upper landing.

Through the open window access to the garden was easy. Guerdon did not wait to get help; and in all probability none of the servants could have been persuaded to come with him. He climbed out alone, and as if by some blind impulse, started to run as hard as he could in the direction of Hal's Planting. He knew that Sir Edric would be found there.

But when he got within a hundred yards of the plantation, he stopped. There had been a great flash of lightning, and he saw that it had struck one of the trees. Flames darted about the plantation as the dry bracken caught. Suddenly, in the light of another flash, he saw the whole of the trees fling their heads upwards; then came a deafening crash, and the ground slipped under him, and he was flung forward on his face. The plantation had collapsed, fallen through into the caves beneath it. Guerdon slowly regained his feet; he was surprised to find that he was unhurt. He walked on a few steps, and then fell again; this time he had fainted away.

Gabriel-Ernest

SAKI

'There is a wild beast in your woods,' said the artist Cunningham, as he was being driven to the station. It was the only remark he had made during the drive, but as Van Cheele had talked incessantly his companion's silence had not been noticeable.

'A stray fox or two and some resident weasels. Nothing more formidable,' said Van Cheele. The artist said nothing.

'What did you mean about a wild beast?' said Van Cheele later, when they were on the platform.

'Nothing. My imagination. Here is the train,' said Cunningham.

That afternoon Van Cheele went for one of his frequent rambles through his woodland property. He had a stuffed bittern in his study, and knew the names of quite a number of wild flowers, so his aunt had possibly some justification in describing him as a great naturalist. At any rate, he was a great walker. It was his custom to take mental notes of everything he saw during his walks, not so much for the purpose of assisting contemporary science as to provide topics for conversation afterwards. When the bluebells began to show themselves in flower he made a point of informing everyone of the fact; the season of the year might have warned his hearers of the likelihood of such an occurrence, but at least they felt that he was being absolutely frank with them.

What Van Cheele saw on this particular afternoon was, however, something far removed from his ordinary range of experience. On a shelf of smooth stone overhanging a deep pool in the hollow of an oak coppice a boy of about sixteen lay asprawl, drying his wet brown limbs luxuriously in the sun. His wet hair, parted by a recent dive, lay close to his head, and his light-brown eyes, so light that there was an almost tigerish gleam in them, were turned towards Van Cheele with a certain lazy watchfulness. It was an unexpected apparition, and Van Cheele found himself engaged in the novel process of thinking before he spoke. Where on earth could this wild-looking boy hail from? The miller's wife had lost a child some two months ago, supposed to have been swept away by the mill-race, but that had been a mere baby, not a half-grown lad.

'What are you doing there?' he demanded.

'Obviously, sunning myself,' replied the boy.

'Where do you live?'

'Here, in these woods.'

'You can't live in the woods,' said Van Cheele.

'They are very nice woods,' said the boy, with a touch of patronage in his voice.

'But where do you sleep at night?'

'I don't sleep at night; that's my busiest time.'

Van Cheele began to have an irritated feeling that he was grappling with a problem that was eluding him.

'What do you feed on?' he asked.

'Flesh,' said the boy, and he pronounced the word with slow relish, as though he were tasting it.

'Flesh! What Flesh?'

'Since it interests you, rabbits, wild-fowl, hares, poultry, lambs in their season, children when I can get any; they're usually too well locked in at night, when I do most of my hunting. It's quite two months since I tasted child-flesh.'

Ignoring the chaffing nature of the last remark Van Cheele tried to draw the boy on the subject of possible poaching operations.

'You're talking rather through your hat when you speak of feeding on hares.' (Considering the nature of the boy's toilet the simile was hardly an apt one.) 'Our hillside hares aren't easily caught.'

'At night I hunt on four feet,' was the somewhat cryptic response.

'I suppose you mean that you hunt with a dog?' hazarded Van Cheele.

The boy rolled slowly over on to his back, and laughed a weird low laugh, that was pleasantly like a chuckle and disagreeably like a snarl.

'I don't fancy any dog would be very anxious for my company, especially at night.'

Van Cheele began to feel that there was something positively uncanny about the strange-eyed, strange-tongued youngster.

'I can't have you staying in these woods,' he declared authoritatively.

'I fancy you'd rather have me here than in your house,' said the boy.

The prospect of this wild, nude animal in Van Cheele's primly ordered house was certainly an alarming one.

'If you don't go. I shall have to make you,' said Van Cheele.

The boy turned like a flash, plunged into the pool, and in a moment had flung his wet and glistening body half-way up the bank where Van Cheele was standing. In an otter the movement would not have been remarkable; in a boy Van Cheele found it sufficiently startling. His foot slipped as he made an involuntarily backward movement, and he found himself almost prostrate on the slippery weed-grown bank, with those tigerish yellow eyes not very far from his own. Almost instinctively he half raised his hand to his throat. The boy laughed again, a laugh in which the snarl had nearly driven out the chuckle, and then, with another of his astonishing lightning movements, plunged out of view into a yielding tangle of weed and fern.

'What an extraordinary wild animal!' said Van Cheele as he picked himself up. And then he recalled Cunningham's remark 'There is a wild beast in your woods.'

Walking slowly homeward, Van Cheele began to turn over in his mind various local occurrences which might be traceable to the existence of this astonishing young savage.

Something had been thinning the game in the woods lately, poultry had been missing from the farms, hares were growing unaccountably scarcer, and complaints had reached him of lambs being carried off bodily from the hills. Was it possible that this wild boy was really hunting the countryside in company with some clever poacher dogs? He had spoken of hunting 'four-footed' by night, but then, again, he had hinted strangely at no dog caring to come near him, 'especially at night'. It was certainly puzzling. And then, as Van Cheele ran his mind over the various depredations that had been committed during the last month or two, he came suddenly to a dead stop, alike in his walk and his speculations. The child missing from the mill two months ago – the accepted theory was that it had tumbled into the mill-race and been swept away; but the mother had always declared she had heard a shriek on the hill side of the house, in the opposite direction from the water. It was unthinkable, of course, but he wished that the boy had not made that uncanny remark about child-flesh eaten two months ago. Such dreadful things should not be said even in fun.

Van Cheele, contrary to his usual wont, did not feel disposed to be communicative about his discovery in the wood. His position as a parish councillor and justice of the peace seemed somehow compromised by the fact that he was harbouring a personality of such doubtful repute on his property; there was even a possibility that a heavy bill of damages for raided lambs and poultry might be laid at his door. At dinner that night he was quite unusually silent.

'Where's your voice gone to?' said his aunt. 'One would think you had seen a wolf.'

Van Cheele, who was not familiar with the old saying, thought the remark rather foolish; if he *had* seen a wolf on his property his tongue would have been extraordinarily busy with the subject.

At breakfast next morning Van Cheele was conscious that his feeling of uneasiness regarding yesterday's episode had not wholly disappeared, and he resolved to go by train to the neighbouring cathedral town, hunt up Cunningham, and learn from him what he had really seen that had prompted the remark about a wild beast in the woods. With this resolution taken, his usual cheerfulness partially returned, and he hummed a bright little melody as he sauntered to the morning-room for his customary cigarette. As he entered the room the melody made way abruptly for a pious invocation. Gracefully asprawl on the ottoman, in an attitude of almost exaggerated repose, was the boy of the woods. He was drier than when Van Cheele had last seen him, but no other alteration was noticeable in his toilet.

'How dare you come here?' asked Van Cheele furiously.

'You told me I was not to stay in the woods,' said the boy calmly.

'But not to come here. Supposing my aunt should see you!'

And with a view to minimising that catastrophe, Van Cheele hastily obscured as much of his unwelcome guest as possible under the folds of a *Morning Post*. At that moment his aunt entered the room.

'This is a poor boy who has lost his way – and lost his memory. He doesn't know who he is or where he comes from,' explained Van Cheele desperately, glancing apprehensively at the waif's face to see whether he was going to add inconvenient candour to his other savage propensities.

Miss Van Cheele was enormously interested.

'Perhaps his underlinen is marked,' she suggested.

'He seems to have lost most of that, too,' said Van Cheele, making frantic little grabs at the *Morning Post* to keep it in its place.

A naked homeless child appealed to Miss Van Cheele as warmly as a stray kitten or derelict puppy would have done.

'We must do all we can for him,' she decided, and in a very short time a messenger, dispatched to the rectory, where a page-boy was kept, had returned with a suit of pantry clothes, and the necessary accessories of shirt, shoes, collar, etc. Clothed, clean, and groomed, the boy lost none of his uncanniness in Van Cheele's eyes, but his aunt found him sweet.

'We must call him something till we know who he really is,' she said. 'Gabriel-Ernest, I think; those are nice suitable names.'

Van Cheele agreed, but he privately doubted whether they were being grafted on to a nice suitable child. His misgivings were not diminished by the fact that his staid and elderly spaniel had bolted out of the house at the first incoming of the boy, and now obstinately remained shivering and yapping at the farther end of the orchard, while the canary, usually as vocally industrious as Van Cheele himself, had put itself on an allowance of frightened cheeps. More than ever he was resolved to consult Cunningham without loss of time.

As he drove off to the station his aunt was arranging that Gabriel-Ernest should help her to entertain the infant members of her Sunday-school class at tea that afternoon.

Cunningham was not at first disposed to be communicative.

'My mother died of some brain trouble,' he explained, 'so you will understand why I am averse to dwelling on anything of an impossibly fantastic nature that I may see or think that I have seen.'

'But what *did* you see?' persisted Van Cheele.

'What I thought I saw was something so extraordinary that no really sane man could dignify it with the credit of having actually happened. I was standing, the last evening I was with you, half-hidden in the hedgegrowth by the orchard gate, watching the dying glow of the sunset. Suddenly I became aware of a naked boy, a bather from some neighbouring pool, I took him to be, who was standing out on the bare hillside also watching the sunset. His pose was so suggestive of some wild faun of Pagan myth that I instantly wanted to engage him as a model, and in another moment I think I should have hailed him. But just then the sun dipped out of view, and all the orange and pink slid out of the landscape, leaving it cold and grey. And at the same moment an astounding thing happened – the boy vanished too!'

'What! vanished away into nothing?' asked Van Cheele excitedly.

'No; that is the dreadful part of it,' answered the artist; 'on the open hillside where the boy had been standing a second ago, stood a large wolf, blackish in colour, with gleaming fangs and cruel, yellow eyes. You may think – '

But Van Cheele did not stop for anything as futile as thought. Already he was tearing at top speed towards the station. He dismissed the idea of a telegram. 'Gabriel-Ernest is a werewolf' was a hopelessly inadequate effort at conveying the situation, and his aunt would think it was a code message to which he had omitted to give her the key. His one hope was that he might reach home before sundown. The cab which he chartered at the other end of the railway journey bore him with what seemed exasperating slowness along the country roads, which were pink and mauve with the flush of the sinking sun. His aunt was putting away some unfinished jams and cake when he arrived.

'Where is Gabriel-Ernest?' he almost screamed.

'He is taking the little Toop child home,' said his aunt. 'It was getting so late, I thought it wasn't safe to let it go back alone. What a lovely sunset, isn't it?'

But Van Cheele, although not oblivious of the glow in the western sky, did not stay to discuss its beauties. At a speed for which he was scarcely geared he raced along the narrow lane that led to the home of the Toops. On one side ran the swift current of the mill-stream, on the other rose the stretch of bare hillside. A dwindling rim of red sun showed still on the skyline, and the next turning must bring him in view of the ill-assorted couple he was pursuing. Then the colour went suddenly out of things, and a grey light settled itself with a quick shiver over the landscape. Van Cheele heard a shrill wail of fear, and stopped running.

Nothing was ever seen again of the Toop child or Gabriel-Ernest, but the latter's discarded garments were found lying in the road so it was assumed that the child had fallen into the water, and that the boy had stripped and jumped in, in a vain endeavour to save it. Van Cheele and some workmen who were near by at the time testified to having heard a child scream loudly just near the spot where the clothes were found. Mrs Toop, who had eleven other children, was decently resigned to her bereavement, but Miss Van Cheele sincerely mourned her lost foundling. It was on her initiative that a memorial brass was put up in the parish church to 'Gabriel-Ernest, an unknown boy, who bravely sacrificed his life for another'.

Van Cheele gave way to his aunt in most things, but he flatly refused to subscribe to the Gabriel-Ernest memorial.

The She-Wolf

SAKI

Leonard Bilsiter was one of those people who have failed to find this world attractive or interesting, and who have sought compensation in an 'unseen world' of their own experience or imagination – or invention. Children do that sort of thing successfully, but children are content to convince themselves, and do not vulgarise their beliefs by trying to convince other people. Leonard Bilsiter's beliefs were for 'the few', that is to say, anyone who would listen to him.

His dabblings in the unseen might not have carried him beyond the customary platitudes of the drawing-room visionary if accident had not reinforced his stock-in-trade of mystical lore. In company with a friend, who was interested in a Ural mining concern, he had made a trip across Eastern Europe at a moment when the great Russian railway strike was developing from a threat to a reality; its outbreak caught him on the return journey, somewhere on the further side of Perm, and it was while waiting for a couple of days at a wayside station in a state of suspended locomotion that he made the acquaintance of a dealer in harness and metalware, who profitably whiled away the tedium of the long halt by initiating his English travelling companion in a fragmentary system of folk-lore that he had picked up from Trans-Baikal traders and natives. Leonard returned to his home circle garrulous about his Russian strike experiences, but oppressively reticent about certain dark mysteries, which he alluded to under the resounding title of Siberian Magic. The reticence wore off in a week or two under the influence of an entire lack of general curiosity, and Leonard began to make more detailed allusions to the enormous powers which this new esoteric force, to use his own description of it, conferred on the initiated few who knew how to wield it. His aunt, Cecilia Hoops, who loved sensation perhaps rather better than she loved the truth, gave him as clamorous an advertisement as anyone could wish for by retailing an account of how he had turned a vegetable marrow into a wood pigeon before her very eyes. As a manifestation of the possession of supernatural powers, the story was discounted in some quarters by the respect accorded to Mrs Hoops' powers of imagination.

However divided opinion might be on the question of Leonard's status as a wonderworker or a charlatan, he certainly arrived at Mary Hampton's house-party with a reputation for pre-eminence in one or other of those professions, and he was not disposed to shun such publicity as might fall to his share. Esoteric forces and unusual powers figured largely in whatever conversation he or his aunt had a share in, and his own performances, past and potential, were the subject of mysterious hints and dark avowals.

'I wish you would turn me into a wolf, Mr Bilsiter,' said his hostess at luncheon the day after his arrival.

'My dear Mary,' said Colonel Hampton, 'I never knew you had a craving in that direction.'

'A she-wolf, of course,' continued Mrs Hampton; 'it would be too confusing to change one's sex as well as one's species at a moment's notice.'

'I don't think one should jest on these subjects,' said Leonard.

'I'm not jesting, I'm quite serious, I assure you. Only don't do it today; we have only eight available bridge players, and it would break up one of our tables. Tomorrow we shall be a larger party. Tomorrow night, after dinner – '

'In our present imperfect understanding of these hidden forces I think one should approach them with humbleness rather than mockery,' observed Leonard, with such severity that the subject was forthwith dropped.

Clovis Sangrail had sat unusually silent during the discussion on the possibilities of Siberian Magic; after lunch he side-tracked Lord Pabham into the comparative seclusion of the billiard-room and delivered himself of a searching question.

'Have you such a thing as a she-wolf in your collection of wild animals? A she-wolf of moderately good temper?'

Lord Pabham considered. 'There is Louisa,' he said, 'a rather fine specimen of the timber-wolf. I got her two years ago in exchange for some Arctic foxes. Most of my animals get to be fairly tame before they've been with me very long; I think I can say Louisa has an angelic temper, as she-wolves go. Why do you ask?'

'I was wondering whether you would lend her to me for tomorrow night,' said Clovis, with the careless solicitude of one who borrows a collar stud or a tennis racquet.

'Tomorrow night?'

'Yes, wolves are nocturnal animals, so the late hours won't hurt her,' said Clovis, with the air of one who has taken everything into consideration; 'one of your men could bring her over from Pabham Park after dusk, and with a little help he ought to be able to smuggle her into the conservatory at the same moment that Mary Hampton makes an unobtrusive exit.'

Lord Pabham stared at Clovis for a moment in pardonable bewilderment; then his face broke into a wrinkled network of laughter.

'Oh, that's your game, is it? You are going to do a little Siberian Magic on your own account. And is Mrs Hampton willing to be a fellow-conspirator?'

'Mary is pledged to see me through with it, if you will guarantee Louisa's temper.'

'I'll answer for Louisa,' said Lord Pabham.

By the following day the house-party had swollen to larger proportions, and Bilsiter's instinct for self-advertisement expanded duly under the stimulant of an increased audience. At dinner that evening he held forth at length on the subject of unseen forces and untested powers, and his flow of impressive eloquence continued unabated while coffee was being served in the drawing-room preparatory to a general migration to the card-room.

His aunt ensured a respectful hearing for his utterances, but her sensation-loving soul hankered after something more dramatic than mere vocal demonstration.

'Won't you do something to *convince* them of your powers, Leonard?' she pleaded; 'change something into another shape. He can, you know, if he only chooses to,' she informed the company.

'Oh, do,' said Mavis Pellington earnestly, and her request was echoed by nearly everyone present. Even those who were not open to conviction were perfectly willing to be entertained by an exhibition of amateur conjuring.

Leonard felt that something tangible was expected of him.

'Has anyone present,' he asked, 'got a three-penny bit or some small object of no particular value – ?'

'You're surely not going to make coins disappear, or something primitive of that sort?' said Clovis contemptuously.

'I think it very unkind of you not to carry out my suggestion of turning me into a wolf,' said Mary Hampton, as she crossed over to the conservatory to give her macaws their usual tribute from the dessert dishes.

'I have already warned you of the danger of treating these powers in a mocking spirit,' said Leonard solemnly.

'I don't believe you can do it,' laughed Mary provocatively from the conservatory; 'I dare you to do it if you can. I defy you to turn me into a wolf.'

As she said this she was lost to view behind a clump of azaleas.

'Mrs Hampton – ' began Leonard with increased solemnity, but he got no further. A breath of chill air seemed to rush across the room, and at the same time the macaws broke forth into ear-splitting screams.

'What on earth is the matter with those confounded birds, Mary?' exclaimed Colonel Hampton; at the same moment an even more piercing scream from Mavis Pellington stampeded the entire company from their seats. In various attitudes of helpless horror or instinctive defence they confronted the evil-looking grey beast that was peering at them from amid a setting of fern and azalea.

Mrs Hoops was the first to recover from the general chaos of fright and bewilderment.

'Leonard!' she screamed shrilly to her nephew, 'turn it back into Mrs Hampton at once! It may fly at us at any moment. Turn it back!'

'I – I don't know how to,' faltered Leonard, who looked more scared and horrified than anyone.

'What!' shouted Colonel Hampton, 'you've taken the abominable liberty of turning my wife into a wolf, and now you stand there calmly and say you can't turn her back again!'

To do strict justice to Leonard, calmness was not a distinguishing feature of his attitude at the moment.

'I assure you I didn't turn Mrs Hampton into a wolf; nothing was farther from my intentions,' he protested.

'Then where is she, and how came that animal into the conservatory?' demanded the Colonel.

'Of course we must accept your assurance that you didn't turn Mrs Hampton into a wolf,' said Clovis politely, 'but you will agree that appearances are against you.'

'Are we to have all these recriminations with that beast standing there ready to tear us to pieces?' wailed Mavis indignantly.

'Lord Pabham, you know a good deal about wild beasts – ' suggested Colonel Hampton.

'The wild beasts that I have been accustomed to,' said Lord Pabham, 'have come with proper credentials from well-known dealers, or have been bred in my own menagerie. I've never before been confronted with an animal that walks unconcernedly out of an azalea bush, leaving a charming and popular hostess unaccounted for. As far as one can judge from *outward* characteristics,' he continued, 'it has the appearance of a well-grown female of the North American timber-wolf, a variety of the common species *canis lupus*.'

'Oh, never mind its Latin name,' screamed Mavis, as the beast came a step or two further into the room; 'can't you entice it away with food, and shut it up where it can't do any harm?'

'If it is really Mrs Hampton, who has just had a very good dinner, I don't suppose food will appeal to it very strongly,' said Clovis.

'Leonard,' beseeched Mrs Hoops tearfully, 'even if this is none of your doing, can't you use your great powers to turn this dreadful beast into something harmless before it bites us all – a rabbit or something?'

'I don't suppose Colonel Hampton would care to have his wife turned into a succession of fancy animals as though we were playing a round game with her,' interposed Clovis.

'I absolutely forbid it,' thundered the Colonel.

'Most wolves that I've had anything to do with have been inordinately fond of sugar,' said Lord Pabham; 'if you like I'll try the effect on this one.'

He took a piece of sugar from the saucer of his coffee cup and flung it to the expectant Louisa, who snapped it in mid-air. There was a sigh of relief from the company; a wolf that ate sugar when it might at the least have been employed in tearing macaws to pieces had already shed some of its terrors. The sigh deepened to a gasp of thanksgiving when Lord Pabham decoyed the animal out of the room by a pretended largesse of further sugar. There was an instant rush to the vacated conservatory. There was no trace of Mrs Hampton except the plate containing the macaws' supper.

'The door is locked on the inside!' exclaimed Clovis, who had deftly turned the key as he affected to test it.

Everyone turned towards Bilsiter.

'If you haven't turned my wife into a wolf,' said Colonel Hampton, 'will you kindly explain where she has disappeared to, since she obviously could not have gone through a locked door? I will not press you for an explanation of how a North American timber-wolf suddenly appeared in the conservatory, but I think I have some right to inquire what has become of Mrs Hampton.'

Bilsiter's reiterated disclaimer was met with a general murmur of impatient disbelief.

'I refuse to stay another hour under this roof,' declared Mavis Pellington.

'If our hostess has really vanished out of human form,' said Mrs Hoops, 'none of the ladies of the party can very well remain. I absolutely decline to be chaperoned by a wolf!'

'It's a she-wolf,' said Clovis soothingly.

The correct etiquette to be observed under the unusual circumstances received no further elucidation. The sudden entry of Mary Hampton deprived the discussion of its immediate interest.

'Someone has mesmerised me,' she exclaimed crossly; 'I found myself in the game larder, of all places, being fed with sugar by Lord Pabham. I hate being mesmerised, and the doctor has forbidden me to touch sugar.'

The situation was explained to her, as far as it permitted of anything that could be called explanation.

'Then you *really* did turn me into a wolf, Mr Bilsiter?' she exclaimed excitedly.

But Leonard had burned the boat in which he might now have embarked on a sea of glory. He could only shake his head feebly.

'It was I who took that liberty,' said Clovis; 'you see, I happen to have lived for a couple of years in North-Eastern Russia, and I have more than a tourist's acquaintance with the magic craft of that region. One does not care to speak about these strange powers, but once in a way, when one hears a lot of nonsense being talked about them, one is tempted to show what Siberian magic can accomplish in the hands of someone who really understands it. I yielded to that temptation. May I have some brandy? The effort has left me rather faint.'

If Leonard Bilsiter could at that moment have transformed Clovis into a cockroach and then have stepped on him he would gladly have performed both operations.

The Thing in the Forest

BERNARD CAPES

Into the snow-locked forests of Upper Hungary steal wolves in winter; but there is a footfall worse than theirs to knock upon the heart of the lonely traveller.

One December evening Elspet, the young, newly wedded wife of the woodman Stefan, came hurrying over the lower slopes of the White Mountains from the town where she had been all day marketing. She carried a basket with provisions on her arm; her plump cheeks were like a couple of cold apples; her breath spoke short, but more from nervousness than exhaustion. It was nearing dusk, and she was glad to see the little lonely church in the hollow below, the hub, as it were, of many radiating paths through the trees, one of which was the road to her own warm cottage yet a half-mile away.

She paused a moment at the foot of the slope, undecided about entering the little chill, silent building and making her plea for protection to the great battered stone image of Our Lady of Succour which stood within by the confessional box; but the stillness and the growing darkness decided her, and she went on. A spark of fire glowing through the presbytery window seemed to repel rather than attract her, and she was glad when the convolutions of the path hid it from her sight. Being new to the district, she had seen very little of Father Ruhl as yet, and somehow the penetrating knowledge and burning eyes of the pastor made her feel uncomfortable.

The soft drift, the lane of tall, motionless pines, stretched on in a quiet like death. Somewhere the sun, like a dead fire, had fallen into opalescent embers faintly luminous: they were enough only to touch the shadows with a ghastlier pallor. It was so still that the light crunch in the snow of the girl's own footfalls trod on her heart like a desecration.

Suddenly there was something near her that had not been before. It had come like a shadow, without more sound or warning. It was here – there – behind her. She turned, in mortal panic, and saw a wolf. With a strangled cry and trembling limbs she strove to hurry on her way; and always she knew, though there was no whisper of pursuit, that the gliding shadow followed in her wake. Desperate in her terror, she stopped once more and faced it.

A wolf! – Was it a wolf? O who could doubt it! Yet the wild expression in those famished eyes, so lost, so pitiful, so mingled of insatiable hunger and human need! Condemned, for its unspeakable sins, to take this form with sunset, and so howl and snuffle about the doors of men until the blessed day released it. A werewolf – not a wolf.

That terrific realisation of the truth smote the girl as with a knife out of darkness: for an instant she came near fainting. And then a low moan broke into her heart and flooded it with pity. So lost, so infinitely hopeless. And so pitiful – yes, in spite of all, so pitiful. It had sinned, beyond any sinning that her innocence knew or her experience could gauge; but she was a woman, very blest, very happy, in her store of comforts and her surety of love. She knew that it was forbidden to succour these damned and nameless outcasts, to help or sympathise with them in any way. But there was good store of meat in her basket, and who need ever know or tell? With shaking hands she found and threw a sop to the desolate brute – then, turning, sped upon her way.

But at home her secret sin stood up before her, and, interposing between her husband and herself, threw its shadow upon both their faces. What had she dared – what done? By her own act forfeited her birthright of innocence; by her own act placed herself in the power of the evil to which she had ministered. All that night she lay in shame and horror, and all the next day, until Stefan had come about his dinner and gone again, she moved in a dumb agony. Then, driven unendurably by the memory of his troubled, bewildered face, as twilight threatened she put on her cloak and went down to the little church in the hollow to confess her sin.

'Mother, forgive, and save me,' she whispered, as she passed the statue.

After ringing the bell for the confessor, she had not knelt long at the confessional box in the dim chapel, cold and empty as a waiting vault, when the chancel rail clicked, and the footsteps of Father Ruhl were heard rustling over the stones. He came, he took his seat behind the grating; and, with many sighs and falterings, Elspet avowed her guilt. And as, with bowed head, she ended, a strange sound answered her – it was like a little laugh, and yet not so much like a laugh as a snarl. With a shock as of death she raised her face. It was Father Ruhl who sat there – and yet it was not Father Ruhl. In that time of twilight his face was already changing, narrowing, becoming wolfish – the eyes rounded and the jaw slavered. She gasped, and shrunk back; and at that, barking and snapping at the grating, with a wicked look he dropped – and she heard him coming. Sheer horror lent her wings. With a scream she sprang to her feet and fled. Her cloak caught in something – there was a wrench and crash and, like a flood, oblivion overswept her.

It was the old deaf and near senile sacristan who found them lying there, the woman unhurt but insensible, the priest crushed out of life by the fall of the ancient statue, long tottering to its collapse. She recovered, for her part: for his, no-one knows where he lies buried. But there were dark stories of a baying pack that night, and of an empty, bloodstained pavement when they came to seek for the body.

Among the Wolves

VASILE VOICULESCU

'We were talking about big game and major hunts, gradually aban-doned here though our mountains still teem with huge bears, proud stags, ominous black goats and dangerous boars; the lynx and the marten, however, fewer in number.

'The auroch alone is missing in the old hunting fauna of this country. It's a pity we didn't breed them again, as other countries did' – the host added.

'I have long been saying so,' another man put in. 'This is a spot where impassioned hunters could easily meet the emotions and adventures of big game hunting, no need to go tearing to Africa or India.'

The talk kept coming back to the decadence of this vital and ancestral activity: hunting. Man had brought it from the depths of the stone age when he had had to fight alone an unequal battle with the cave bear and the native lion. Most of all with the elk, the bold stag of primitive eras, more dangerous than all the beasts together.

Someone asked a question about the elk. The host instantly produced sketch-books with copies from drawings found in caves presenting wonderful primitive hunting scenes. He also brought books about the role and importance of hunting in the prehistoric period. Leaning over them we began to realise that the struggle with wild creatures far stronger than ourselves, forced us into becoming human beings in order to get the better of them.

The host explained that for food man could find plenty of booty weaker than he was, as well as all the fruits of the earth. But against the lion invading his cavern, against the bear with whom he was competing for shelter, or against the mammoth who simply crushed him, hunting was bound to become the supreme art, both knowledge and witchcraft, technique and culture, sacrifice and tense energy, using puppets and magic ritual as displayed on the walls of altars, such as they appear in all the paintings of prehistoric caves. As still practised by present day savages.

Here and there,' he continued, 'far-sounding echoes are still to be heard in the magic practices and superstitions of rural hunters: the charmed bullet, the magic salves, talismans, auspicious or ill-fated days, and other ceremonials of hunting going as far as purification. A true huntsman does not smoke tobacco and abstains from drinking spirits, at least while hunting.

'But no-one troubles to store and treasure the dust of this shattered culture, formerly the embodiment, the essence of human ideal,' he concluded with a sigh.

Deeply moved, our thoughts were turning back along the paths cut by palaeolithic men, to the caverns strewn with bones of bears and lions pacified and buried with incantations and charms by the clan's wise men.

After a brief silence, a lawyer put the book down and asked permission to tell a personal experience that he was just beginning to understand in all its implications.

'I was justice of the peace in a rural district,' he began, 'all hilly, wooded country at the foot of the mountains. Angry rivers had formerly torn the earth apart so that huge precipices with horizontal layers of purple clay interspersed with white grit-stone gave a shocking impression of primeval archaism. Nowhere have I seen the sky rent by such deep, mysterious sunsets, shedding over regions petrified in immemorial time, the yellow anaemic blood of eras long gone by. I wouldn't be surprised to hear that the black hollows yawning in the steep sides of the precipice were openings of caverns full of bones of the past such as the ones in the books we've just been looking at. The district was still rich in game, mostly wolves and foxes, even martens and lynxes, but shooting did not interest me. In those days, I was merely thinking of my position, of my promotion, and a quick release from that place. However, I had begun collecting rudiments of common law and samples of local customs in view of a study meant to keep me busy.

The low bowing and the fear in people's looks were not the only surprise. Such kow-towing met all of us who belonged to the administration. And reasonably too. I dealt out penalties, didn't I? There was something more, however, that impressed me: a kind of reverence, a veneration of a different kind greeted me, not granted to my colleagues the medical man and the sub-prefect. I soon understood. I was a wise man, a magus. The judge was considered over and above the others, invested with spiritual powers. I did not beat people like the gendarme or the county chief. Nor did I grab sick children out of their mothers' arms, like the doctor, to send them to hospital. As a judge a single written line of mine could tie or untie whatever the others devised: fines, infringement of the law, law-suits. My mere signature was enough to rid the offender of all the sins that had brought him before me. Nor could the clergyman do this, who, as a matter of fact, was wrangling with and suing the villagers.

One day I acquitted a peasant charged with poaching in forbidden season and shooting forbidden game. To cap it all: a doe. The gendarme had caught him in the act of flaying it.

The man protested that he hadn't shot it nor trapped it, but redeemed it from the fangs of wolves who had been driving it hard. Actually, upon enquiry, no bullet marks had been found, just the traces of fangs deep sunk into the prey's neck torn and mangled by beasts. The people of the village, however, appeared discontented with my verdict. Some with whom I was on friendly terms ventured to say so. The man had taken me in. He had been poaching and should have been punished. The fact that bullet marks had not been found was no proof at all.

'What are you talking about?' I said. 'You've all seen the doe's neck mangled by wolves' fangs.'

'Yes, but the wolves were working for him. He set them on.'

'Set them on, did you say?' I asked in wonder. 'You won't tell me that wolves are as good as hounds in these parts.'

'It's just as you say,' they confirmed. 'The beasts wait upon him as if hired. They chase and kill the game by order. Nay, place it at his feet. How else could he get it out of the pack's jaws, if not by agreement? They would tear him to tatters, too.'

Quite true. At the hearing I never thought of asking the accused how he had managed to get the prey from the wolves.

On this occasion I learnt that my man was known as a wolf-tamer, subjecting them by means of charms and magic, and using them like a master.

They called him the Wolfer and he was considered ta be one of the freaks of nature. I became interested and went to see him. He could have been of help in my research into peasant tradition, as well as an intersting human type.

He was living like an outcast away from the village, in the wilderness, in a kind of half-hovel, half-cavern, dug into the clay of a desolate hillside. He had no wife, no child, nothing whatever. He was alone like a hermit. People said he couldn't bear any tame animal usually found in human households to live by his side. Cattle would run away frightened at the sight of him and dogs would scuttle away howling.

In fact no live creature came to meet me as I entered his yard. Poverty, I said to myself, that's all. Just a few hens bathing in the dust. I called. He took his time in coming. He was glad to see me. A vigorous old man, lean, tall and bony, gloomy yet eyes sharp and singeing, thick hair falling upon his brow, broad hands with fingers spread out like paws. The long olive-coloured face was almost glabrous, framed by a collar of thin prickly beard under the jaws. There was something secret, sad, yet vehement in this face.

So I understood why he was the terror and the curse of the village, for they actually hated and hooted him. He looked abnormal, the Lombroso criminal type. People said that a fierce reeking smell came out of his body and that none could bear either his smell or his gaze. I tried to sift the truth from the blame that people were piling upon him; they accused him of much evil and foul deeds, more especially that he was purposefully sending the wolves to work havoc among the cattle of the farmers. Nay, he sometimes would himself turn into a wolf, attacking the men to tear them to pieces.

The Wolfer received me awkwardly but decently, no kow-towing, with a dignity and self-control that impressed me. I stepped up to him. You could actually feel a strong smell. I wonder if any of you ever skinned a serpent. Well now, he had a sharp smack, as of arsenic. But I think it came from a fur jacket that he was wearing, as well as from the fur waistband wrapped tight against his slim waist, as slim as a young man's.

He asked me inside his den. There was a fire burning in the grate and a pot of weeds was boiling. The bench too was covered with hides of beasts. Hides everywhere: of bears, of wolves, of does.

I asked why he had shot them. He said they were old ones, mostly inherited from his father and grandfather. Some, since he had formerly been carrying a gun like every huntsman, long ago. But now, in his old age, unable to take aim, he had given up shooting. He would lay snares and set traps, occasionally catching a fox grown vicious for fowls; or still more seldom would he recapture a prey from the wolves, by clubbing at them, as it happened with the doe for which he had been driven to law by his enemies. But as he grew older it was ever more difficult. His strength on the wane, he was waiting for the wild beasts to tear him to pieces some day.

I took the opportunity of his talking about wild beasts, openly confessing my interest in his relations with wild things, wolves in particular. That's what I had come for. The man considered me without blinking and was silent. I pleaded to have come out of real friendly feeling for him, in no way to spy or sound him. That I too was experimenting a kind of magic or incantation to call up the spirits of the dead – I was actually practising spiritualism – and I asked him to impart the secret ol his knowledge and strength. He pleaded that the world's slander held no truth, that he didn't know and couldn't do anything beyond what other men could do. But that he had the knack of talking to wolves in their own language and making himself understood.

'You know the speech of the wolves, do you?'

'Yes sir. I learnt it as a small child.'

'How did you and who from?'

'From grandfather and from father, they both knew.'

'Did they, really?'

'They did. Grandfather and father were foresters, always had been. They lived at the heart of the forest and reared wolves that they caught when cubs. I was born and bred among wolf whelps, eating side by side with them, playing and wrestling till my folks came late at night, from the wilderness. Here, you can still see the marks of their fangs and claws.'

He bared his arms, hairy stumps, all sinews, knots and lumps.

'What about your mother?' I asked.

'I had no mother,' was the brief answer.

'And your wife?'

'My wife is a bushy hollow in the woods.'

I realised that along this line everything was sore to the touch. I changed the subject.

'What did your people do with the wolves?'

'They kept them just for company,' the man said with a bitter smile.

'Just that much?'

'Nay they would also keep away men and beasts from the den.'

I went on considering him inquiringly.

'Occasionally they would help them catch,' the man completed his answer to my enquiry.

'But,' he added, 'as soon as they grew up and felt the urge of love, they would break the chains and run back into the forest, forgetful of human friendliness and a settled life.'

'So they actually were like dogs to you.'

'Wild things, nevertheless, sir; no way of thoroughly taming them. Father's hands and legs were all marks and sores, bitten in by them. They had to be crammed with meat to allow you anywhere near them, to fondle them and get the prey out of their jaws.'

Confession after confession. The Wolfer went as far as to promise to take me one suitable night to show me his skill with the wolves.

He chose the night before St Andrew's Day when wolves were to get their yearly portion of booty. They were each granted one special man, woman or child that they were allowed to eat. No more! There was no reckoning for cattle and other booty. They could have as many as they liked. As regards man alone the wolf had to be content with his appointed portion. It was a kind of right – I set this down for my study – a fragment of the old code of laws governing primitive hunting. I sounded him concerning other superstitions and heresies. He answered truthfully and intelligently.

I was moved by the haunted and abused man standing before me; it was not pity for the loneliness he had been driven into by an adverse society, but rather an active interest for his toughness in the struggle for life, for his firmness in opposing a hostile world of people who were actual brutes to him.

As I was leaving he wished to present me with a fur cap full of freshly laid eggs. I refused. He quickly rummaged in a trunk and produced a few marten hides, sheer beauties. I did not take them. He realised that I was not the kind to be after presents, so he did not insist.

It was settled that on the eve of St Andrew's Day I should call on him. I did not want the village to get wind of what I was doing and interfere in my affairs. That was about three weeks ahead.

I can't say I had forgotten about our meeting. But my interest had subsided to such an extent that I was loath to face the cold and go out. I had other worries now. I was actually waiting for urgent summons from Bucharest pending my transfer to the law courts. A possible trip to Bucharest in order to hasten my promotion, was a real bother since there was no-one to leave in charge for a couple of days.

So the day promised to the Wolfer had quite slipped out of my mind.

One night I was suddenly wakened by the shrieking and hooting in the village and all the farm hands bustling about. Two wolves had boldly entered the country court residence where I was staying and tried to steal the usher's pig. That made me keep my word, so that the following night, my gun across my shoulder, I made for the Wolfer's den.

'I got your message,' I shouted joking. 'You were right to send it, I had a mind to stop bothering you.'

'Why no, sir,' he said with glistening eyes, 'no bother at all. Please to come in till the dark dispels, for the moon shall soon rise.'

I walked in. In the gleam of a rushlight I then saw that which I hadn't noticed before: on the whitewashed walls, large and small figures of wolves, stags, foxes and wild boars, some drawn in charcoal, others in red clay, in various positions. Some were running, others were laid low, some in unlikely attitudes like standing up on their hind legs or up in widely-branching trees. In the midst of these images there was a huge man with a gigantic club, as if he were driving them on. His outline went beyond the wall, stretching out upon the low ceiling, like a protecting divinity.

There was a wonderful firmness and skill in the drawing, as if by some really gifted hand.

'Childish nonsense,' the man said, watching my amazement with displeasure. 'I'm in my second childhood, so that in the winter, to while away the time, I play as I used to in father's hut.'

Looking around I saw on the stove and in various corners other animal figures made of clay. These were coarser, such as those that are sold at fairs. Some were lame, with one leg missing, some had holes in the ribs, some were pierced with pikes.

I tried to examine them more closely. But the Wolfer stopped me.

'Ready, your Honour,' he solemnly announced, rising in front of me and obscuring the view. 'The moon's out and we'd better be going, it's a good bit to walk.'

I had to leave alone the clay idols and follow him. He had only taken an enormous club. He wore a long mantle of wild animal hides, wolves' I think, which, reeked with that insufferable sharp smell now all over the man.

We walked some two hours, in a roundabout way, climbing up and down hills and hillocks, now barren, now thick with tangled woods till we reached a hill top dominating the valleys. Now that I think it over, I don't believe we got very far, but the man took me round about to conceal his tracks, as beasts do. Or maybe – But the place we stopped at was sunk in silence, solitude and frost, as on a lifeless planet. The stunning moonlight making everything look even more fantastic, was enveloping, isolating, secluding it even more from the rest of the world.

The Wolfer helped me climb a wide-branched oak tree where he had contrived a small bed out of a few armfuls of maize stalks, in between two strong branches. Then he, too, climbed higher *up to the top*.

Nothing budged in the freezing moonlight that glazed the whole visible world in its frost. My heart alone was nervously thumping.

Suddenly, from above, bitter weeping bubbled forth, a sorrowful yelping, rapidly changing into a monstrous, prolonged, modulated howl, gurgling and gushing. Had I not quickly grabbed at something and planted myself squarely in the tree's branches, I should have tumbled down. I looked up. Perching upon a branch that he clung to with both arms, the man rose above the crown of the tree. His face was bent upon a thing that he was holding in both hands out of which came that frightful wailing. He stopped a few minutes, the surrounding stillness seeming to prick its ears expectantly. Then the strange lullaby began again, a dramatic appeal, a kind of scream of the wilderness and a perplexity at the same time. Then the tragic chanting was quiet again, in expectation.

From afar a loud dirge-like call, as if from a wooden horn, sounded fiercely.

The man called again. From another corner of the world a still more horrible howl answered. Soon a dialogue or rather a polylogue grew ever stronger, a savage mimicking between the Wolfer and the Unseen whose sorrowful tones approached on padded feet, drawn by the ever more urging clamour of the Wizard.

Suddenly, with all my instincts awake, I felt a presence. I looked down. At the foot of the tree a wild beast was looking up, considering us. Swiftly another wolf slipped alongside, silently. The man went on calling long and mournfully to the four winds, wherefrom answers came ever more dismal, lamentations close or distant as if spinning round in a blizzard, hoarse chanting, cries, ho there! strangled in hungry gullets, like the shrieks of boundless desolation, of endless hopelessness.

The tree was soon surrounded by a pack of wolves, placed in a circle, sitting on their hind legs as if in conference. Necks tense, eyes shining, they were softly yelping between their teeth, with rumblings and flourishes, in different registers and tones, flat and sharp notes, in conversation with the man. He was now modulating his incantation in short syncopated rhythms as if in a predicament, from sepulchral grave sounds to the velvety voice of the flute, and the fearful shrillness of crime. Down below savage vocalising was alternating with thoughtful silence.

What was the man saying? Was he telling them a tale? Was he scolding them? Promising something? Sharing out the spoils, each one his lot? Because the wolves, gullets turned upwards, kept changing places, creeping upon their bellies, springing to their feet; then started wailing, chattering their teeth as if dancing to the master's tune. I couldn't tell how long this circus-like show lasted. I was more than dizzy and bewildered. I sat there hypnotised, stunned, my hands clinging fast to a branch, the gun useless on my knees. I didn't feel the cold but I must have been frozen to the bone, for I was rigid like an icicle. I then came to my senses. At a move the gun started slipping down. I tried to catch hold of it, but I toppled over with the pile of maize stalks on which I had turned to stone; rolling over several times, I was down at the root of the tree surrounded by wild beasts who all rose at the same moment, their hairs bristling.

Before any of them had broken the circle and jumped, the Wolfer had dropped from the top right into the midst of them – tempestuous, the club raised like a sceptre, with a fearful roar.

As I lay looking up at him, he looked enormous, his fluffy coat shaggy and the pointed cap obscuring the moon that formed a kind of halo round his head. Eyes agog glowed with a kind of flame, as well as his outstretched hands, particularly his fingers: a sort of phosphorescent essence as that of glow-worms. And the strong scent, the insufferable reeking that no-one could abide, now still sharper, exuded from his body with unbearable force.

The wolves were stunned; the man stuck his head again into a pot – I could now see clearly – and swiftly started producing ever shorter, more commanding sounds, like the panting, smothered gurgling of a savage gullet. Hearing this the wolves, their tails sagging, began to draw back, loosening the loop around us.

'Climb instantly up the tree,' the Wolfer ordered me in a low voice, half his muzzle out of the pot still astir with howling echoes.

I tried to stand up but could not. There was a sharp pain in my ankle.

'I can't,' said I moaning, 'I've broken my ankle.'

The man crouched down, with his back close to me. 'Cling to my back, quick.' – And he crouched into as low a heap as he could, that I might reach him and put my arms round his neck: I was then still slim and no weight.

The man rose, myself clinging to him, he shook himself to give me a good seat along his broad back and made his way with the burden on his back, never stopping those magic sounds and the many-voiced converse with the wild things no longer in a loop but now gathering into a pack again, the large beast heading it.

I contracted my knees and raised my feet that my toes should not trail on the ground, stumbling against stones or roots. So I clung to him deeply breathing in that magic scent that held the beasts in check, of which I now felt the full magic power. His hands went on sending forth the phosphorescent blaze, through the fingers mostly. I could see it before us when he reached out and rolled the club towards the wild things which drew back step by step, receding in front of him.

A few hesitations and the pack gave up. The magic poise required that there should be no blood. A single drop from man or beast would have broken the magic. Nothing could have stopped a catastrophe. But the Wolfer had won.

The howling, sounding ever more remote, smothered by moonlight and silence as by a shroud, gradually vanished beyond our horizon. What followed I don't know. I think I fainted with strain and pain, or possibly simply fell asleep. What I do know is that I woke up in my own bed at the justice's residence. It was broad daylight and the usher had brought me coffee in bed, as usual.

How the man had slunk in unseen and unheard bearing me on his back, remains a mystery. If it hadn't been for the pain in the ankle I should have been certain of having dreamt it all.

The medical man found that it was a mere sprained ankle. He wrapped it in a tight bandage and I could walk, my foot in a snowshoe, leaning on:a stick. I couldn't keep to my bed. There had been a wire that very morning summoning me urgently to Bucharest for transfer. I packed my things and left like mad.

'What about the Wolfer?' the host asked.

'I can't tell you more. I left everything behind, never looking back, never giving it another thought. Once in Bucharest, entering a big career, I had to turn wizard myself, for a different kind of wild beasts, men with whom, as you know, I waged a hard battle.

'But your talk of magic hunting brought back all that former stress and led me to penetrate some of the mysteries that I experienced.'

'What was the blaze in the man's eyes and fingers? What do you think?'

'I couldn't say now. But then and there, as I lay prostrate in the midst of wild things, all my instincts alive and tense, I remember subconsciously feeling that the flame was the essence of the man's willpower exasperated by dire predicament, the sum total of the magic fluid collected and condensed from the person who was making the extraordinary effort to rout the danger.

'Without that magic force we should have been lost. Later I no longer thought of this, I forgot. But I now begin to understand again. As in the old hunters' magic, my man had grown and broadened out of himself, beyond his narrow wild nature, in order to take in and understand the wolf, assimilate him as it were. By thus magically knowing him could he subject and master him, in no other way. An enormous activity in spirit that we can no longer accomplish. The primeval magus was thus becoming the wolf's archetype, the great spiritual wolf beyond; before him the ordinary pack withdrew in fear, as men will at the sight of an angel. Prehistoric man did not hunt beasts, but chased dangers, shot his arrow at hostile mysterious forces, laid snares for purposes of existence.'

'You're exaggerating, your Honour,' a friend put in. 'I think that your man's blaze was common phosphorus, a rot such as produced by the wood of certain trees; he had soaked his hands and face ift it, to keep the beasts at bay. I have read this somewhere.'

'Quite possible, but the blazing was none the less magic,' the president agreed, quietly rubbing his ankle where the memory of pain, long ago experienced, was reviving.

The Shadow of the Wolf

RON WEIGHELL

It was not at all uncommon, upon arriving at 221B Baker Street, to hear the strains of Sherlock Holmes's violin. Often he would be playing some melancholy air to suit his dark mood; at times the ear might be assailed by the atonal sawing that often accompanied some profound introspection; less often by the endless repetition of some complex phrase as an aid to analysis of its structure. I was, however, surprised to hear a jig or reel that leapt and sang for very joy.

I found Holmes cross-legged in an armchair, violin bow poised, a contented smile playing about his thin lips. Indeed so contented was the smile that for an instant an unpleasant possibility suggested itself to me. Holmes stopped playing just long enough to shake his head and say, as if in answer to my unspoken question: 'No, Watson, I have not returned to my old ways and sought 'surcease from sorrow' in the seven-per-cent solution.'

'Then it must be the Arnot case,' I offered. 'You have solved it!'

'Oh that. Yes, it is solved. It was the sundial, Watson! They had turned it.'

'Of course! So when the old man sat in the garden and noted the hour in his diary, he wrote down his murderer's alibi!'

'And signed his own death warrant.'

'Then who was it, Holmes? Which one of the brothers?

'Both of them, Watson. By their clever ruse, each implicated the other, for the sundial was far too heavy for one to have moved it alone. However, you are wrong in supposing that to be the reason for my good mood. Read this Watson, it arrived a little while ago.'

He held out a telegram speared on the end of his bow. I took it and read:

MR SHERLOCK HOLMES. COME AT ONCE IF YOU CAN. ONE MAN DEAD, OTHERS WILL DIE. WEREWOLF RESPONSIBLE.

FREYA STURLESON, TARN LODGE

I noted that the telegram had been dispatched from Crowford in the county of Yorkshire.

Holmes, who had been watching keenly for my reaction, said innocently: 'It has the charm of brevity, has it not? If you look in the index lying beside me, you will see what we are up against.'

I did so and read: ' "The change of a man or woman into a wolf, either through magical means, or judgement of gods'. But Holmes, this is foolishness.'

'Read on, Watson.'

' "A form of madness, Lycanthropy, Kuanthropy or Boanthropy, depending on whether the victim thinks himself transformed into wolf, dog or cow." '

'Now be so good as to read this.'

He handed me one of the sensational journals to which he devoted so much attention.

'Let me see – "Tarn Lodge slaying – horrible death of young man – found with throat and face terribly torn – police have no clues as to culprit's means of escape. Window open, but no prints on the snow outside." Holmes, the telegram . . . '

' . . . was sent from Tarn Lodge. You see Watson, there has undoubtedly been a crime, and a very interesting one at that. I rather think this case satisfies my requirement of an outré and macabre element in full. Do you think your practice could spare you for a few days?'

'I do.'

'Splendid; then let us consult our Bradshaw. We must brave the wild North Country.'

Tarn Lodge proved to be a sombre Jacobean pile standing in extensive grounds. That winter was a particularly harsh one, and the forbidding look of the house was not mitigated by the bleak, snow-locked landscape nor the now frozen expanse of tree-encircled water which gave the house its name. The sky was clear, but the country lay an unbroken carpet of white, the trees plumed and swathed with snow.

The door was opened by a steely-eyed butler who ushered us into a chilly hall, dominated by a statue of a jackal-headed deity of Egypt carved in black basalt. As we entered, a quite remarkable figure descended the wide stair.

She wore a long flowing garment such as I had sometimes seen worn by devotees in Indian temples. Her long hair was suffered to fall in a wild mass of curls about her face and shoulders, and many strings of beads hung about her neck, along with a heavy pendant of bronze. Her whole appearance should have been unseemly for a Western woman, but she was magnificent, her features calm and very dignified under their mantle of dark tresses. When she spoke, however, her voice was grim and clearly offered no welcome.

'Mr Holmes and Dr Watson, I presume? I am Mrs Sturleson,'

'Good day, Mrs Sturleson,' said Sherlock Holmes. 'I perceive that you are a Tantrika, and have visited Rajasthan recently.'

The woman gasped, but quickly recovered her composure and said, 'How clever of you, Mr Holmes! Let me guess; the pendant . . . '

' . . . which is peculiar to the sect of that area, and whose significance you clearly understand, judging by the colour of the cord on which you wear it.'

'And you guessed I had been there myself because of the colour of my skin.'

'Forgive me for saying so, Mrs Sturleson, but you are clearly not pleased to see us, suggesting that it was not you who summoned us.'

'That is correct. My stepdaughter sent the telegram. I do not approve of her action.'

'There has been a murder – '

'My stepson will reincarnate to fulfil his destiny with or without your assistance, Mr Holmes.'

I could not keep silent at this.

'His death does not seem to have upset you unduly.'

'Upset? He has gone to a higher plane, that is all.'

The sound of footsteps on the stair brought a frown to Mrs Sturleson's face.

'My stepdaughter is on her way down. Should you require anything, I will be in the study.'

Hardly had she departed when a woman of a very different stamp descended the stair. She was much younger, a fresh northern beauty with golden hair and ruddy cheeks, and was dressed in black. She seemed to be struggling against deep distress.

'Mr Holmes, I'm so relieved to see you. I am Freya Sturleson. It was I who summoned you.'

'A most tantalising missive,' said Holmes. 'The murdered man was your brother, I take it?'

She bowed her head at this, but nodded and straightened her back. 'Yes. I was the one who found him.'

'You are very courageous,' I interjected. 'If this is too upsetting – '

But she would have none of it.

'No, I will not rest until the matter is solved. It was for this reason that I called you. I must be strong for John's sake. Come, I will show you the room where it happened.'

She led us to a room whose windows looked out onto the frozen tarn. Bloodstains on the carpet left no doubt where the terrible event had occurred. Holmes was suddenly the hunter, stalking around the room, crouching over the hideous stains, gauging their distance from the window. Miss Sturleson left the room and returned with the butler.

'Dodds found the body. Tell them all you know, Dodds.'

'Were the windows open?' asked Holmes.

'They were, sir. A cold wind blowin' in and master John just lyin' there covered in blood.'

'Quite so – the report said no prints were found outside.'

'There'd been no fresh snow that night, and it did not snow for a day after. You could have seen where a sparrow had walked. It were clear and untrodden all the way to the Tarn.'

'No wildlife at all then. That is most instructive. And outside the other windows?'

'The same, sir. Not a mark in the snow.'

'Thank you Dodds. Your assistance has been invaluable.'

Turning to Miss Sturleson, Holmes asked: 'I take it the house was thoroughly searched?

'Very thoroughly, I assure you. We ordered an immediate examination of every room, including the attics.'

'So, now I must ask why you believe the culprit to be a werewolf.'

She smiled grimly and replied: 'Because I have seen it, Mr Holmes.'

I have rarely seen Sherlock Holmes as stunned as at that moment. Then his expression changed to one of mingled intense interest and pleasure.

'Come, sit down and tell me what you saw, in as much detail as you can. Leave nothing out.'

'It happened the night before we found poor John. I was out walking in the grounds with my pet dog when it began to growl and ran off into the bushes. Then there was a cry of pain and I saw something come out of the bushes and lope off. Poor Loki was dead, Mr Holmes, dead and horridly torn just as my dear brother John was torn. I only glimpsed the monster that did this, but it moved on its back legs, yet crouched over, and it gave me the impression that its top half was that of a wolf. I may as well tell you, Mr Holmes, that I believe it to be the astral body of my stepmother in wolf form.'

Holmes showed no more visible reaction to this than someone who has been bidden the time of day.

'I am most interested,' said Holmes, 'pray continue.'

'She once told me that each of us possesses a subtle body capable of assuming a form shaped by thought and emotion. My father is a bed-ridden invalid, and we are very close. My stepmother is a very jealous woman, and is envious of every call on his attention; she hates me deeply. My brother's recent return gave her another rival. But you will think me mad.'

'I think nothing, Miss Sturleson, save that the time has come to meet your father.'

She led us back through the hall and up the stairs to the very top of the house.

'Forgive me,' I said, 'but if your father is an invalid, would it not be easier to locate his room on the ground floor?'

'There is a good reason for his choice of room, as you will see, Doctor.'

She opened a door and gestured for us to enter. The room was a species of studio, with a skylight that let in little radiance, as the expanse of glass was covered with snow.

In the grey light stood many canvases covered by dust-sheets. Under the skylight sat a giant of a man, lean-jawed, grizzled of beard and mane, staring at us balefully with deep-set eyes whose unhealthy, ivory yellow tinge gave him the malevolent gaze of some beast of prey. He lay upon an upholstered, reclining chair with winged dragons for front legs, double footstools supported by gryphons, and a movable reading desk whose stem was a coiling serpent. The desk held a half-finished watercolour of the Fenris Wolf of Norse legend. Within arm's reach on either side stood canvases depicting in gruesome detail wolf packs at hunt and the kill. Miss Sturleson ran to him and they embraced tenderly. He whispered some words and she left the room.

'Mr Holmes,' bellowed the man, 'welcome to my house. I fear yours has been a wasted journey. My daughter meant well in bring-ing you here, but it is useless, unless you can defeat the power of an ancient curse.'

'I make no claim to supernatural powers, yet I have helped in many cases where all hope seemed lost.'

'Then hear this, Mr Holmes. In the dark forested regions of Nor-way my ancestor was savaged by an albino wolf. Thereafter, his village suffered periodic depredations by some wild beast. When at last the creature was wounded, he was found maimed and bleeding in his bed. From that day, my family has been under the shadow of the wolf. Mr Holmes, the curse has returned to plague this house, and I fear for my wife and daughter. I have done terrible things in my attempt to fight it, but to no avail. It was I who killed my son. Oh, I see the look on your faces. You do not believe in werewolves. Well, you will learn. I only wished my daughter might be spared this. All my children – it is too cruel. Please guard her, and my wife, Mr Holmes. And when the time comes, put an end to me.'

Holmes allowed himself the briefest of smiles.

'Let us hope things may never come to such a pass. I have yet to resort to these measures. By the way, Mr Sturleson, you have a rare gift for art. Might you not choose a less depressing subject? Excuse us.'

As we left the room, Holmes said quietly: 'Yes, it has some similarities to that case, Watson, but this is a good deal simpler than the affair of the Hound.'

'Would you say so? I would – but Holmes, how?'

'Not mind-reading, my dear fellow. You could hardly fail to note that the ancestral curse and the savage beast were reminiscent of one of our strangest cases. But come, there is no time to be lost. We must make a search of the house and be certain that nothing has been overlooked.'

During the hours that followed, Sherlock Holmes stalked through every room, examining, measuring, comparing the internal and external dimensions of the house to eliminate the possibility of hidden spaces.

'Do I take it from your search for a hiding-place that you suspect some unseen hand in this, Holmes?

'I have reached no conclusions yet, Watson. I merely seek to exclude impossibilities.'

'And whatever remains, however improbable, must be the truth.'

Holmes shrugged. 'I suppose so, Watson. Though when I said that I did not have werewolves in mind! Now as to our course of action – shall we watch the suspects? What use would we be against – what did she call it – the astral body? Is the doting father more mobile than he pretends? There are too many variables here. So let us forget the culprit and guard the most likely victim. Let us see. First Miss Sturleson's pet is killed, then her beloved brother. It is not unreasonable to conclude that she is herself the next victim. I think we could do worse than to keep an eye on the young lady's room tonight.

We ascertained that the room next to Miss Sturleson's was vacant, and it was agreed that I should wait there with my revolver at the ready. Holmes insisted on taking up a position outside the house, where he could watch the only other means of ingress, the window.

On taking up my post, I looked out of my window. It was a bitterly cold night, the moon large and bright against driving rags of cloud that ran before a north-east wind. There had been a light fall of snow earlier, deepening the carpet on the lawns to a frozen crust that broke with sharp detonations audible through the panes as Holmes trudged into view and took up his position by the wall.

Two hours later I looked again, and he had not moved an inch. Had I not seen his arrival, I would have taken him for a statue.

I fear that I had dropped into a fitful doze when a shrill cry rang through the house. I was on my feet and out of the room, revolver at the ready, before I had realised that the cry had not been that of a woman. Miss Sturleson and her stepmother were already on the landing. Even as we stood undecided, Holmes came bounding up the stairs, the blade of an unsheathed sword-stick glinting in the lamplight.

'It came from the studio, Watson!'

By the time I reached the top landing, Holmes was already battering at the studio door. From beyond the unyielding panels came cries of agony and fear. We threw our combined weight against the door, but it held. Before our second assault a silence fell in the studio. Again the door withstood our charge. At our third attempt the frame splintered and we fell into the room. At once Holmes closed the door and jammed a chair under the handle to prevent the women from entering.

I will never forget the sight that met our eyes. I had thought Marie Kelly's room in Miller's Court a shambles, but this was worse. Sturleson's remains lay half on the floor, half on that weirdly magnificent couch. In the moonlight everything glittered blackly with blood. I have seen terrible injuries in war, but nothing to equal the carnage of that place. On every side the gaping jaws of wolves slavered from blood-spattered canvases. A superstitious dread fell upon me then, for what had been done in that room was the work of a beast, not a human being.

Holmes looked even more shocked than I. Carefully skirting the growing blood pool, he peered out of the window and shook his head.

'I do not understand, Watson. This was not – well, it is too late now; we must go and check the house and grounds.'

Pausing only to place Dodds at the door to prevent the women from entering, we established that all the other servants were accounted for and free from bloodstains. Since it would have been impossible to commit such an atrocity and remain unstained, and the women had been with us outside the door, all known occupants of the house were eliminated. We conducted another painstaking search of every room, then donned our overcoats and made a circuit of the ground outside the house, paying particular attention to the side overlooked by Sturleson's window. Save for Holmes' own prints, the unbroken surface of the snow made it clear that not so much as a bird had alighted there in hours.

'This is incredible, Holmes. No-one has left the house, and none of the occupants could have committed the act. This is impossible . . . '

I said this in the firm expectation that Holmes would chide me for overlooking some obvious clue, but he did not appear to hear me. He stood with head bowed, utterly crestfallen.

'This is my worst hour, Watson. I fear that the faculties hymned in those sensationalised accounts of yours have not been in evidence, and a man is dead because of it. I have allowed my mental processes to be dulled by a shadow out of the pit.'

'The Hound, Holmes?

'No Watson, the shadow falls from a greater distance than Dartmoor: Tibet, Watson, Tibet. I had not intended to mention it, for it is another account for which the world is not yet ready. I believe I mentioned that I was honoured to receive an invitation from the Dalai Lama to enter Lhasa and converse with him. I learned a good deal from that wise soul, Watson, but I like to think that the meeting was of mutual benefit. His Holiness wished me to locate and learn all I could of a mountain-dwelling creature they called Metoh Kangmi, also called the Supkpa, or – '

'The Yeti!' I cried.

'His Holiness had read my monograph *Upon Tracing of Footsteps*, and was particularly impressed by my work on the use of plaster of Paris as a receiver of impress. He hoped that I might further his knowledge of that shy creature. There is, I believe, a legend to the effect that the Compassionate Spirit from whom the Tibetans descend was once incarnated as a monkey, and the High Lama felt there may be some responsibility to carry the word of Buddha to those strange mountaindwellers. One day I may tell you of my experiences at the Roof of the World, Watson. Suffice it to say that I ascended the highest mountain on Earth, and there confronted a creature around which hangs an aura of terror and superstitious dread.'

Holmes turned and looked about him, his face gaunt in the moonlight.

'It is the snow, Watson, the snow and the howling wind and the threat of some fearful thing waiting in the darkness. These have brought it all back to me, and I have allowed the shadow they cast to eclipse my powers.'

'I can understand that, Holmes. Any man would react in the same way. But you have a duty to the slain. Think of Mr Sturleson only hours ago, his fear for his wife and child. It is still in our power to save them. We can ensure that his last fear is never realised; that *both* his children should not suffer this curse.'

I had hoped that I might stir Holmes by these words, but the effect upon him surprised even me. He straightened up, turned to me with the old fire in his eyes and slapped me on the shoulder.

'Watson, once more you have performed the function for which you are so eminently suited: a conductor of light. Your words have made the whole puzzle much clearer.'

Turning away, he stood for some moments with fingertips to his lips, quite oblivious of the biting cold. I became aware that the first flakes of a fresh snow storm had begun to settle on our shoulders.

'Yes,' he muttered, 'whatever remains, however improbable, must be the truth. It does fit the facts – '

'Holmes, I do not see – '

'Oh you see, Watson, and more to the point, you hear, but as yet you do not understand. Perhaps it is better that you do not. If I am correct, our adversary is a fearful one. Oh yes, Watson, I know the identity of the murderer. The difficult, indeed the vital, question still to be answered is not who, but where.'

'You have lost me, Holmes.'

'I sincerely hope not, Watson. Before this night is out your presence may prove invaluable. Yes,' he went on, looking up into the sky, 'it must be tonight, or we can do nothing for another month. Come, let us go inside.' As we made our way back to the door, Holmes became quite excited.

'You know, Watson, I have given my life to rationality, suppressing the animal in order to raise the intellect. So in this case I have failed miserably. Deductive reasoning will not serve our turn, Watson. Sometimes one must assume the thought processes of one's quarry. Often that has meant thinking like a thief or a murderer, or a traitor or a thug. In this case it means descending to the level of the beast.'

'A beast, Holmes?

'Or, as Miss Sturleson so perceptively named it, a werewolf.'

The change that came over Holmes as he muttered these incredible words was remarkable. He began to pace the house restlessly, dropping to all fours at times to examine the carpets. I swear he sniffed his way around the scene of the first murder like some predator on the hunt for blood. Suddenly he stiffened and froze. Nothing moved but his eyes for about thirty seconds. Then he smiled grimly and stood up.

'I think I understand now, Watson. We have our solution. Do you still have your revolver about you? Good, then let me take a swordstick from the hall. There is no time to lose.'

It soon became clear that we were making our way to the attic studio.

'But Holmes,' I exclaimed, 'these rooms were thoroughly searched at the time.'

Holmes seemed not to hear me. We entered the studio, now foul with the smell of blood.

'It is so simple, when the mind is applied in the correct way. Think like a wolf, Watson. You need a suitable hiding-place: where do you go? A world of snow-clad valleys, crevasses, icy peaks.'

'But no-one has left the house, Holmes. Where is the world?

'In the sky, Watson, in the sky.'

Dragging a table across the floor, he leapt on to it, pushed open the skylight and was gone. An arm appeared and helped me up into a blast of icy flakes. By the time I climbed unsteadily to my knees, Holmes was already walking up the slope of the roof. I crawled after and found him looking down at a wide expanse of rooftops. Through the blizzard I could discern chimney stacks encrusted with glittering crystals; broken water pipes hung with fantastic stalactites of ice; the steep cloven ways between the roofs already half-filled by the windblown drifts. Holmes leant close and shouted over the blast.

'Icy peaks, Watson. Snow-clad valleys. Deadly crevasses. We have entered his world!'

Then began a search of the roofscape of Tarn Lodge. No-one could have guessed from the ground how many ridges, valleys, sloping expanses of icy tiles and chimney stacks lay concealed from sight. It was, indeed, a hidden world in the sky, a treacherous terrain offering many hiding places for a deadly adversary, bounded on every side by a sheer drop to reward a misplaced step.

That occasion was perhaps the only time I have ever seen Sherlock Holmes truly afraid. Who can say what memories of his encounter in the fastnesses of Tibet were rekindled by the savage landscape around us. Gaunt and pale, he bared the blade of the sword-stick and edged down into the first valley. I drew my revolver and followed. Knowing from my army experience that it would be impossible to flush out a hidden enemy if we kept together, I gestured to Holmes that we should spread out. I made my way up the nearest ridge and squinted against the stinging flakes to survey the expanse before me. Visibility was very poor, and every shadow might conceal – what? A madman; or an animal? Or would we encounter something worse? Directly below me a convergence of pitched roofs formed a crooked valley that turned this way and that. I slid down into it and trudged forward, revolver at the ready.

How small a space would accommodate our quarry? I moved forward with painful slowness, expecting to be attacked at every turn. Emerging onto a flat stretch of roof commanding a wider prospect, I glimpsed a movement behind a chimney stack. Was it Holmes closing in from the other side? I could not risk a shot until I was certain. At that moment Holmes came into view, his back to me, picking his way up a steep wall of tiles. I shouted, but my voice was lost in the wind. Then a figure emerged from behind the chimney and closed on Holmes with the slow, purposeful movement of a hunting beast along the shadow of the wall. As I raised my revolver the creature launched itself at the defenceless back of my friend.

I caught only a glimpse through driving snow, so I am not certain to this day what I saw. Was it an emaciated, naked human figure matted about the head and shoulders with a massive growth of hair? Or something whose upper torso and head were abnormally large and furred with a thick white pelt? Was it a grizzled head or the muzzle of a wolf? Whatever it was carried a mantle of snow upon it, concealing much of the form at which I aimed the revolver and fired twice. One at least of the bullets found its mark, for the figure twitched in mid-leap. Then it was upon Holmes.

What saved him from certain death at that moment was his years devoted to the art of fencing. In the split second before the creature landed on him, no ordinary man could have levelled the sword-stick with deadly accuracy and dropped to a crouch as he did. The forward momentum of his assailant ran it onto the full length of the blade, bowled Holmes over backwards and carried the creature cart-wheeling over his head to plunge over the edge of the roof. By the time I got there, Holmes was peering down into the snow-swirling depths.

'What was it, Holmes?' I asked.

'It was Sturleson's *other* son, Watson.'

Once more in the warmth and comfort of our Baker Street rooms, Sherlock Holmes stirred up a good blaze in the hearth and settled back in his armchair.

'It was you who solved the mystery, Watson, when you referred to Sturleson's fears for *both* his children. Perfectly good English, but not what Sturleson actually said. Can you remember his words? "All my children". And there was also something about doing terrible things in order to lay the "curse". A tyro could have picked up on these things, but my mind was distracted. There was at least one child more than we knew, but more than that. There was one child more than his own daughter knew about, for Miss Sturleson would surely have mentioned it. Someone, then, of whom he was so ashamed that he had not even told his own children. The curse was lycanthropy. The terrible thing he had done was to put the child into an asylum, and the poor creature, now adult, had escaped.'

'But Holmes, the body on the ground looked a pathetic specimen, yet the thing that attacked us was more like a ferocious beast than a man. I can think of no more fitting description for what I saw than a werewolf! How can it be?

'Oh Watson, Watson! The vanity of humankind! Our time on this planet has been but the blink of an eye. Only yesterday our ancestors emerged from caves and gazed out over dense forests and endless plains that teemed with the claws and teeth of sudden death. Every living thing was a potential threat or a potential victim, every day a struggle for survival which depended upon the ruthless wielding of deadly weapons. I say to you, Watson, that each of us stands hardly more than a hand's span from nature red in tooth and claw. The real wonder is not that there was indeed a curse of Tarn Lodge, but that such things are not more common. The are deeps in each of us, labyrinths wherein the beast still lurks.'

Holmes paused to light his pipe, blew out the pungent smoke luxuriously and smiled.

'If I have one fault, Watson, it is that I have not devoted sufficient attention to literature. Did not a great poet give us fair warning?

' "Some people have accused me of misanthropy; and yet I know no more than the mahogany that forms this desk of what they mean; lykanthropy I comprehend, for without transformation men become wolves on any slight occasion." '

The Clay Party

STEVE DUFFY

From the Sacramento *Citizen-Journal*, November 27, 1846
Disquieting news reaches the offices of the Citizen-Journal from our correspondent at Sutter's Fort, where the arrival of a party of settlers embarked on an untried and hazardous new crossing has been anxiously expected since the beginning of the month. November having very nearly elapsed with no word of these prospective Californians as yet received, it is feared by all that their party has become stranded in the high passes with the onset of winter. There is a general agreement among mountain men and seasoned wagoneers alike that the route believed travelled by these unfortunate pilgrims is both unorthodox and perilous in the extreme, it being the handiwork of a Mr Jefferson Clay of New Hampshire, a stranger to these parts with no reputation as a pioneer or a capable navigator. We hear anxious talk of a rescue party being recruited, once the worst of the snow has passed . . .

From the *Diary of John Buell*, 1846
May 17, Independence, Missouri: Embarkation day. At last! Set out at nine sharp with our fellow Californians – for so we shall be entitled to call ourselves, in but a little while. A great clamour of oxen and horses along Main Street, and the most uproarious cheering from all the townsfolk as they bid us farewell. It is sad to reflect that among these friendly multitudes there should be faces – dear faces, friends and relatives among them – that we shall never see again; and yet the prospect of that providential land in the West recalls us to our higher purpose, and strengthens us in our resolve. We carry the torch of Progress, as our mentor Mr Clay has written, and it is most fitting that he should be at the head of our party as we depart. We are forty-eight in number: seven families, a dozen single men, our great wagons pulled by sturdy oxen. Surely nothing can stop us.

Elizabeth concerned at the possible effects of the crossing on little Mary-Kate; also, that the general health of her mother is not all it might be. Again I remind her that the balmy air of California can only strengthen the old lady's general constitution, and that no other place on God's earth affords such opportunities for our daughter and ourselves. This she accepts, and we are fairly bound on our way. So it's 'three cheers for Jeff Clay, boys', as the wagoneers sang out at our departure – and onwards into the West. Lord, guide us in this great undertaking!

May 26: The plains. An infinite expanse of grassy prairie, profoundly still and empty. Surely God created no more unfrequented space among all His mighty works. Thunder in the nights, and storms away off on the horizon. Mud along the trail, thick and treacherous, so that we must double-team the oxen on the inclines. The rate of our advance is measured, yet perfectly steady. If only there were some sign by which we could mark our progress! I long for mountains, such as we knew back home in Vermont. Elizabeth's mother no better; she eats but little, and is silent as these endless brooding plains. Mary-Kate in excellent health, thank God.

May 31: The Big Blue, and our first real reverse. River swollen with much rain: unfordable. We are obliged to construct a temporary ferry. It will take time.

June 3: On our way again. It was the Lord's own struggle crossing the Big Blue, and we were fortunate not to lose more than a couple of our oxen, but now at least we have an opportunity to make up for lost time. Mrs Stocklasa now very weak, though generally quiet and uncomplaining. Elizabeth says little, except to cheer me up with her words of tender encouragement, but I know her every waking hour is filled with anxiety for her ailing mama. Perhaps at Fort Laramie we shall find a doctor.

June 16: Laborious progress up the Platte; mud still obliging us to double-team on the slightest incline. Found Elizabeth outside the wagon this evening after settling Mary-Kate for the night, wringing her hands in a perfect storm of tears. She fears her mother's mortal crisis is approaching. God grant it may not be so. Throughout the night she watches over her, soothing her when she wakes, speaking to her in that strange language of her homeland. It gives the old lady much comfort – which may be all that we have left to give her.

June 18: With a heavy heart I must record the most sorrowful of all tidings: Elizabeth's mother died around sunset yesterday. The entire party much distressed and brought low by this melancholy event. We dug her grave at a pretty spot on a little knoll overlooking the valley, with up ahead the still-distant prospect of mountains. Would that she had been destined to stand on their peaks with us, and gain a Pisgah view of the promised land! The Lord giveth and the Lord taketh away. One of the wagoneers has inscribed with hot-iron a simple wooden marker for her grave:

JULIA STOCKLASA
BORN 1774, WALLACHIA; DIED 1848, MISSOURI TERRITORY
BOUND FOR CALIFORNIA – TARRYING HERE AWHILE

It is a curious thing to come across in such a lonely place, the humble marker atop its little cairn of rocks; and a sad enough sight for us who mourn, to be sure. But may it not be the case that for those Westerners yet to pass along this trail, it will speak, however haltingly, of home and God and goodness, and may even serve as a first, albeit melancholy, sign of civilisation in this great American wilderness? It is hard to envisage this now, as the wolves cry out in the night-time, and Elizabeth starts into wakefulness once more, her features drawn and thin, her eyes reddened with much sorrow. But it may be so.

June 30: Fort Laramie, at the foothills of the mountains. Revictualling and recuperating after our grim passage across the plains, for which we paid with much hardship and great sorrow.

July 4: Celebrations in the evening, sky-rockets and dancing to fiddle music; all marred somewhat by an altercation between our leader Jefferson Clay and certain of the mountain men. These rough-hewn, barbarous individuals are much in evidence at the fort, paying homage to the independence of our fair Republic by drinking strong whiskey till they can barely stand. Some of these fine fellows engaged Mr Clay in conversation, in the course of which he showed them the maps laid out in his booklet *California, Fair Garden of the West*. Herein lay the roots of the discord. The mountain men would not concede that his route – a bold and imaginative navigation of the Great Salt Desert and the mountain passes beyond – represents the future of our nation's westward migration. Harsh words were exchanged, till Mr Clay suffered himself to be led away from the scene of the quarrel. I was among those who helped remove him, and I recall in particular his strong patrician countenance flushed with rage, as he shouted at the top of his voice – 'It's the nigher way, I tell you! The nigher way!'

July 5: On our way again. We were happy enough to arrive at Fort Laramie, but I guess we shall not miss it overmuch.

July 12: Another black day for our party: Mrs Hiderick dead of a fit in the night. Hiderick, a silent black-browed German Pennsylvanian, buried her himself before sun-up.

July 20: Hard going. Storms bedevil us still, and we are pretty well accustomed now to our night-time serenades of rolling thunder and the howling of far-off coyotes and wolves. Even Mary-Kate does not stir from her childish slumbers. On nights when the storms are at their worst, the oxen stampede, half-mad from the thunder and the lightning. Regrouped only with much labour. And then the endless sage, and the all-enveloping solitude of the plains. The passage through to California must indeed be a great prize, to be gained at such a cost.

July 25: The Continental Divide, or so we reckon. From here on in, Oregon country. A thousand miles out, a thousand still to go, says Mr Clay. It is comforting to know that the greater part of our endeavours are now over. I say this to Elizabeth, who I know is grieving still for her beloved mama, and she agrees with me.

July 27: A curious conversation with Elizabeth, late last night. She asked me if there was anything I would not do to protect our family. Of course I said there was nothing – that her safety, and the safety of our beloved daughter, must always be foremost in my mind, and if any action of mine could guarantee such an outcome, then I would not hold back from it for an instant. She said she knew it, and rallied a little from her gloom; or tried to. What can all this mean? She pines for her mother, of course; and fears what lies ahead. I must seek to reassure her.

July 28: The Little Sandy river. Here we arrive at the great parting of the ways; while the other wagon trains follow the deep ruts of the regular Oregon trail to our right, heading North, we shall strike out south along Mr Clay's cut-off. A general air of excitement throughout the company. Even Elizabeth rallies somewhat from her melancholy reveries.

July 31: Fort Jim Bridger. Supplies and rest. Elizabeth and Mary-Kate the subject of some wonderment among the bachelor gentlemen of the fort, when taking the air outside the wagon this morning. It is quite comical to see such grizzled individuals turn as silent and bashful as a stripling lad at his first dance. Such is the effect of my schoolteacher lady, and our little angel!

August 2: Bad feeling again in the fort. Cagie Bowden came to our wagon this morning, with news that Mr Clay was once more in dispute with the mountain men last night. Bowden says that together with Mr Doerr & Mr Shorstein he was obliged to remove Mr Clay from the proceedings; also, that in their opinion he was every bit as drunk as the mountain men. Let us not tarry overlong in this place.

August 3: On our way once more, along the cut-off. Thus we reckon to save upwards of three-hundred and fifty miles, and should reach Sutter's Fort within six or seven weeks.

August 9: Ten, fifteen miles a day, when we had reckoned on twenty. Reasonable progress, still we must not fall behind our schedule. Difficult terrain ahead.

August 17: A wilderness of canyons. Impassable except by much labour. Entire days wasted in backing out of dead-ends and searching for another route. We are falling behind, and the seasons will not wait. Mr Clay delivered the harshest of rebukes to Cagie Bowden for suggesting we turn back to Fort Jim Bridger and the northern trail. (And yet it is only what some of the others are saying.) Too late now in any case.

August 23: Lost for the last six days. Only this morning, when Mr Doerr climbed a tall peak and scouted out a surer way, were we freed at last from the hell of the canyons. Much time lost here. Mr Clay is now generally unapproachable except by a very few. He will not suffer the Bowdens to come nigh him. It is regrettable.

August 27: Into the trackless wastes along the Wasatch. Two and three miles progress in a day. Aspen and cottonwoods choking up the canyons; cleared only with superhuman effort. Weary to my very bones. Elizabeth tells me not to over-exert myself, but there is no choice. I brought my wife & baby daughter into this place, and now they must always be at the forefront of my thoughts. We *must not* be caught here in the wilderness when winter comes.

August 29: Some of the other families have proposed that we abandon the larger wagons, which they believe cannot be driven through this mountainous territory. They called a meeting tonight, at which Mr Clay overruled them, assuring the party that we have passed through the worst of the broken land, and speaking passionately of the ease and speed with which our passage shall be completed once we leave behind the canyon country. Cagie Bowden pressed him on the details, upon which he became much agitated, and attempted to expel the Bowdon wagon from the party. On this he was overruled, by a clear majority of the settlers. He retired with

much bitterness to his wagon, as did we all. A general air of fore-
boding over all the party.

August 30: Seven of the single men missing this morning; gone
with their horses. The party is fractured clean down the middle. No-
one looks up from his labours save with a grave and troubled face.
Double-teaming all day. Elizabeth urges me to rest tonight, and
cease from writing. God grant we shall one day read these words,
settled safe in California, and wonder at the tribulations of the
passage across.

September 1: Out of the canyons at last! and on to the low hilly land
above the salt flats. Six hundred miles from our destination. A chance
to recoup lost time, and fresh springs in abundance. Charley and
Josephus, the Indian guides we engaged at Fort Bridger, went from
wagon to wagon warning us to take on board all the water we might
carry, and to hoard it well – no good springs, they said, for many
days' march ahead. On hearing of this Mr Clay had the men brought
to him, and cursed them for a pair of craven panic-mongers and
Godless savages. Hiderick was for lashing them to a wagon-wheel
and whipping them – restrained with some difficulty by the rest of us
men. Heaven help us all.

September 2: A note found stuck to the prickerbushes by the side
of the trail, by the Indian Charley scouting ahead. He brought it to
me at the head of the wagon train, and with some difficulty Bowden
and I pieced it together. We believe it to be the work of several of
the single men who cleared out last week – it tells of hard going
up ahead, and warns us to turn back and make for Fort Bridger
while we have the chance. I was for keeping it from Jefferson Clay
till we had spoken to the other families, but nothing would do
for Bowden but to force the issue. Once more Clay and Bowden
wound up at each other's throats, and were separated only by the
combined exertions of all present. An ill omen hangs over this
party. Ahead lies the desert. Into His hands we commend our spirits,
who brought His chosen ones through forty years of wandering to
the promised land.

September 3: Slow passage across the face of the great salt desert.
Hard baked crust over limitless salty mud, bubbling up to the surface
through the ruts left by our wagon wheels. The wagons sink through
to above the wheel-hubs, and the going is most laborious. Again we
fall behind, and the season grows late.

September 4: Endless desolation – no safe land – no fresh water.
This is a hellish place.

September 5: Disaster in the night. The oxen, mad with thirst, stampeded in the night; all but a handful lost out on the salt pans. Four of the wagons have been abandoned, and the families must carry what they can. All have taken on board as much as they can carry, and the overloaded wagons sink axle-deep into the mud. Surely God has not set his face against us?

September 7: Passage still devilish slow; no sign of an end to the desert. Bitter cold in the night time – we huddle with the dogs for warmth, like beasts in the wilderness. Little Mary-Kate screams in disgust at the bitter salt taste that fills her pretty rosebud mouth. Vainly she tries to spit it out, as her mother comforts her. Would that I could rid my own mouth of the bitter taste of defeat. ~~I have led them into this hell~~ (*remainder of sentence erased – Ed.*)

September 9: Off the salt pans at last. Oxen lost, wagons abandoned, and no prospect of a safe retreat to Fort Bridger. To go back now would surely finish us off. In any case, the provisions would not last – Bowden says they will barely serve for the passage through the mountains. He is for confronting Clay, once and for all, and holding a popular vote to determine who should lead the party from here on in to California. I counsel him to wait till our strength is somewhat recouped. None of us have the belly for such a confrontation at present.

September 13: Ahead in the distance, the foothills of the Sierras. White snow on the hilltops. Dear God, that it should come to this.

September 20: No slackening in our progress, no rest for any man; but we are slow, we are devilish slow. Without the oxen and the wagons we lost out on the salt pans our progress is impeded mightily, and much effort is expended in the securing of provisions. Clay now wholly removed from the rest of the party; like a general he rides alone at the head of the column, seeing nothing but the far horizon while all around him his troops suffer, close to mutiny. Around our wagons each night, the howling of wolves.

September 23: Desperation in the camp, which can no longer be hidden. The remaining single men have volunteered to ride on ahead, that they might alert the Californian authorities to our plight; they set out this morning. All our chances of success in this forlorn undertaking ride with them.

October 2: The Humboldt river. According to Charley the Indian guide, we are now rejoined with the main trail, and done at last with Clay's damned cut-off. No sign of any other parties along the banks of the river. It is late in the season – they will be safe across the mountains and in California now. A note from the men riding on ahead was discovered on the side of the trail, and brought straight to Clay. He will not disclose its contents. I am persuaded at last that the time has come to follow Bowden's counsel, and force a reckoning.

October 3: A catastrophe. The thing I most feared has come to pass. Last night Cagie Bowden led a deputation of the men to Clay's wagon and demanded he produce the note. Clay refused, and upon Bowden pressing him, drew a pistol and shot him through the chest. Instantly Clay was seized by the men, while aid was summoned for the stricken Bowden; alas, too late. Within a very little time he expired.

I was for burying him, then abandoning Clay in the wilderness and pressing on. Hiderick would have none of it, calling instead for frontier justice and a summary settling of accounts. His hotter temper won the day. Hiderick caused Clay's wagon to be tipped over on its side, and then hanged him from the shafts. It was a barbarous thing to watch as he strangled to death at the end of a short rope. Are we no better than beasts now? Have our hardships brought us to such an extremity of animal passion? Back in the wagon, I threw myself to the floor in a perfect storm of emotion; Elizabeth tried to comfort me, but I could take no solace even from her sweet voice. I have failed her – we have all failed, all of us men who stood by and let vanity and stupidity lead us into this hell on earth. Now on top of it all we are murderers. The mark of Cain lies upon us.

October 4: In all my anguish of last night I forgot to set down that the note was found on Clay's body after all, tucked inside his pocketbook. It read – 'Make haste. Indians in the foothills. Snow already on the peaks. Waste no time.'

October 11: Forging on down the valley of the Humboldt. Such oxen as remain alive are much weakened through great exertion and lack of fodder, and to save their strength we walk where we can. No man talks to his neighbour; our gazes are bent to the trail ahead, and our heads hang low. Why should we look up? Snowcaps clearly visible atop the mountains in the West.

October 23: In the night, a great alarm: Indians, howling down from the hills, attacking our wagons. Four wagons lost before we knew it – nine men dead in the onslaught. They have slaughtered half of the oxen too, the brutes. As they vanished back into the hills, we heard them laughing – a terrible and callous sound. I hear it now as I write, and it may be that it shall follow me to my grave: the mocking of savages in this savage land. Savages, I say? At least they do not kill their own as we have done.

October 31: Our progress is so slow as to be hardly worth recording. Oxen dying between the wagon-shafts; if we are to make the crossing into California, I believe we shall have to rely on the mules and upon our own feet. Thunder atop the peaks, and the laughter of the Paiutes, echoing through these lonely canyons. They do not bother us much now, though; even the wolves leave us alone. We are not worth the bothering.

November 4: Very nigh to the mountains now – can it be that the Lord will grant us safe passage before the winter comes? Dark clouds over all the white-capped peaks. One more week, Lord; one more week. At night on our knees by the bunks we pray, Elizabeth and I – God grant us another week.

November 8: In the high passes. So close! Lord, can it be?

November 9: Snow in the night, great flakes whirling out of a black sky. We pressed on without stopping, but in the morning it commenced again, and mounted to a perfect flurry by midday. The oxen are slipping, and the wagons wholly ungovernable. We made camp by the side of a lake nigh to the tree-line, where some party long since departed made four or five rough cabins out of logs. For tonight we must bide here by the lakeside, and pray for no more snow.

November 10: Snow all through the night. Trail impassable – neither man nor beast can battle through the drifts. Exhausted, hope gone. Wind mounting to a howling frenzy, mercury falling, sky as black as lead. We have failed. The winter is upon us and we are lost in the high passes. God help us.

From the Sacramento *Citizen-Journal*, February 2, 1847

Our readers, anxious for fresh news of the wagon-train of settlers trapped in the mountains, will doubtless remember our interview with Mr Henry Garroway, one of the outriders sent on ahead of the party who arrived in California last November, with the first of winter's storms at his heels. Mr Garroway, it will be recalled, announced it as his intention to lead a rescue company at the earliest opportunity, made up of brave souls from the vicinity of Sutter's Fort, kitted out and victualled by the magnanimous Mr John Augustus Sutter himself. Alas, grave news reaches us from the fort: the ferocity of the January storms has rendered even the lowest of the Western passes wholly impenetrable. Drifts higher than a man on horseback have been reported as the norm, and even the most sanguine estimate cannot anticipate the departure of any rescue party until March at the earliest . . .

Addendum to the *Diary of John Buell*
(undated, made by his wife, Elizabeth)

I had not thought to take up my dear husband's pen and bring the story of our family's tribulations to its conclusion; however, should this diary be all that remains of us, then it may serve as a testament – to much bravery, and also to wickedness beyond measure.

We have been snowed in at the lakeside for nigh on three months now. Things have gone hard with us since the beginning: our provisions were scanty on arrival, and dwindled soon enough to nothing. I have seen people trying to eat shoe-leather and the binding of books; bark and grass and dirt they have eaten, twigs and handfuls of leaves. We were thirty-five on our arrival, thirty-two adults and three nursing children including my angel Mary-Kate. Now we are reduced to three.

The hunger swallows all things. Whole days will pass, and we think of nothing save food, how it would be to fill our bellies to repletion. There is a narcotic in it; it lulls one into a dangerous inactivity, a dull vacant torpor. I have seen this look settle upon a score of people; in each case the end came very nigh after. Daily I look for it in myself. I must be strong, for my angel's sake.

The provisions ran out before the end of November: the last of the oxen were slaughtered and eaten by then, and the mules too. One of the children was the first to die, Sarah Doerr's little Emily; soon after her, Missy Shorstein, and her father the next day. Our sorrow was great – we had no way of knowing that all too soon death would become a familiar thing with us. It is hard to mourn, when horror is piled upon horror and the bodies are beyond counting or remembrance; but it is necessary. It is the most human of emotions, and we must remain human, even in this uttermost remove of hell.

From the start it was clear that some would not last the year out. A great depression settled over our camp like a funeral pall, and many succumbed to its all-embracing pressure. It was most prevalent among the men – not least in my dear husband John. From the first he reproached himself, and for many days after our arrival, half-crazy with remorse, he would not stir from his bed of leaves and moss in our cabin. Many times I spoke with him, and sought to assure him he was not to blame for our predicament; but he would not be consoled, and turned his head away to the wall. Greatly I feared for his life; that he would give up the will to live, and fade away like so many of the others.

But my husband John Buell was a strong man, and a brave one, and soon enough he arose from his bed and was about the general business. He managed to trap some small animals for the pot; hares and crows and the like. He helped weather-proof our cabin, and the cabins of our neighbours. And around the middle of December, when folks were dying and all hope seemed forlorn, he came up with a plan.

Together with three of the other men – Bill Doerr, Martin Farrow and young Kent Shorstein – he purposed to cross the mountains on foot and fetch help. The Indians, Charley and Josephus, would accompany them, guiding them safe through to California. It was a desperate plan, fraught with much peril and offering but little chance of success, but it was voted the last best hope of our pitiful assembly, for all were in agreement when the plan was presented for approval. Here I must be honest, and record that in private I counselled against the expedition – I wept and pleaded with John, that he should stay with us and not throw his life away on such a rash and impetuous undertaking. He would not listen, though: it was as if he saw in this reckless plan a last chance, not just for our beleaguered party, but for himself – as if he might thus redeem himself in my eyes, when all along he was my hero and my one true love.

They set out in the second week of December; and soon afterwards Hiderick set forth his awful proposal to the remainder of the party.

Now I must be brave, and set forth the facts of the matter without flinching. Hiderick said that the rescue party were doomed to failure, and would undoubtedly die in the mountain passes; we should not rely on them for assistance. I could have struck him – that he could thus impugn my husband, and his brave allies, when he had not the courage to do aught save cower in his cabin! But I must tell it aright, and not let myself be sidetracked.

Hiderick said that we were doomed, and should not make it through to the spring, save for one chance. He said that we were surrounded by fresh meat, if we had only the brains to see it, and the nerve to do something about it; he said he was a butcher by trade, and would show us what he meant. If I live another fifty years I shall not forget what he did next.

He went to the door of the big cabin and flung it wide open. The snow rose up in drifts all around, parted only where a path had been cleared between the cabins. All around were the graves of those who had already succumbed to the hunger and the cold; maybe nine or ten by that time. We could not dig them in the ground, for that lay ten feet beneath the snowdrifts, and was frozen hard as iron. Instead we lay them wrapped in blankets in the snow, where the cold would preserve them till the spring.

Hiderick pointed to the nearest of the graves – little Missy Shor-stein's. 'There's your meat,' he said, in his thick guttural voice. 'Like it or not, it's the only vittles you'll get this side of the thaw.'

There was an uproar. Old man Shorstein struck Hiderick full in the face, and swore he would take a pistol and spill Hiderick's brains on the snow before he ever disturbed the grave of his daughter. Hiderick wiped the blood from his cheek, licking his hand clean in a way that made me sick to watch, and merely said, 'You'll see. None need eat his own kin, if we handle it right.'

But Mr Shorstein himself was in his grave before Christmas-day, and two others with him. Two more the next day, and three the next – and soon after that the first of the families took to eating the dead.

Hiderick dressed the bodies, and distributed the parcels of meat. Like a terrible black-bearded devil he passed from cabin to cabin; always he would knock upon our door, and always I would refuse to answer. Sometimes the ghoul would show his grinning face at the window; I would hold little Mary-Kate close to my bosom, and pray for our deliverance. Five of the seven families partook; let the record show that the Buells and the Shorsteins never ate human flesh. It is not my place to judge them – Mama told me more than once that survival runs close to the bone, closer than anything save the blood. But the flesh of our friends and fellow-Christians! Dear Lord, no. I trapped what I could, enough for Mary-Kate at least: back in Ver-mont when I was but a little child, Mama had showed me many ways to catch the small creatures of hills and woodland. Still the hunger was always with us, and Mary-Kate grew awful thin and pale; yet no unholy flesh passed our lips. As for the rest of them, they ate or fasted according to their consciences, and yet even for those who chose to partake there was scarce enough meat to grow fat on, so little was there left on the bones of the dead. They cheated death for but a little while, but at what cost, Lord? At what cost?

Even this grisly feasting was all but through by the January, and folk were dying again almost daily, when out of the mountains staggered Kent Shorstein and the Indian Josephus, carrying between them the body of my dear brave husband John Buell.

We buried John in the snowdrifts out back of the cabin. Kent Shorstein told me of the great hardships endured by the five of them up in the mountains; he said that they lost their way searching for a pass that was not entirely blocked, and so within a week they were starving and nigh to death themselves. Doerr and Farrow were for killing the Indians, and eating their flesh; on this Charley rose up and ran Martin Farrow through with a knife, and Bill Doerr shot Charley dead on the spot. Josephus would have killed him for it, but John and young Kent restrained him. Best if they had not, maybe, for next morning when they awoke they found Doerr eating Charley's liver by the campfire. Kent and my dear John refused to join him in the gruesome repast, and instead they entreated Josephus to lead them away, back to our camp by the lake. The last they saw of Bill Doerr was him raving and singing to himself among the pine trees, waving a gobbet of meat on a stick.

Poor Kent Shorstein told me all this from his sickbed; he shivered like a man with the ague, and I was not surprised when two days later, his body was taken for burial by his grieving sisters. Soon they too had joined him at rest; and then began the grimmest passage of my travails.

With John dead and the last of the Shorsteins gone also, there now remained of the party only Mary-Kate and I who refused to eat the flesh of the deceased. Hiderick was now pre-eminent among us; he roamed from cabin to cabin like a robber baron, adorned – I can scare bring myself to speak of it! – adorned with a gruesome sort of necklace, fashioned from small knuckle-bones and vertebrae strung on a leather strip. He said they were from the mules and the oxen, though everybody knew this to be a lie. Who though could reproach him? He fed them, and they depended on him. On his shoulders he wore a cape of wolfskin – the wolves surrounded the camp but would not come close, for I had set up snares all around as Mama showed me how to do, and we still had ammunition enough to shoot them.

It was the practice of the families to place over the bodies of their loved ones a marker made of wood, together with a small tag hung round the neck, lest anyone should eat his own kin. In the cases of the Shorsteins and us Buells, this marker served to warn away the ghoul Hiderick entirely. Imagine then the distress and the horror with which I found, when going to pray awhile at John's graveside, that the bodies of Adolph and Bella Shorstein had been dragged from their sacred resting-place around to Hiderick's cabin, whither I dared not go. What to do?

In the presence of all those remaining in the party – few enough, Lord, few enough! and yet sufficient to deal with Hiderick, had they but dared – I confronted him with the foul deed. He merely laughed and said, 'Hain't I got to put meat on the table? They ain't so particular about their food now, I reckon.' No-one would take my part in it; they slunk away like so many starving jackals, licking the bloody hand that feeds them. I took Mary-Kate back to our cabin, and wept throughout the night. I vowed to myself: she is my angel, and I will do what I must to protect her. Let the others throw in their lots with the ghoul, I said, and see what comes of it.

Death came of it, I believe as much of shame as hunger in the end. People could scarce bear to look at one another, and took to their beds, and come morning they were dead; only Hiderick seemed to thrive on his grisly diet. He ruled over all, and grew fat on the bodies of his erstwhile subjects.

Josephus would have taken my part, for he too – let his name be recorded among the virtuous! – never ate of the cursed meat; but he was gone. After bringing John back to the camp he spent a night resting, then another day crouching out in the snow beneath the mightiest of the trees around the camp, muttering to himself some words of heathen prayer. The wolves came right up to him, but did not touch him; for his part, he hardly seemed to heed their presence. At dusk he came down from the treeline to knock on my cabin door and tell me he was departing. Would I come with him, he asked? I said I could not, and showed him Mary-Kate asleep in her rough cot. He nodded, and said a curious thing: 'You are best fitted of all of them to look after her, maybe. I will see you again.' Then he looked at me for the longest time, so long that I felt uncomfortable and averted my eyes from his keen and curious gaze – upon which he turned on his heel and departed. That night – I am sure it was him – he left the dressed-out carcass of a deer at our door. We never saw him again.

Now we are through February and into March, and still no sign of a thaw, nor any hope of rescue. Instead the snow redoubles, and my traps are empty come the morning. There were upward of a dozen souls remaining in our party when John's companions dragged him back into camp. Today, there are but three remaining, Mary-Kate and me – and Hiderick.

Oh, unutterable horror! That such things could exist under the sun! The deserted camp is like some awful frozen abattoir. Long streaks of blood disfigure the white snowdrifts. Here and there lie the horrible remains of some devil's feast – a long bone picked clean, a shattered skull – and barricaded inside our cabin we hear, Mary-Kate and I, the ravings of the maniac outside.

This afternoon – I can scarce bear to set the words down. I must be strong. This afternoon, he came to the cabin door and hammered it till I opened. He was stripped to the waist, I thought at first; then I realised I could not see his mop of greasy black hair and bristling beard, and thought he wore some sort of leathern cap over all. What it was –

What he wore was the skin of my dear husband John Buell, stretched over his head and shoulders like an awful mask. He was laughing like a madman, and bawling at the top of his cracked and shrieking voice: 'You like me? You like me now, huh? I fitten enough for you now, maybe?'

I raised John's pistol level with my eyes, and said, I know not how I managed it but I said: 'Get out.' He scarcely heard me, so filled with the spirit of devilishness and insanity was he. I did not hesitate. I fired the rifle. The load flew so close by his head – closer than I had intended it to, I think – that it served to rouse him from his madness. He stared at me, but all I could see were the features, blackened and distorted, of my dear sweet John. The horror of it – the horror –

'Get out now,' I said.

'I'll come fer you,' he said, and I swear there was nothing in his voice that was halfway human any more. 'I'm your husband, now, don't you see, and I'll come fer you. You'll want me by and by, I reckon. I got meat – got good meat – ' and he raised his hand to show me some hideous gobbet of flesh – please God let it not have been *his*, oh merciful Lord please! He brandished it before him like a dreadful prize.

I fired again, and this time the bullet took the greater part of his ear off. He dropped the stinking piece of carrion and screamed; with the incredible clarity of great stress and panic, I saw his traitor's blood spilling out on the white and blameless snow. Like the basest coward in creation he scuttled back to his shack, shrieking and cursing all the while. For the time being he is quiet; but I doubt not that he will come for us, maybe tonight when the moon is up. My bullet only wounded him, he will survive. But shall we, Mary-Kate and I?

Alone; abandoned; forsaken. How shall I protect my darling babe from this madman, from this wolf at the door? All that drives me on is the remembrance of Mama, those nights she lay nigh death in the wagon, how she clasped my hand in hers and gripped it and told me that I would survive, though she might not. I said mama, mama, no, it shan't be, you're strong, you're so strong, and I am weak, but she said I would change. When the time came I would change. I do not know whether she was right, but I feel at the end of myself.

The moon is up. Its broad full face smiles down on this stained defiled earth. The howling of the wolves echoes out across the frozen lake and through the deserted cabins, up into the snow-choked trees. Four bullets left. Not near enough, I fear, but one each for me and Mary-Kate at need. Grant me the strength to do what I must, to survive this night!

From the Sacramento *Citizen-Journal*, April 27, 1847

THE MIRACLE OF THE MOUNTAINS
Child found in the wilderness
Guarded by wolves – horrors strewn all about
Full particulars

The incredible and shocking news, so long awaited, from the rescue party led by Mr Henry Garroway who rode to the assistance of the wagon train trapped all winter long in the mountains, is setting all California ablaze. Wild rumours have been bruited on all sides, and it is incumbent upon the *Citizen-Journal* to set down the facts as we have learned them, *directly from Mr Garroway himself*.

The party set out from Sutter's Fort in the last week of March, and battled through mighty snow-drifts to the far side of the peaks, where lay the encampment of the unfortunate settlers stranded by the winter storms. The first of the outriders drew up short on reaching the outskirts of the camp, so appalling was the scene which lay before their eyes. Together the would-be rescuers prayed for strength and marshalled their forces, before entering into a scene of horror no pen can describe, fit only for some grim courageous Dante of the New World.

Five cabins of rough construction lay before them, their roofs alone visible above the snow. No sign of chimney-smoke, or indeed of any human activity, could be seen; instead, between the cabins, there were bloodied trails, as of the aftermath of a great slaughter. One veteran member of the party, Mr Frederick Marchmont of Sacramento, swears that the carnage wreaked upon that place surpassed in horror anything seen by the most hardened of frontier campaigners; not even the savage Apache, he avers, could have left in his wake so much bloodshed and butchery.

Great was the dismay with which the rescuing party gazed upon this devastation; heavy were the hearts of all as the search from cabin to cabin began. Horrible to relate, all about the cabins were portions of human flesh and bone, torn as if by wild animals; so atrocious was the general aspect of the place that several of the rescuers were all but unmanned, falling to their knees and praying to the Lord that this bitter cup should pass them by.

Imagine, then, the wonderment with which the assembled men of the rescue party heard, in all that great stillness of desolation, the crying of a little child!

From a private letter of Elizabeth Buell to her daughter Mary-Kate, held within the Garroway family

My darling, I believe they are coming soon. Last night I heard them, ever so far off, up in the peaks – I smell them now, their scent travels on the thin spring wind. Tomorrow they will arrive, and they will find you.

It will be the cruellest and most bitter thing to leave you, crueller even than the burying of my own dear husband, your loving father John Buell. I saw his body once Hiderick had done with it: oh, my child, pray you never have to look on such a sight! Hard it was to look upon; till now, the hardest thing in that long season of sadness and hardship that began with the death of your grandmother, Julia Stocklasa, at the commencement of all our wanderings.

Your father, as he lay raving in his cabin by the lakeside, called this a godless place; and then cursed himself for a blasphemer. God has abandoned us, he screamed into the night; better say that God was never here, my darling. Better say that we rode beyond His grace into some strange and ancient land, where the old gods still hold sway, where blood and death and the animal passions yet contend for mastery of the earth. Your grandmother knew it, Mary-Kate; as she lay on her deathbed she whispered it in my ear. Remember, she said, you will change at need. You will change, she said, and I did not know what she meant at first. Then she told me of the shape-shifter women of her homeland, those that go out into the woods on nights when the moon is full, and the change comes upon them. She told me what to do. I did not believe her at first, but perhaps only in the uttermost desperation can such things ring true. I did what she told me, and everything changed, my darling – everything, save my love for you.

I thought I could come back, after it was done. For it was only to protect you, my darling, that I did what I did that night of the full moon when Hiderick came for us; little did I care for my own life, only for yours, since to stay alive would be to keep you safe from harm, and that was all that mattered to me. How could I know that what is done, is done, once and for all; that *there can be no changing back*? How could I live among men again, after such a fearful alteration? Now I have other family, and must leave you to your own kind.

They wait for me among the trees, my new kin, tongues lolling from their strong jaws as they grin and pant, coats wet from the melting snow. How it feels to run with them, to fling myself into snowbanks and roll and play and lie together – this you can never know, my darling. Josephus, who helped save you, knew: straight away I recognised him, after the deed was done and the rest of the wolves came down to the camp to look upon the slaughter. I looked into his eyes as I lay there full changed, streaked and clotted still with Hiderick's reeking blood, and he looked back into mine. This time I did not turn away.

Did I do wrong? I did what I had to do. Did I betray my dear husband? At least I did not fail our beautiful and most perfect daughter, first in both our affections and ever dearest to us. So how bitter, my darling, to leave you for these men to find. They will take you across the mountains, whither your father and I cannot follow: we shall remain here as you ride away. At least you shall find your home in the new Eden: east of Eden is fit enough for such as we, who have the stain of blood on us.

Perhaps this land, that has so much escaped God's grace, may still be subject to His justice; perhaps I will be punished for what I have done. As if there could be a worse punishment than knowing you to be alive and well in that promised land beyond the mountains, and I not able to see you, or hold you in my arms and hear your pretty laugh.

Hark! They are coming down from the mountain. I must go, and leave you now. All my love goes with you. Be good, my darling; be kind, be honest, be faithful, and know that your Mama will love you always. Listen for me, nights when you lie abed and the moon is up. The pack are waiting for me. I must go –

The Tale Untold

GAIL-NINA ANDERSON

There was a man, they say, not rich or poor but a man who worked for his living, who needed to gather a cartload of heather. So he made a day of it, hitching his horse to the cart and travelling to the moor where the heather grew in great abundance. And with him went his young wife, already with child but not so far advanced in her term that she could not help in his task. So they loaded up the cart and were going back as it grew dark, and the man said to his wife,

'Now you must take the reins and drive the cart, for I shall leave you for a little while. For protection, take the pitchfork, but if anything attacks you, be sure to beat it off with the sides of the fork. Do not stab at it with the prongs.'

And of course, something did attack her – otherwise what would be the point of putting such a warning into a tale? Within a few moments of the husband disappearing (and why did she never ask his reason?) a great grey wolf leapt at the cart and the poor woman beat and beat at it with her pitchfork, but still it got so close that it grabbed her apron between its teeth and tore it to shreds. Then she just shut her eyes and stabbed straight at it, and the wolf howled out in fury and pain and ran away.

Soon the woman's husband returned, less than sympathetic – indeed, snappish and annoyed. And she would have cried at his lack of care for her, except I don't think she was that sort of woman. Instead she looked closely at him and she noticed the threads of linen between his teeth and she cried out, 'It was YOU!'

Well, not those exact words. She was Scandinavian so she said it in her own language, but with as much force as you can put into any tongue, for she was shocked to the marrow of her bones and her baby.

'It was *you*,' she said, but she was already calculating the situation in which she found herself (I told you she was that sort of woman.)

'Well I'm glad, because now you can never turn into a werewolf again.'

That's the thing with folktales – down to the nub of the story and no description, no analysis, not even any motivation. Who was she, this woman? Did she have long, thick hair plaited neatly under a head-scarf? Was she already weatherworn from working outside? Had she had many suitors and made a poor choice, or had her wolfish husband been the only one to ask for her hand?

And had she, up until this moment, ever regretted her marriage?

No, I don't think so. That's the funny thing about the tale. They should by all rights be the moral centre, hero and heroine, working to keep their cottage secure and warm against the wild world and any strange things that threatened their domestic comfort. They should have known every trick, inherited every piece of old wives' (and husbands') wisdom designed to keep the goblins at bay, placate the elves, stay on the good side of the fairies. In the way of things they – the status quo – should have triumphed and been rewarded with a beautiful baby, fair of face and sturdy of limb. Or with three wishes. Or with a well of pure water that never ran dry. Something practical like that.

But this is a folk tale, not a fairy story. It may have been collected, in several variants, but it's not been improved, romanticised, rounded off. It doesn't give us more than the narrative core, puts no flesh on the bones, doesn't admit of *and then* . . . So what happened next?

Here's what happened before. She was not one of those lily girls with long pale hands and skin like moonbeams. Nor was she a nut-brown gypsy with passion lurking deep in her dark, dark eyes. There were few of either type in the village, and amongst the marriageable maidens she was the pick of the crop. Perhaps, when he came looking for a young wife, he was disappointed to find that life was, after all, going to be ordinary, just as it had been for his father and mother.

He was a catch, bonny and strong, broad-chested and blue-eyed. The son of the miller, he had gone for a soldier when still a lad, and returned now, miraculously unscathed, with money in his purse, and the promise of the mill that would one day be his, and the light of experience in his eyes. He could have chosen any girl, but why should he not choose her? She was good-natured and brimming with health, hard-working and had a dowry besides. When he went to war, had he encountered women more tempting, with lily maids and dusky temptresses for the taking? Was her smiling red mouth no temptation?

So he was not the most ardent of wooers, but his soldier's stories captured her father's ear just as something about him caught her eye, and they were married just as was right and proper. Their house was small, but furnished with gifts from both families, so they spent their first night together in a wooden bed with a soft, fat mattress, which is more than many young couples can hope for.

What passion did he hope for? What passion did *she* hope for? She was happy and healthy, not over-shy and as knowing about the ways of a man and wife as a girl brought up on a farm must be. She unplaited her soft brown hair and put on her new linen shift and was ready to lie with him, already thinking about the tiny clothes she would knit for her first baby if it was born in the winter. And because her mind was on babies and because she did not, after all, have any notion of romance, she was only a little surprised to discover that their love making took him further away instead of bringing him nearer. Perhaps it was always like that with men, she thought. But it was sweet enough to cradle his head on her breast as he slept.

And she saw his red cheeks and his broad shoulders and thought what a good father she had chosen for her children. And what she did not see was that part of him had slipped away that night, though he never left her bed. He had already lost something she couldn't understand – his shadow, perhaps, or that part of him which came to life only in dreams.

And men in those days would have warned you to protect your dream self, for it could be spirited away to somewhere unknown, unhomely. And women in that village would have told you that the best guard against such enchantments was a stout bed, a soft mattress and above all a happy young wife. These were the anchors against wandering off, the ropes that tied a man to home and hearth, village and family, all the places where he should be and the things that he must be, or where would it end?

But after that first night the bride was pregnant, and what could be a surer sign that all was as it should be? And if her husband often left her bustling about with her mother and sisters and neighbours, that was only suitable too. After all, a man still young who has seen something of the world may not wish to be cooped up with village women and their unchanging domestic universe. So he spent time with the village men, telling them tales of where he had been and what he had seen that was far from hearth and home. And if the stories grew ever more fantastic, they did not think him a liar. After all, though they had no lily maidens and dark-eyed succubae for the asking, did they not have their own dwarves and elves and rumours of things that kept them indoors when the moon was full and the trees rustled as though they would pull up their roots and walk?

But one story he never told them, which was strange as it grew and grew in his memory each night, even as he lay beside his plump, contented wife who no longer bothered to unbraid her hair. It concerned a village he had marched through, where there was no war but a good bivouac and a friendly welcome for the soldiers at the inn. Many of the village men had served their time fighting for the local lord, had travelled and come home with strange scars and foreign wives, so they were not afraid of these visitors, but drank with them as the air in the inn grew closer and shapes danced in the firelight. He had drunk as much as he could, feeling safe among his companions and seeing so many smiling faces.

And among them was a boy, young and slim, curly-haired and golden-skinned, always on the edge of the flickering light. He did not laugh, but looked as though he would drink in every word the soldier spoke, about his father the miller, his going for a soldier and his adventures done and to come. And the miller's son thought that if the boy had a sister who could look at him in the same way, then he might never go home, but come back to this village when his time for soldiering was done and settle here instead.

But he never did go back there. By the next morning he was glad to shake off the drink and the memories of the night and march away as fast as he could. There had been a moon, just one sliver off being full, yet huger than he had ever seen it in the sky. There had been cool hands and feverish flesh in the woods outside the inn, and feelings he had never known before. And there would have been guilt, but some things are too strange even to be put into words, and so this was the tale he never told. But it left him with a hunger that chased him through his dreams.

Do you pity the young wife, who had done everything as it should be done, as her mother would have done it, yet was rewarded with a husband who turned out to be a werewolf and attacked her even after she had spent all day gathering heather for him? But she got *her* reward – she had named the thing he was and could never again be, she had restored the status quo. And if he left their home and their village soon after and was never seen again, did she even have room to care? He had not, after all, been such a good bargain. She knew there were more vigorous young men who would come looking for such a handy wife, who had seen off a beast and still kept her good-nature, her health and her dowry. Her mattress was still soft, and besides, she soon had a fine young baby son to care for. If she had thought about it (and I doubt she did, for she was not that sort of woman) she would have admitted that she loved her beautiful curly-haired golden boy far more than she had ever cared for his father.

Loup-garou

R. B. RUSSELL

I first saw the film, *Loup-garou*, in 1989, in a little arts cinema in the centre of Birmingham. I had driven there for a job interview and, as usual, I had allowed far more time for the journey than was required. I had reasoned that it should take me two hours to travel there, to park, and to find the offices of the firm of accountants where I desperately wanted a position. The interview was at two thirty, so I intended to leave home at midday. I had worked it all out the night before, but then became concerned that the traffic might be against me, and I decided to allow another half-hour for the journey. That morning I checked my map but no car parks were marked on it and so I added yet another half hour to the time I would allow myself. Leaving at eleven o'clock seemed prudent, but I was ready by half-ten and rather than sit around the house worrying, I decided to set out.

I know my nervousness about travelling is a failing, but I've always lived and worked in this small provincial town and it is not a day-to-day problem. On this occasion it was made very obvious to me just how irrational my fear of being late for appointments really was; the traffic was light and the roads clear and I was in the centre of Birmingham by a quarter to twelve. I found a car park with ease and was immediately passed a ticket by a motorist who was already leaving, despite paying to stay the whole day. I parked, and as I walked out on to the street I could see the very offices that I wanted directly opposite. I had two and a half hours to kill.

For no reason other than to pass the time I looked into the foyer of the cinema which was immediately adjacent to the car park. Pegged up on a board was the information that a film called *Loup-garou* was about to start, and that it would be finished by two o'clock. It seemed the perfect solution to my problem.

I doubt if there were more than five or six people in the cinema. It was small and modern and the seat into which I settled myself was not too uncomfortable. I was in time to watch the opening credits slowly unfold. The sun was rising over a pretty, flat countryside, and the names of the actors, all French, slowly faded in and out as the light came up over fields and trees. It was beautifully shot, and a simple, haunting piano piece repeated quietly as the small cast were introduced, and finally the writer and director, Alain Legrand. I noted the name carefully from the information in the foyer when I left the cinema two hours later.

The film was incredibly slow, but each scene was so wonderfully framed, and the colours so achingly vivid that it was almost too lovely to watch. The sunlight, a numinous amber, slanted horizontally across the landscape as we were introduced to the hero, a boy who was walking from his home in the village to a house only a half-mile distant. The camera was with him every step of the way. There was a quiet voice-over, in French, that was unhurried enough for me to understand it. The boy was kicking a stone and noting that he had a theory that four was a perfect number, as exemplified by a square. Therefore, if he kicked this stone, or tapped the rail of a fence, he had to do it three more times to make it perfect. If, by some unfortunate mischance, he should repeat the action so that it was done, say, five times, then he would have to make it up to sixteen – four times four. The penalty for getting that wrong was huge; the action would need to be repeated again and again to make it up to two hundred and fifty-six, or sixteen times sixteen.

It was a rambling dialogue, and a silly little notion such as any young lad might have, but I was immediately struck that it had been an affectation that I myself had had as a teenager. Predisposed toward our hero on the strength of this, I was rather looking forward, as he was, to seeing his sweetheart, if the director would ever allow him to arrive at her house. When he eventually knocked at the door, predictably we had to wait for the mother to answer it, and for him to be shown into the comfortable, dark kitchen. He had to wait, of course, for the girl who, he was told, was brushing her hair upstairs and would not be long. He talked to the mother, stroked a cat and looked out of the window. Finally the object of his affections descended the stairs.

At this point I sat forward in my seat. The young girl looked exactly as my wife, Yvonne, had looked at that age. She was pretty, with startlingly blue eyes, and long blond hair. I was delighted by the coincidence.

They took their time, of course, in going outside to where the sun was now higher in the sky. I felt a frisson as they sat close together on the bench outside the door, and, unseen by the mother, he tenderly kissed the nape of her neck as she bent down to look into a box of buttons. I marvelled at the film-maker's art. As the boy's lips brushed the girl's skin she slid her hand through the buttons in a way that was incredibly sensual. Then she picked out a heavy green one, shaped like an apple, and asked him if he knew that it had once belonged to the costume of a famous clown?

Up until this point I had enjoyed the coincidences I had found in the film, but this was stretching them too far. My mother had also had a very similar button in a sewing box, which was also said to have once belonged to a well-known clown. I did not know what to make of its appearance in the film.

The hero and heroine then decided to take a walk through the fields, talking of love and their future. And then, in the woods, there was the most delicately handled love-making scene, shown to us through carefully concealing trees. When he eventually walked home we had another voice-over where he declared his love for the girl whom he inevitably calls Yvonne.

After a few more meetings between the two of them, the only scenes involving several other actors are played out on a day of celebration; their last at school. Here another character is introduced, an older boy who clearly has an interest in the heroine. I immediately cast around for the equivalent character in my youth. There had been jealousies in my relationship with Yvonne when we were still at school, but I had finally married my childhood sweetheart. Completely lost to the apparent reality of the film I hated this potential suitor with a passion. Suddenly it is revealed, in a scene where Yvonne tentatively kisses this second boy, that we had been watching the earlier love-making scene at a distance through our hero's eyes!

The film then changed in style. In an instant the long, beautifully framed scenes from a single static position were replaced by abrupt, short images from what appears to be a hand-held camera, and which were presumably meant to be from our hero's viewpoint. It conveyed the black rage within him. He was retracing the journey to Yvonne's house from the start of the film, but this time at a run. He was looking all about him in desperation. When he arrived at the farmhouse he hammered at the door and when the mother answered it she told him that the girl had gone out. He rushes off across the fields and into the woods, and as the hurried camera-work shows his journey the viewpoint subtly moves down from the eye-level of a young man to that of an animal running, finally, over the floor of the woods. For only a few moments we see the love-making couple once again. The hero rushes upon them and there are terrible screams and the wild movement of the camera makes it impossible to see what is happening. The screen goes black, and just as the audience is getting restless and wonders whether the film has finished, or if the reel has not been replaced by the project-ionist, the picture slowly comes up to show an incredibly languid sunset, and the hero, looking dirty and ragged, crying uncontroll-ably, walks slowly back to the village.

We are back to the earlier, slow direction. He slips unnoticed into a dark garage, and in the dim light we see him loop a length of rope around the rafters. The music has started by this time, a variation on the opening theme, and in front of one long apparently unedited shot we watch him climb a chair, tie the rope around his neck, and kick the chair from under him. By now it is so dark that we can't make out the details of his horrible death, and the music has taken the place of the sounds in the garage, but the imagination makes up for what is not shown.

I was emotionally drained by the film. I emerged into a Birming-ham afternoon light, initially affected by the closing scene and not thinking particularly of the earlier coincides. The rage that had been in the hero as he rushed to find the lovers seemed to grow in my own breast and it was a while before the shock passed. Eventually I remembered and was able to reflect upon the uncanny similarities between the hero's circumstances and my own. I could not work out what was real, what was my imagination and what was the film-maker's art. I was standing on the pavement outside the cinema, angry at the injustice of the film. To this day I do not know how I managed to compose myself for an interview thirty minutes later, and how I made the shortlist.

When I arrived home that evening and related the events of my day, the film assumed more importance than the interview. Yvonne listened to my description patiently, amused, and said that she too would like to see it. I had written on a flier taken from the cinema *Loup-garou* and the director's name, 'Alain Legrand'. She pointed out that *loup-garou* meant werewolf, which I had not registered at the time. 'You've been watching horror movies then,' she asked, and I had to agree that it was horrific.

Having unburdened myself to my wife, and, I am embarrassed to admit this, having cried while re-telling the story, I felt remarkably better, and with a little distance was able to be amused by the coincidences of the film. Perhaps I had made too much of them. As I lay in bed that night I told myself that if there was anything super-natural about the apparent coincidences, anything at all, then it was there to show me how lucky I was to have made my childhood sweetheart my wife. I looked at her as she slept beside me, at her tangled blond hair and fine skin, the shape of her nose and at her soft, parted lips. For the first time that day I thought of the hero as an actor rather than as myself, and I slept soundly.

I did not get the job when I was called back for the second interview, and in retrospect I am glad that I didn't. At the time I was disappointed, but my life carried on comfortably and pro-vincially, and city life has never since appealed to me. On my return to Birmingham for the ill-fated second interview I looked in the cinema but the film they were showing was apparently a Norwegian 'comedy of manners'. It didn't appeal, and I did not have the time to watch it.

Almost immediately *Loup-garou* became something of a joke amongst our friends. I had explained what had happened one evening to another couple at a dinner party, and my wife saw a tear in my eye as I explained the plot, and a great deal of fun was had at my expense. I played up to it, and berated my wife for leaving me for another in her filmic existence, and letting me, presumably, attack her and her lover and then commit suicide. My wife was quite fascinated by the idea of the film, and between ourselves we resolved that we would try and see it. Obscure French art films don't often appear on the provincial film circuit, though, and it was some years before I saw any reference to it anywhere.

For a while I bought a few books about werewolves, fiction and non-fiction, but it struck me that the power of the film didn't derive from the legends, but the way in which the film had been put together, and my fascination for the subject quickly waned. My interest in foreign cinema grew, though, along with my video collection, and soon I was quite knowledgeable on the subject of art-house European cinema. In my researches I found a reference to *Loup-garou* in the biography of the director, Alain Legrand, which claimed that the film had never been distributed because it had fallen foul of the censors (because it appeared to condone under-age sex). A few years later it appeared on the internet in a French language film database which claimed that not only had it never been distributed, but had never even been edited. These claims were repeated, word for word, on other databases, and although a large reference book on European cinema later corrected these errors, those entries remain unrevised on the internet. The reference book added that those critics that had seen *Loup-garou* reported that it contained some of the most beautiful, as well as some of the most amateurish, camera-work they had seen. The only other reference that I discovered in the intervening years was on a 'werewolf' website, where it was described as 'disappointing', and 'hardly to be described as a werewolf film at all'. Nowhere could I find any reference to it being made available in any form. Without any hope of success I programmed the details into an internet search-engines with no result, and left it as a permanent 'want', which I refreshed every year without success.

And then only a couple of weeks ago I had an email notification that the film was available on an auction website. A private seller had a DVD to sell that he admitted was an unauthorised copy from an unreleased studio video. I didn't hesitate to put £50 on as my max-imum bid, and despite there being no other apparent competition, with a day to go I raised it to £100. I watched the end of the auction on a Sunday evening, waiting for the flurry of last-minute bidding, but none came. I won the DVD for the minimum bid of £5.

It arrived in the post two days later, sent by a Frenchman living in London. There was no accompanying receipt and the DVD was blank, with no artwork. We had decided to make an occasion of watching it, and planned to wait until the children were in bed. We had opened a bottle of wine in readiness, but a nagging headache that Yvonne had earlier complained of became worse, threatening to develop into a migraine, and she decided to go to bed.

I decided to watch the film anyway. I knew that I'd be happy to see it again in a few days time when Yvonne was feeling better, but after all this time I could not wait.

In the quiet house that night I sat down before the television, and pressed 'Play' on the remote control. The credits came up as they had done in the little cinema over fifteen years before. The picture jumped a couple of times at the beginning but settled down after that and the quality was good. The sound was clear, and the music was just as haunting as I remembered it. A part of me was worried that it wouldn't be quite as I remembered, but it still looked beautifully shot, and I waited to see the young boy walking out towards the farmhouse. He duly appeared, and explained in the voice-over about his obsession with the number four. A shiver ran through me.

When the camera panned slowly around Yvonne's family kitchen I noticed a number of things that I hadn't seen the first time; the first being that their dresser was similar to one that my wife's family had once owned. The mother, too, looked a lot like her own mother. I drew in a breath as the young Yvonne started to come down the stairs, but suddenly found myself completely bewildered.

The girl that appeared was certainly not the girl that I remembered. This actress had dark hair, and was slightly plump as opposed to the skinny little thing from before.

As though wilfully ignoring my confusion the actress assumed the role as though it had always been hers.

Outside the door they sat on the bench as I remembered, and the whole scene with the buttons was repeated exactly as I had retold the story to others over the years. As far as I could tell, the walk across the fields and into the woods was the same, scene for scene, and the love-making was carefully, and enigmatically, handled as before. I could understand now that there might be some who would protest that the actor and actress were under-age, but almost everything was inferred by the viewer; suggested but not shown by the director.

Disillusioned at my apparent inability to remember the film correctly I watched the scenes with the alternative suitor without quite the same passion as before. I had retold the story of the film on so many occasions and nobody had ever said that I had changed any details, therefore I must have reported it wrongly from the very beginning – immediately after I had seen it!

I was too annoyed with myself to enjoy the rest of the film, and suddenly it seemed to drag interminably. I made myself watch it, wondering if I'd even bother showing it to Yvonne, when the final scenes eventually appeared. The attack on the love-making couple was as sudden and almost as unexpected as before. But again I had got the details wrong. It was not the hero but the other boy who made his way back to the village, and into the darkened garage. He climbed the chair and fixed the rope. Barely perceptible in the dark, and with the sound masked by the music, he hanged himself as before.

The credits came up and I turned it off. I put the DVD back in its blank case and decided to go and get myself ready for bed. I locked up the house and turned off all but the landing light, where I stopped to look in at Yvonne, who was sleeping.

I sensed that something wasn't quite right, though, and walked into the room.

There, in our bed, was a dark-haired woman. I stood quite still, not wanting on any account to wake her. I found myself trembling though, and backed out of the door, not knowing what to do. There, at the top of the stairs was our wedding photo, and I had problems standing as I saw myself, in a picture from twenty years ago, standing at the side of a pretty, plump, dark-haired woman.

I must have fallen asleep on the sofa that night, and the next morning was the usual whirlwind of getting the children's breakfast and taking them to school before I myself carried on to work. I murmured something to the darkened bedroom before I had left the house, trying not to think who was lying under the blankets.

I am not sure how I got through the day. All that I could think of was that my wife had changed. This was a ludicrous proposition, especially as the wedding photograph showed that it was my error. I certainly didn't feel mad, but through the whole day I examined every possibility, and the only one that made any sense was that I had made an error of vast proportions. This did not convince me, of course, and it was with the greatest trepidation that I made my way home that evening. I parked in the garage and stood in the dark, not wanting to go indoors. Despite the turmoil that my mind was in, I realised that I was not thinking about the dark-haired woman in my house, but of my confusion between the heroines of the film I had seen. It was when I found myself thinking about the last scene of the film that I decided to go indoors.

My daughter greeted me in the hall as though nothing was at all amiss. Indeed, she announced brightly that 'Mummy is feeling better and is up, out of bed.'

I walked through to the kitchen where the dark-haired woman was up and preparing dinner. My other daughter walked out with a cheery 'hallo' as I walked in, and the woman saw me with a smile. She walked over to me and took my hands in hers.

'You watched that film last night, didn't you?' she asked.

I agreed that I had.

'I understand,' she said. 'We were meant to watch it together, but after all these years you couldn't wait to see if it was the same as you'd remembered it. I hope you don't mind, but when I got up this afternoon I wasn't up to anything other than sitting in front of the television. I decided that I might as well watch the film as well. And you were right; it's a wonderful film, but you didn't remember the end properly, did you?'

I shook my head.

'But you were right about Yvonne . . . she *is* just like me.'

And she hugged me, and although I could not see her face I knew that she was crying. I should have felt love for her, but all that I could think of was the dark garage, and the rage that was growing within me . . .